FIERY WITCH
THE FAIRY QUEEN

BY:

TJ BERRY

FOX FIRE PUBLICATIONS, LLC 2020
SIXTH BOOK OF THE CLAIMED SAGA

Acknowledgements

To my mother, the original storyteller in my life and example of a strong woman in my life. To my sisters, who have often been my rocks and my biggest supports/fans. To my friends and friends who became family, thanks for all the love and support. To one of the greatest women to ever touch my life without me ever meeting her…the one, the only, THE Notorious RBG, Supreme Court Justice Ruth Bader Ginsburg…for being an inspiration to young girls everywhere. To all the passionate women in my life…you inspired the person Jamina is…you are such an amazing force of nature and I love you all! And last but certainly not least, to (The Notorious JHD) my best friend, one of the best mom's I know, and one of the most remarkable women I've had the pleasure of knowing, JH DeMond…thank you for sharing the world of Fox Fire with me…it's been an awesome ride so far!

Fox Fire Publications would like to thank www.SelfPubBookCovers.com/ andrewgraphics for this amazing cover.

The Fairy Queen Chapters

Chapter 1: Party

"It's going to be great," Zoë hums in my ear.

"It'd be even greater if I could actually go down to the party, where all of my friends are," I say. She moans an affirmative, moving the brush across my cheek again. "I can't possibly be that red…I'm constantly pale." Another favorable sound comes. "Can I, at least, open my eyes?"

"Absolutely not," Shay demands, walking up behind me.

"Did you get the…?"

"Yeah, yeah," Shay cuts her off. "Here you go."

"Thank you," Zoë replies. She gasps. "Oh, these are perfect."

"What? What are perfect?" I ask as she takes hold of my left ear. "Earrings…?" She puts one through my ear.

"Not just earrings," Zoë purrs.

"THE perfect earrings," Shay joins. This time, I groan a positive response. "Now…?" she asks Zoë, I suppose. "Okay, open your eyes," Shay says with a jubilant bounce to her voice. "Wait, wait, wait," she barks as my eyes make it up to the point that I see a tiny sliver of light. I sigh. "In front of the mirror," Shay whispers. Two soft hands take each of my arms. They pull me to my feet and guide me across the floor. Thankfully, they guide me the entire way. We're in Shay's room, and this is the first time she's allowed me in here, despite it being right next to Tony's room.

"Open," Zoë commands.

"Are you sure this time?" They both give me a shake. I sigh and open my eyes. I'm standing at a full-length mirror, and I look amazing. They brushed my hair down, parting it in the middle, but angled toward the back. Most of it is bound into a ponytail, draped over my left shoulder in large, dangly baby-doll curls. I'm wearing a pearl-colored, silky dress with two thin straps tied together in little bows over my shoulders and a low heart-shaped neckline.

The dress wraps around me, coming in to a snug fit around my waist before billowing out in ruffled pleats that stop just above my knees. I'm wearing tiny little peep toe high-heeled shoes with straps moving up my ankles that are the same color as the dress…so is the polish covering my toenails… I check. …and fingernails. I didn't notice it earlier but so do my lips, although they appear to be a little pinker.

I turn left to see the earr… "Oh my God," I moan, taking in the massive square cut diamond hanging from my right ear. I turn to the right and see its match. "These are…"

"…borrowed," Shay says with a mom-tone. "So, take REALLY good care of them." I nod. "What do you think?"

"How…did you guys pull…?" I motion to my reflection. "…this off…?"

"Well," Zoë says. "It's easy when you have such a pretty girl to start with." I purr as she wraps her arms around me at the shoulder.

"I still don't get how they're having an outdoor party in January," I complain as she releases me.

"Huge canopied tent," Shay explains. "…open air heaters every few feet. Throw in a few hundred dancing, hormone-driven teens, and boom, instant outdoor party." She looks down at her phone. "That you are already fashionably late for, so you should head downstairs." I frown as she shoots a wink at Zoë.

I open my mouth to speak, but before I can, Zoë holds her hand up in my face. "Just one more thing, and you'll be perfect." She puts my glasses on being careful not to mess my hair. "There. Perfect. Now, go get 'em."

I steal another glance at myself in the mirror. "Perfect?"

Zoë pulls me away from myself. "Yes." She points. "Go," she orders.

"You two should…?" I start, approaching the door.

"Stay far away from a party filled with a bunch of horny high school boys," Shay finishes.

"That," Zoë adds. "Besides, the two of us and Mitchell are going to a movie." I pull the door open. "Oh, don't let them mope around the house. The point of this party is to introduce them to your friends, since they plan to go back to school to stick close to you." I nod. "Go," she murmurs again tipping her head to the right. I nod.

I step into the hall and hurry to the stairs. I move downstairs at a slow pace, feeling extra awkward trying to walk in heels. "Why are we waiting here?" Tony complains from the first floor with the sound of heavy footfalls across the hardwood floor. I slow down.

"Shay said that we should wait here for some reason," Quincy returns.

More steps, Tony's pacing. "Our guests…have been arriving for the past thirty minutes now," Tony counters as he crosses the floor again. "There's already a crowd. It's rude for us to keep them waiting."

Quincy sighs. "Well, Shay said that Zoë said we'd better not move from this spot."

Tony stops walking. "I don't have to do what Zoë says! We don't work for her; she works for us!"

"Go ahead then, brother," Quincy says. "If you're not worried about what Zoë will say, go outside."

"Shut up!" Tony groans and resumes pacing. Quincy laughs.

I descend the stairs and stop at the landing. Quincy faces the stairs but watches Tony as he turns and stalks past him. Quincy wears a black suit with a slender cut and a black vest fastened up to his diaphragm. He's wearing a white button up shirt underneath with the top two buttons undone and no tie.

Tony wears a black suit with a black button up underneath with only the top button undone. I almost groan at how over the top hot they are.

It's hard to believe that I only met them three months ago. I've been living here with them ever since my mom went missing. Except, my mom wasn't really missing, she'd signed on with an evil cabal… Yes, cabal. …dead set on reviving a 2,000-year-old demigod and taking over the world. She came back to the Witch of Light side of things when said cabal lured me into a trap and tried to kill me.

She helped me, and the Cursed Brothers, stop the evil cabal's dark witch and a horde of daemons… I sigh. …and then told me how to break the curse that forced the Blackshear Brothers to love me. I can't love either of them. If I choose neither of them, eventually they won't be forced to love me anymore. I shiver. *Remember give them nothing. They can't know that you're still in love with them.*

"What are we waiting for?" Tony growls again. Quincy looks up and sees me. His eyes widen, and his mouth falls agape. He reaches back and hits his brother across the arm. Tony turns to him and then follows his line of sight. Tony moves up to stand beside his brother with the same shocked expression.

"Me," I sigh, pushing my glasses up. "…I guess, you were waiting for me."

"Worth the wait," they say in unison. My smile comes down to a smirk. They look at each other and then return to me. I descend the stairs, their eyes on me the whole time. I reach the first floor. I look to Tony then Quincy.

"Shall we?" I pose. Tony nods, and Quincy smiles. Tony turns and offers me his right arm. Quincy turns and offers me his left arm. I take both their arms, and we round the stairs. We walk toward the back of the house. They each push one of the doors open, and we step outside onto their massive stone deck that moves around the left side of the house after starting next to the low-lying garage on the right.

A huge white canopy tent with twelve ropes staked down visible from this side, stands in the center of the yard. Some random, dance-inducing pop song plays extra loud, making me glad that this house sits nowhere near anything. The air is unusually chilly, even for this time of year in North Carolina. I can already feel the heat under the tent from here thankfully.

Several dozen of my friends and several hundred people I don't know huddle underneath the tent and dance to the music. We walk down the eight gray stone steps leading to the ground. The frigid earth gives way because of a little moisture underfoot.

"Are you ready for this?" Tony asks.

I nod.

"She nods unconvincingly," Quincy narrates. I can't put into words how much it annoys me that he knows my tell. He smiles. "S'okay, we'll go ahead, make the announcement, and let you mingle amongst your friends."

"'Amongst?' Are we using 'amongst' now?"

"Yep."

I stare at him and nod again. "Okay."

We three, walking arm-in-arm…in-arm, move over to the DJ's table. We separate, Tony remains on my left and Quincy on my right. Tony extends his hand to the DJ, who places a microphone in it. He, in turn, offers it to me. I press my lips into a line and shake my head.

Quincy takes the microphone from Tony and then renews the offer to me. "You can do this," he says with confidence. I nod and take the mic. Tony places his arms behind his back, and Quincy crosses his over his chest.

"Excuse me," I say into the mic. "Excuse me," I repeat a little louder. Everyone turns his or her attention to me as the DJ turns the music down. "Hey everyone," I pant. I steal a glance at Quincy's smiling face and then Tony's even expression. "On behalf of my family friends, the Blackshears, I'd like to welcome you to their home. Their parents regret that they are unable to welcome you properly, but…" I turn and motion to... "…Quincy…" I turn and motion to… "…and Tony Blackshear are glad that you came out. They look forward to getting to know as many of you as possible in the coming weeks as classmates and eventual friends." I look at Tony, and he nods. "Thank you and…let's party!"

The crowd applauds, and the music picks up again. Everyone resumes dancing. I pass the DJ back his mic and issue a silent 'thank you.' He bobs his head and smiles. I turn back to Tony…and he's gone. Quincy is too. I turn to the house, and they're already on the second floor. They peer out the bedroom window next to mine. I sigh and walk toward the house.

I reach the stone stairs, only almost falling twice on these stupid heels. "Jamie," comes from a voice that warms my soul. I turn and…

"Alex," I moan and throw my arms open to hug him. He wraps his arms around my midsection. "Where have you been? I missed you a ton."

"Well, I don't have a car, and you're living way out here in the sticks now." I laugh. We part, and he pulls his black hoodie out from his body. "Had I known this was supposed to be a dressy deal, I would've…"

"That's no excuse," Stephen says, stepping up beside him. "I mean, look at me," he adds, motioning to his dark gray suit with light gray button-up underneath.

"Look at you, Stevie," I say to his big, chocolaty eyes. "You look so good." The gray of his suit compliments his mocha skin tone perfectly.

He smirks. "Yeah, yeah, but it's Stephen, not Stevie…never Stevie, Jamie-Lynn."

I laugh. "Ugh," I groan, wrapping my arms around Alex again. He hugs me back and laughs himself. "I seriously can't tell you how much I missed you…I feel like we missed out on so much with that whole stupid memory spell thing."

"Easy there, witchy," Meghan says in that bored way of hers. "This one's spoken for and when my bestie gets back from Japan, I'm sure she'd hate to hear that you were pushing up on her man," she finishes with a wag of her finger. "They're bound after all."

"Bound…? Witchy…?" I point at Meghan's beautiful face, framed by her perfect blond hair pressed straight. Her hypnotic blue eyes stay with me, even when I turn to Alex. "She knows?" He nods. "So, you know about your glamour, too?" She frowns. "That'd be a 'no.'"

"What I do know," Meghan starts. "…is that I'd love to see where those smoking hot Blackshear brothers got to." She looks around.

I frown and bite my tongue before I say something about the fact that she's calling my Quincy and my Tony… I sigh. Relax, Jamie. They're not yours. They can't be…but what about…I turn to look at Stephen. He sighs, while staring at the ground and sliding his hands into his pockets.

"I think I saw the taller one," Alex starts. "…over by the DJ, a second ago." Meghan smiles and wanders off in that direction.

"I thought," I begin, still looking at Stephen. "…that you and she were a 'we.'"

"*We* broke up," Stephen admits. "She was worried that I didn't really like her and that it was all whatever this thing is that makes people like her."

"Her glamour," I say with a nod. "You should stop by and talk to my mom when she gets back tomorrow." Stephen and Alex scowl. They look at each other and come back to me. "Trust me. She can explain this whole glamour thing way better than I can. Oh, and make sure you bring Meghan with you. It'd be kind of pointless if it were just you two," I add, taking the first stair up to the patio.

"Where're you going?" Alex asks.

"Ugh, it's so annoying," I groan. "I have to go and wrangle some…" I pause. "…what's literally the opposite of party crashers?" Alex and Stephen laugh. "I'll be back," I say to Alex. "We'll talk some more then." He smiles. I hurry up the stairs and into the house.

#####

Chapter 2: Crasher

"Ow," I complain as I roll my ankle, moving around the banister at the bottom of the stairs. I take a deep breath, and the brief pain subsides.

I look up the stairs and grimace with the thought of how many more times I can injure myself. Remember what your mom taught you about heels. Ignore your heels and stay on your toes. "Just like being in a fight," I whisper as I climb the stairs. I turn to the right as soon as I reach the second floor and move past my bedroom door with well-deserved confidence, considering how fast I took the stairs. I stand in the open bedroom doorway. The room mom chose so that she could keep an eye on me…and them.

The lights from outside create haloed silhouettes of Tony standing on the left side of the window and Quincy sitting on the windowsill to the right.

"I'm sorry," I complain, stepping into the room, although I know they heard me from the moment I entered the house. "Did the party get moved to my mom's room?" They face me. Quincy stands, throws his jacket open, and slides his hands into his pants pockets. Tony clenches his fists at his sides. They both wear tense expressions. They must have been talking about something serious. "Guys, you're kind of freaking me out here. What's up?"

Quincy laughs without any real humor behind it. "We're scaring her."

"What's wrong?" I pose. Tony shakes his head then his eyes move to the floor between us. Quincy takes a step back. "The party's outside," I prod, trying to keep what's obviously a tense situation light. "Lots of pretty girls to dan-"

"…as if we'd give a damn about that!" Tony interrupts.

"Brother," Quincy says in a softer tone and reaches for him. Tony knocks his hand away.

"I'm sorry." Tony clutches his right arm. His Fury Seal must be acting up.

"S'okay," I whisper.

"How…?" Tony asks. "How is it that you don't feel anything for either of us…?" I look away and fight the tears that want to fill my eyes. "The curse seems to have given up its hold on you but intensified on the two of us." I shrug as I turn back to them. "I look at you," Tony says, sounding as if he's in pain. "…and I'm using every ounce of my willpower not to march over there and kiss you."

"I'm sorry," I murmur, not knowing what else I can say to him. "But," I pause and look at Quincy before coming back to Tony. "I just don't feel that way about either of you." Tony scoffs and turns toward the window, left hand sweeping across his mouth. I look at Quincy, and he…smirks into a…he's smiling. Oh no! He knows my tell. If I had kept it at, *I won't choose either of you* or *I can't choose between you* or even if I'd said that *I won't give in to the curse,* he would've let it go, but I…stupid, stupid me… He steps forward.

"I'm going back down to the party," I say while extending a hand to halt him. "You two can come down if you want…" I turn and walk out. "…or not, I don't really care!"

I stomp down the stairs. I'm so angry. I'm not mad at Tony for being so mad at me. I'm not even mad at Quincy for knowing my tell. I'm mad at myself for giving Quincy hope, hope that he might share with his brother. The more they hope, the more it makes me hope…hope that in some strange and fantastic way, I'll be able to choose one of them, and the other will somehow be perfectly happy with that. That somehow the curse will be lifted all at the same time. That kind of stupid, outrageous hope isn't fair. It's not fair, because it's not real.

I'm outside again before I even realize it. Some girls from my biology class walk by and wave. I return the gesture while making my way down the patio stairs. "So," Alex starts from behind me. "I take it, the owners of this sick house, aren't coming down?"

I press my lips into a line and shake my head. "Well, it might be for the best," Alex says. "From what you've told me, you and them…" I put my right pointer finger over his mouth, tap my right ear with that same finger, and then point to them in the window. He nods. He extends his right hand, as if asking me to take it. I do. I follow him onto the dance floor, across it, and then out the other side of the tent. He lets go of my hand. I frown.

"It's less noisy out from under the tent," he explains. "Plus, Sora always tells me it's hard to zero in on one conversation or one sound when there's a loud noise between you and what you're trying to listen to.

"So…" Great, Alex has that sympathetic ring to his voice. "Do you want to talk about how you're secretly in love with both brothers but can't have either of them?" I groan and wrap my arms around myself, partly to comfort myself from the point that he just brought up, but also because out from under the tent it gets cold fast. Alex unzips his hoodie and slides it off.

"Lex, you don't have to…"

"Shut up," he reprimands as he throws it over my bare shoulders. "And don't call me that." I slip my arms through it and laugh.

"Won't you be cold though?" He shakes his head.

"I don't know. Lately, I don't really get that cold." He scratches the side of his head. Where have I seen that before? "I mostly just wear the hoodie because it's my style, you know?"

"You don't have a style, Alex." He laughs, and it makes me laugh all over again. I really did miss him. He's my best friend, and I let my mom throw away four years we could've spent together.

"Isn't this sweet?" a voice that chills my soul asks from behind me. Alex looks past me. "He's quite the gentleman, Bunny," Rais follows up.

I turn to him. "Rais!"

He steps out of the shadows wearing a black vest with buttons that stop just above his diaphragm with his black tie tucked into it and above his black slacks. He also has a white button up shirt with oversized cuffs and a tiny collar. His hair is still messy chic, but he's cut his muttonchops back to thin lines that run the length of his chiseled jaw. His grayish-blue eyes probe every inch of me and then move to size Alex up. The stubble remains on his cheeks and around his mouth. If I didn't know he was a monster and that this is just his human face, I'd say he was handsome.

"You remembered," he breathes, placing his right hand over his heart. He shows off three rings on each of his fingers from his pointer to his ring finger, including an impressive silver wolf's head on his middle finger. "I'm touched."

"What are you doing here?" I grumble between clenched teeth, while moving to stand between him and Alex.

"Jamie, who is this guy…?" Alex asks. I open my mouth to respond, but Rais appears between us. I look to the tent and then back to Alex, who now holds Rais's attention. "What…?" Alex barks.

Rais tips his head to one side and stares at Alex. He faces me. "Nothing," he says. "I just thought I saw something interesting in you, kid, but I was wrong. You're completely dull."

Rais gives me his full attention. "To answer your question, I came to see you, Bunny." I frown. "I came to tell you…Liz is dead."

I gasp. "Did you…?"

"Nah, it wasn't me, Bunny," he says with a casual swagger. "It was her boss. He was disappointed in her for not only failing but for getting Siemon, Agatha, and Thulani killed and breaking her contract with your mom."

"And who's that?" Alex asks in my place. "Who was Liz's boss?"

Rais glares at him over his shoulder. "Listen up, little wolf, why don't you go wee on a tree while the big kids talk?"

Alex growls, actually growls, and takes a step forward. Rais's eyes shift from beautiful gray blue to red with black replacing the whites.

"Stop it," I snap. Rais turns to me, and the black drains away as his pupils shift from crimson to blue. "Alex, I'm fine. I'll come find you soon." He frowns and stares at me, before cutting his eyes to Rais. "I'm fine. Really." Alex nods and walks toward the tent. "Alex." I slip my arms out of his hoodie. He extends his hand to stop me, but I toss it to him anyway. He holds it up and backs away.

"Hubba-hubba," Rais says, staring at me. Now, I feel like wrapping my arms around myself for a completely new reason. "You look amazing," he breathes looking me over.

"Speak your peace before I burn your furry little butt to a pile of ashes."

"So, you've been checking out my butt, have you? Don't you think you're a little young for me?" he asks, cupping his chin.

I push my glasses up and extend my other hand to him. "One..."

Rais holds up his hands in submission. "Okay, okay, but just for the record, I'm only twenty..." I frown. "...when I stopped aging, that is."

"Two..."

"Look, I just came to tell you that Liz was dead and that from now on..." He points at my heart. "...I'm on your side."

"You're what?"

"On your side," he says, stepping closer. I look up at him. "See," he breathes. "If I wanted to hurt you, I could've killed you and been on my way by now."

"That means you should be up for sainthood, right?"

He laughs and scratches the side of his head, similar to how Alex just did. "There's another reason, too, to be honest with you." He reaches down, collects my right hand, and holds the back of it close to his heart.

"What are you...?"

"I find you...interesting...Bunny," he whispers. He holds my hand in both of his, caressing the back with his thumbs. "I want to know you. I want to get to know you and find out what makes you tick."

"So, you can use it against me?" I try to pull my hand away.

He rubs my hand again and shakes his head. "No." He sounds as if I hurt his feelings. "So, I can determine if I'm an idiot or not, for wanting to protect you...even from the guys whose side I'm supposed to be on."

"...even from the guys on whose side...you should be," I whisper. He smirks. I stare into his eyes that seem so sincere, but how can I believe him? He just tried to kill me like six weeks ago.

He leans in close. Too close. "This close," he whispers. I gasp...actually, gasp. "I was this close to ripping out your throat." He huffs, and I can feel his breath against the nape of my neck.

"What stopped you?" I pant.

"This," he says, tugging on the Crescent Moon's chain. "This belongs to my clan..." I frown. "...my great-great-grandfather gave it to an Aldien...I guess that Aldien gave it to your boyfriends' father, and they gave it to you."

"My mother gave me this," I grumble. I try to tug my hand away again.

"How you came to have it isn't really important. The fact that you have it, and it responds to you IS important." I swallow a lump. "The fact that you are able to wear that pendant, and it benefits you means that my clan is destined to be by your side." His voice dropped into a sexy octave like how Quincy's voice does. Oh no, Quincy and Tony…if they find him here… Why am I suddenly worried about his safety? Or am I worried about their safety because I've seen how strong he really is?

He smirks, showing the slightest hint of fang. "It's time for me to go, Bunny. I think your wolf friend told your boyfriends I was here." I nod. "I meant what I said though. I'm on your side. I should warn you though. Devon's been told to watch you, too."

"Devon…? The fire guy…?"

He nods. "Only he's just following orders."

"And how do I know you're not?"

"Not just watching. I'm here talking to you, aren't I?" I frown. "Until next time, Bunny." He kisses the back of my hand and releases me. "Bye-bye now." He vanishes.

I sigh. In the exact spot Rais just disappeared from, Quincy and Tony appear. They look around.

"Where is he?" Tony growls. I frown.

"Your friend Alex told us about Rais," Quincy says. "Did you scare him off, or is he…?"

I sigh again and clutch the Crescent Moon Pendant in both hands. I nod once. "We need to talk."

#####

Chapter 3: Tell

"Where's Alex?" I ask, crossing my arms and leaning against the massive desk that their father used to sit at every night, writing about them in his journals. Random thoughts like that keep coming to me, since their library has become like my second home. I spend almost as much time here as I do in my bedroom. "You guys said he told you I was with Rais, right?"

"Told us might be a bit of a stretch," Quincy says from behind the bar. He hasn't touched a single bottle since I asked him not to drink anymore, without really asking him to do it.

"What do you mean?"

"He," Tony says, tracing the edge of the desk with his finger. "…walked over to the patio, looked up at us, and asked '*Who's Rais?'*" He lifts his eyes to me. His eyes are cold, devoid of feeling. I'm afraid of that look. It's how I imagine he'll look at me if he gives up on me. I never want him to look at me like that for real.

Quincy walks over. "Yeah."

"Where is he?"

"Gone," Tony returns still with a frosty tone. "Like the rest of the party guests, I suppose." I nod. "What were you thinking?"

"What?"

"Rais could've done anything to you, and we wouldn't have known until it was too late."

"How'd he get past the barrier?" Quincy asks.

"We weakened it, remember? I told you guys about Alex and how he's from a family of skinwalkers, plus there's Meghan, and she's…"

"Still," Tony snaps. "It was stupid, and he could've hurt you."

"I'm fine and stop calling me 'stupid!'"

"Stop acting stupid, and I will!"

I just want to punch him in his *stupid*, handsome face right now. I groan and step from between them with my arms crossed over my stomach. I stumble as I step away, tweaking my ankle again. I kneel to undo the straps on the left shoe.

"Rais said he's on our side," I say, looking up to them while moving to the other ankle.

"Yeah," Quincy comes back. "You said that. What's that supposed to mean? He's on our side?"

"I don't know," I admit, while kicking of the shoes.

"Then tell us exactly what he said," mom says, storming into the library. She still has her big suitcase with her. She's wearing black. That is pretty much all she's been wearing since we got her back. This time its black jeans, underneath a leather jacket and black low-cut, V-neck shirt. At least, it's not black leather pants and a corset. She releases the bag, and it continues to sit straight up on its four tiny wheels. "Well…?"

"Did you find out anything about the crystal?" Quincy asks…while pouring a drink. I scowl and focus on not lashing out with my magic, although a few bottles rattle on the table. I can't believe he started drinking again just because I rejected him. He replaces the bottle and grabs his glass…and offers it to mom. She takes it without looking at him and drinks from it.

"Later. I want to hear what my daughter was doing with that sadistic skinwalker," she says, lowering the glass.

"How did you…?"

"Guilty," Tony says, raising his left hand.

I huff. "He said that he came to talk. He made some rude comments to Alex. He told me whoever Liz was working for killed her for losing you, and then he told me that he was on our side…my side," I correct. Mom frowns. Tony same. Quincy same. Crap.

"So, En Quosque killed Liz?" mom whispers.

"Yeah, apparently." She draws her lips into her mouth and nods.

"That still doesn't answer the obvious question," Quincy starts. "We didn't need to know that Liz was dead, and he didn't have to tell us."

"So, why did he?" Tony joins.

"I don't know…" I shuffle. "He just…"

"What?" mom snaps.

"…he said he thinks I'm interesting, okay? And…" I twirl the Crescent Moon Pendant by its chain. "…he said this belonged to his clan. He said that his ancestor gave it to an Aldien a few hundred years ago."

"He did?" mom asks. I nod. "What does that have…?"

"He said that the fact that I wear this pendant and that it's 'of benefit' to me means something. It means that his clan is meant to stand at my side." I can practically hear the anger in Tony's breathing. "And I'm guessing he's the Alpha of his clan for him to be talking so big."

"Probably," Quincy admits. "Usually, only Alphas talk about 'my clan' like that."

"Do you believe him?" Tony asks in a growl. I take a step away from him and closer to Quincy. He sighs. "I'm calm. Do you believe him?"

"I didn't get any magical warnings or anything if that's what you mean."

"No," mom cuts in. "Did YOU believe him?"

"He tried to kill me less than two months ago."

"That doesn't answer the question," Quincy says.

"He's with En Quosque."

"Still doesn't answer the question," Tony grumbles.

"He's dangero…"

"ANSWER THE QUESTION!" mom yells.

"YES, OKAY?" I let go of the pendant. "Yes, I believed him! I'm the stupid girl who believed the guy who's all the things I just said! Okay?" All three of them fall silent. They each stare at the ground in their own way…Quincy with his hands in his pockets, Tony with his hands behind his back, and mom with her arms over her chest. "Screw this!" I grumble, heading toward the door. Quincy appears in front of me. "MOVE!" He holds one finger up and sucks his teeth several times in a negative way.

I glare at Tony, who's standing on my left. "You're right," Tony says. "Everything you just said about him is correct. Everything you just said is exactly why you shouldn't believe him."

I shake my head. "Fine. I don't believe him. Can I go now?"

"In a minute," mom says. "Quincy, Tony, could you give us a minute? I want to have a conversation with my daughter."

"That's code for you're gonna talk, and I'm gonna listen."

"Exactly and please, lose the attitude."

"Not likely," I moan while crossing my arms. Tony slips out, and Quincy behind him, but he pauses in the door, looking at me. There's something in his stare. It brings me down a little bit. It makes me feel less angry. He nods and steps out, pulling the doors closed behind him.

"Absoluta silentium," mom says. I frown. She sighs. "I don't know why you're always angry with me."

"You should've told me, that's why, mom." I motion to the door. "You should've told me about Quincy and Tony, about the curse, about En Quosque, about everything."

"You are still very young," mom grumbles.

"Apparently, not too young to be left in a house with two guys who are both in love with me." She inhales so loudly; I hear her across the room. "What did you want to talk about?" She frowns this time. "I know it wasn't so that you could *check my attitude* or whatever." She nods. "It's about the crystal, isn't it?"

"Of course." She moves over to her bag, and I meet her. She unzips the back compartment and removes a small wooden box with a circle containing about two dozen intersecting lines creating a lot of triangles. She puts the box on top of her bag. "Open sesame," she hums.

"SERIOUSLY?"

"Simple is always best," she returns as the sigil flashes red, and there's an odd wooden thunk. The lid opens all on its own. Inside is the weird oblong black crystal as solid and menacing as the day Alex and his kitsune, Gwen, dropped it off. "This thing radiates power. That's why I'm keeping it in this sigil leeching box." She looks at me. "It never takes any of the power away though, just keeps it from being detected." I nod.

"So, what's next? I mean, you tried our cousins in Georgia, right?"

"Actually, I took it to Devi…daughter of Sharon."

"Why don't I know them? Are they witches?" She shakes her head. "What wolves? Old vampires?"

"Fae," she says and closes the box. The seal on top flashes red again and the same wooden thunk sounds. "Devi is the current Fairy Queen." She looks at me. "She's the mother of your little friend, Twee."

"I haven't seen Twee since the day she disappeared…the same day you disappeared," I add under my breath.

"She was there. She asked about you." She slips the case back into her bag. "I told her that barring the curse that could possibly end our bloodline, you were fine." I turn my back on her. "I'm taking this to New York."

"New York? You just got back!"

"I know, baby-girl. I'm going to go see Maria. I'm going to try and help her find her daughter."

"Her daughter?"

Mom nods. "Angela's been missing since October."

"But Maria's a powerful Witch of Light, her daughter…"

"…had no discernible power. At least, her mom didn't think she had the gift." I sigh. That would suck. I mean, mom's like a major badass in the witch world, and if I didn't have any of her gift… "Angela had just started at Columbia. After her afternoon classes, she went to work one night and told Maria she was going to a club with her boyfriend after. No one's seen Angela or her boyfriend since."

"When are you leaving?"

"Well, Anne called me and said something about wanting to talk to me about Meghan." I grit my teeth in an *oops, my bad* kind of way. "So, you finally told Meghan what she is?"

"Well, between the whole crystal giving a psychotic human powers, and her best friend being a kitsune, I figured she had a right to know." Mom shakes her head. "She broke up with Stephen, because she thought her glamour was the only reason he liked her."

"Who's Stephen?"

"You remember Stephen. Sheriff Harper's son…you said you loved his style and his big brown eyes, remember?" She nods. "I figured we should tell them. Maybe, get them back together."

She nods. "I never liked Anne. Power-hungry, elf-whore…"

"Mom!" I moan.

"Okay, okay. I've already changed my flight for tomorrow afternoon. So…" She points up. "…head up to bed. We have a long day ahead of us."

"I'm not that…"

"Trust me. The Belfour Clan is always a headache and a half." My head tweaks. "Anne's maiden name." I nod. "Bed," she repeats and points upstairs. I turn toward the door. "Don't forget your shoes." I turn back to her. "I might've failed you on the whole smart mouth thing, but I know I taught you to pick up after yourself." I walk over to the shoes and pick them both up by the straps.

"I'm sorry," she breathes as I grab the door handle. I look at her. "You're right. I should've told you everything right from the start." I tap the doorknob and then open it. Her silence spell shatters as the door opens.

I pull the door closed and lean against it for a second. "So many problems," I moan, while walking upstairs. I pull the earring from my right ear and then my left. "Borrowed," I whisper. I wonder who she borrowed them from…or from whom she borrowed them. "Ugh," I groan aloud. Once a book nerd, always a book nerd. I stare at the earrings in my hand. I'll have to give them back tomorrow.

I turn right at the top of the stairs. Tony's standing outside my bedroom door. He has one hand behind his back and the other gripping the doorframe. He still looks angry. He always looks angry, ever since I turned them down.

"Tony," I whisper. He sighs and stares at me…I see past the anger though. He's hurt. He doesn't know what to do. "Are you going to say anything?"

"We need to talk," Quincy says stepping out of my room without his jacket. I look at him and then to his brother.

"Why does everyone want to talk to me all of a sudden? I just wanna go to bed at this point." Quincy nods. Tony takes his hand from behind his back and he has "…one of your dad's journals?"

"Yes. This one he started just before he placed the seals on us." He opens it and turns it to face me. He points to it. "This passage describes the curse on us…"

"…it says *gift*," I read. Quincy takes my shoes from me by the straps and tosses them into my room. "Thanks." I take the fragile, yellowing pages, bound in dusty, brown leather, from Tony. I pull my glasses down and read over them. "…*In a way, I am gifting my sons to the White Witch…if ever she need break their hold on her…she and only she can.*" I look up from the handwritten pages. "We already know this. Not choosing either one of you, breaks your hold on me…rather than making you pine away until I find a husband."

"Keep reading," Quincy whispers, slipping his hands into his pockets.

I sigh. "*…if her will is strong, but her heart cannot be cruel…the spell on the next page should…*" I look up. "Spell? There's a spell that could…?" I start, flipping to the next page, but Tony takes the journal from me and wraps it up in its leather binding. "Wait, what kind of spell can undo a curse…or a gift…or whatever your dad called it?"

"A powerful one," Tony admits.

"He thinks," Quincy adds.

"I know," Tony returns. "We're trying it tomorrow."

"Who's we?" I ask.

"The three of us," Quincy answers. I shake my head. "We can't do it without you."

"And your dad did everything he did for a reason, including binding the two of you to my family and…"

"And," Tony grumbles. "…he included a way to undo that binding for this situation."

"And what situation is this?"

"WE…still love you…but you rejected both of us, and that was supposed to break the spell…but it didn't."

"Easy, brother," Quincy sighs. Tony steps away, moving toward his bedroom. "It's worse for him…because he has two active seals, not just one." I stare after him.

"I'm sorry," I mutter.

"Prove it," Tony snaps. He turns and points the journal at us. "Do the spell. All it takes is your will, a little of your magic, and the two of us. No potion required…no talismans needed." I sigh. "Please, Jamie." Quincy wipes his mouth and looks away.

"Fine," I complain. "I don't think it's the smart move, but…we'll try it." Tony nods. "We'll wait 'til after mom heads to the airport." Tony frowns. "She's going to visit her friend Maria in New York."

"Okay," Tony sighs. "Goodnight, Jamie…brother."

"Goodnight," I whisper. Quincy waves at Tony just before he vanishes, his door slamming behind him. Quincy moves out of my doorway. I catch his arm. "Hey…" He cuts me off with his right pointer finger pressed against my lips. I look down at his finger, held against my lips, before staring into his eyes and nod. He lowers his hand. "…how is he really?" I whisper.

"Worse than he's showing. I'm not telling you that you should tell him the truth…but it might help." I shake my head. "Jamina…"

"Stop," I mouth. "Just stop it." He moves closer, staring into my eyes hungrily. My eyes dart down to his lips and back again. He continues moving forward, and I back up until my butt meets the doorframe. "Quincy, I can't…"

"That's why the curse didn't end." He takes my right hand…diamond earrings and all…and holds it up to his heart. "…because you still love us…" My eyes dart down to his lips again and back up to his emerald-colored eyes. "…because you're in love with…"

I close my eyes and hold myself against the doorframe. "Please," I mutter. His right-hand caresses my cheek. "Please."

"I won't," he moans into my ear. I swallow a guilty knot as his warm, pleasant breath sends a shiver down my spine. "He's desperate. I can understand his feelings though."

"I know," I return. "It IS different this time, isn't it?" He nods. "You should…"

"Yeah," he sighs and steps away. He moves toward his room.

"Quincy," I whisper. He stops and turns back. I stand in front of him. "How do you always know?"

He frowns.

"What's my tell?"

He smirks.

"I mean, I thought it was something in my face, but then you caught me when you weren't even looking at me. Then, I thought it was something in my voice, but…you even call me out when I nod or shake my head." He draws his lips into his mouth. "So, what's my tell?"

"You don't have one," he admits. "You…" His eyes close, and he somehow finds my right hand again. He holds the back of it to his heart…his impossibly loud…thumping heart…under his gorgeous, firm chest. "…lie to me…" I shake my head. "…tell me a lie, right now."

"Um, I think about Alex in a romantic way ALL the time." I snatch my hand out of his…I slip the diamond earrings into my left hand and place my right palm against his chest. "My favorite color is brown." I gasp when I feel it again. "Your…your heart skips a beat when I lie?" He nods. I shake my head and try to look away as a tear rolls down my cheek.

"Goodnight, Jamina," he says and takes a step back.

"Does it hurt?" He pauses. "Does it?"

"A little," he concedes. "But it's nothing that…"

My arms wrap around his neck before he finishes talking. I hold him as hard…as tight as I can. "I'll never lie to you again," I whisper. "I promise." He scoffs a laugh, and I feel his warm breath on my neck again and a shiver moves through me again.

He places his right hand on the small of my back. "No pain," he whispers and then his lips curl up into a smile against my cheek.

#####

Chapter 4: Glamour

"Are you sure you're ready for this?" mom asks.

I bob my head. Not really thinking about Meghan right now though. I can't seem to tear my mind away from what Quincy told me last night. He feels physical pain when I lie to him…no, I think he might've been lying about that. I don't think it's just when I'm lying to him. I think he feels it when I lie in general.

"I wonder what's taking so long. They passed through the barrier a few minutes ago."

"I'll go check," I say, since I was already walking toward the door. What does it mean…? Quincy feels it in his heart when I lie…does that mean he's more connected to me than Tony is?

I reach the library door. "He does not seem like her type," Stephen says in a mocking kind of way. I wonder what they're talking about…

"And what is her type exactly?" Meghan barks. Wow, I thought Alex was exaggerating about them fighting ever since they broke up.

"Her type's probably the older brother," Stephen replies. Crap, they're talking about me…and them… "And since he already likes her…" I pull the door open more.

"Shut up," Meghan snaps.

I peek just my head out the door. "Guys!" I wave them over. Alex is the first one in motion. I smile. He does too. He's in a hoodie and jeans again. Does he ever wear anything else? I figured hanging with Meghan and his kitsune being the little fashionista she is…he'd pick up some style. I check out Stephen's V-neck sweater and leather jacket. Or, at least, he could pay more attention to Stephen.

Meghan follows Alex and Stephen after her. I back up and let them walk into the library. They look around, taking in the décor. Stephen nudges Alex and tilts his head toward the bar. Meghan takes a couple of steps closer to the leather couch. I take her distraction as a chance to get past her anxious, overprotective best friend thing. I move closer to Alex.

"Hey, Alex," mom says as I wrap my arms around him. Oh, he gives great hugs.

"Hey, Mrs. Baggett," he answers and puts a light swing into our embrace.

"I told you, Alex, you can call me, Daphne." He nods and looks at me. I smile again.

"Stephen, Meghan," mom says. "It's good to see you two." *Good to see them?* Last night, she seemed kind of annoyed about having to talk to Meghan's mom, and she didn't even remember who Stephen was. She moves away from the desk, claps her hands, and does a weird pointing thing with both her index fingers together. "So, I should start by asking, how much do you know about your family, Meghan?"

"Well, I..." Meghan starts. She turns away from the sofa and spots Alex and me. "Well, I know that..." She looks at us again. "I know that my dad is from New..." She looks at us again and scowls. "Will you take your hands off my bestie's boyfriend?"

"Well," I start, knowing that this will probably annoy her more. "He was MY bestie..." I pause because I realize that maybe I went too far with the Meghan impression on bestie. "...a long time before he was Gwen's boyfriend." Meghan takes a step toward us. I start to let Alex go to defend myself.

"Easy," Alex says with his hand extended toward Meghan. "I told you, Gwen's my girlfriend, and I love her." Alex gestures to me. "Jamie's like my sister." I laugh and give him a shake. Finally, somebody gets it!

"So, you were saying that your father's from New York?" Meghan nods. "What do you know about his side of the family?"

"Just that he has a sister, my aunt Maria and then there's my cousin, Angela," Meghan replies. "And that the rest of his family are all dead." Mom makes a contemplative noise...is it a comment on Meghan's lack of family knowledge or the fact that her dad's family is dead?

"And about your mom's side?" I ask in mom's place. I step away from Alex.

Meghan shrugs. "Only that she's an only child, like me. Why?" The Crescent Moon Pendant tells me that Quincy's on the other side of the door. That's funny. I thought they said that they didn't want any part of this. Quincy pushes the door open and moves to one side. He allows a woman...who looks like a slightly...and I do mean SLIGHTLY older version of Meghan to enter. "Mom?" Meghan moans.

"Hey, baby," Meghan's mom hums as Quincy pulls the door closed behind her. She stares after him for a second. She puts her hands on her hips, making her red suit jacket open and showing of her...ahem...assets that give my mom's a run for their money. Her skirt matches the jacket, in terms of color and tightness. Her short haircut hangs straight and down to her shoulders. Just like her daughter's, it's the color of gold. She looks at mom. "So, I see your boys are still absurdly gorgeous." Mom groans and shakes her head.

"You know Quincy and Tony?" I ask, feeling a little irritated by her calling them absurdly gorgeous. Only I can say that about them...could say it about them.

"Know them? Hell, if I had my way, Quincy would've been Meghan's daddy."

"Gross," Meghan and I complain at the same time.

Meghan's mom arches her eyebrows and lets them fall. "So," she continues. "What've you told them so far...my former best friend?"

"Former...?" Meghan and I say again at the same time. "...you guys were best friends?" I stare at Meghan, and she looks right back at me. I take it that she knew about as much about this as I did.

"Yep," mom replies with her patented arms over her chest stance.

"What happened?" we say in unison again.

Meghan's mom looks at her. "I'll give you a hint," she starts. "...six-one...hundred and eighty-five pounds of brown haired, green-eyed gorgeousness with a stare that's probably responsible for the polar ice caps melting."

"Quincy," we whisper at the same time. I cut my eyes to Meghan...she does the same. *He's mine...back off, Blondie!* Stephen groans and turns his back on Meghan. He walks over to the doors. Is he leaving? Is it that bad between them?

"We hadn't really said anything," mom says, answering Mrs. Powers's question. "I asked her what she knew...and clearly you didn't tell her much."

"About as much as you told yours...being all Claimed and all," she counters. Wow, I thought Meghan and I had issues.

"Um, we just came to find out about Meghan's," Alex says and then looks at me. "...um...glamour?" I nod to verify.

"Right," mom and Meghan's mom say at the same time. "First of all," her mom continues. "I...am not human. I am a Mage-Warrior Elf...like my mother and grandmother before me." Meghan frowns. "And like my daughter is now." Meghan seems a little lost...okay...so, a lot lost. Who can blame her though? "And despite what some people in this room believe," she continues, glowering at mom. "I did not marry your father because he was a White Witch."

"A WHAT?" I snap at the same time Meghan does.

Mom steps forward. "Yep, Matthew Charles Powers was a very powerful Witch of Light, just like his sister, Maria is."

"I-I knew that her Aunt Maria was," I stutter. "...I had no idea that your dad was, too."

Meghan sighs, looks away, and her eyes flutter. "You don't talk about him," she whispers. "You NEVER talk about him. It's always about whatever guy you're dating this month."

"Because," her mom replies. "...talking about Matthew hurts too much. I date a lot of guys...because none of them compare to your father." She walks over to Meghan and hugs her.

"So, what does this have to do with my...glamour?" Meghan asks and wipes her eyes.

"Admittedly, when I first started dating your father, I," she breaks off and bobs her head. "...only did because I was hoping that he could kick start my powers again."

"Kick start your powers?" Stephen asks. Meghan's mom looks at him and nods.

"Yes." She steps closer to Meghan. "See, your great-great-grandmother fought and defeated the dark witch, Bethany il Cuore Nero."

"Bethany?" Alex whispers. He shakes his head. "Should that name mean something to us?"

"Bethany il Cuore Nero," Meghan's mom repeats. "Don't you kids do your homework?" She motions as if it is something, they should come to...but unlike me...they weren't brought up on bedtime stories about the great Witch of Light Covens or the Fairy Queen and her one-hundred seven children.

"You never told me anything about any of this," Meghan grumbles.

"Human," Stephen says.

"Just learned that my father was a skinwalker while dating my kitsune girlfriend a few months ago," Alex explains.

I figure I should prove that my whole generation of supernaturals isn't completely lost. "It was a pretty epic battle," I start. "...in the supernatural world." Meghan, Alex, and Stephen stare at me as if I'm their drunk uncle who just fell down the backstairs. "In pop culture terms, it'd be like if Taylor Swift, playing the part of Meghan's ancestor, and Katy Perry, filling the role of Bethany the Black Hearted, had a grudge match live on television." Meghan and Stephen nod.

"Okay, did you understand a single word of that?" Meghan's mom asks. Mom shrugs and shakes her head. "Point being," she continues. "Bethany il Cuore Nero or Bethany Triste was bad...tried to conquer the world using dark magic bad. My great-grandmother Evangeline of the Light..." I can hear the reverence in her voice, despite the fact that she mixes it with pride. "...went toe-to-toe with Bethany. She won, but the fight drained her powers to the point that even her children were left nearly powerless."

"And you thought hooking up with my dad would give you your powers back?"

"No." She rushes over to Meghan. "No, I thought it would give you, your children, and your children's children their powers back." Meghan scoffs and moves past her mother, heading for the door. "I was wrong...not wrong about the powers thing because honey you shine brighter than our bloodline has in generations."

Meghan growls at her mother and cuts one of those *if only I had something sharp* looks at her. "I was wrong because of why I approached your father, but the more I got to know him, the more in love with him I fell." Meghan reaches for the doorknob. Her mother catches her free hand. "If you believe anything, believe that I loved your father with my heart and soul."

"Whatever," Meghan murmurs while opening the door. She slams it behind her.

Her mother goes over to Stephen. "Well, you're her boyfriend, right?" She points at the door. "Go after her!"

"Ooooo," Alex and I moan at the same time.

"What?"

"She broke up with me," Stephen says. "She thought that her glamour made me like her, sooooo…"

"You're kidding, right?" Stephen frowns and walks toward the door. Alex steals a glance at me and follows him. I follow Alex.

Alex, fists clenched, stops at the door. He turns to Meghan's mom. "That was kind of harsh. They've been arguing ever since they broke-"

"That's just it," she interrupts. "If they've been arguing…if he does anything, besides exactly what she wants him to do…then her glamour, isn't affecting him." She watches as the door closes behind Stephen. "And I'm guessing that's because she feels the same way about him."

The door opens again. Stephen stomps in muttering something. He walks over to the couch and falls onto it. He rocks back and then forth. He stares at the floor in front of him. Alex, having watched the entire performance, goes over to the door. He pulls it open. "Crap," he grumbles. I move to follow, but his outstretched hand stops me, even though, he steps out into the vestibule.

I turn to Stephen and motion to the doors. "What's going on?"

He flails his arm in that direction. "She's out there talking to the tall one."

"The tall one?"

"Yeah, Mrs. Powers."

"Stephen, I told you, you can just call me, Anne."

Stephen nods and nibbles his lower lip, while wrenching his hands. Oddly, I feel like doing the exact same thing. I mean, Meghan's…well, Meghan, and she's chatting up Quincy…my Quincy. He's not my Quincy. He's…crap, Stephen's staring at me.

"You look like I feel," he whispers. I cross my arms over my stomach and look away.

"Another McCabe witch under their spell, huh?" Anne asks and nudges me with her elbow.

"Um, no," I snap. "I'm a Baggett witch…my name's not Jamie McCabe! It's Jamina Lynda Baggett…Baggett!"

"Oh, she's all attitude like you were, Daphne," Anne says like a complaint.

"Tell me about it," mom replies with just as much venom. I groan. Great, best friends reunited. Yay.

"I'm gonna go check on Meghan and Alex," I say…and I just lied. At least, it wasn't to Quincy…just about him. I want to see if Meghan's making any progress with him. I sigh and take the door handle with my left hand while clutching the Crescent Moon Pendant in my right. Quincy's angry…so is Tony…but that's a constant lately. I snatch the door open.

"…sit around discussing with my brother about how much I'm in love with the girl he's in love with," Alex says to Quincy as I step into the vestibule. Quincy looks as though he's about to break Alex in half…and Meghan looks as though she's going to swoon…yes, swoon like a proper Southern Belle…the second he does. Quincy does that fast-moving thing and steps over to Alex.

"What are you guys doing?" I ask, trying to stop any of that from happening. Quincy sighs and looks me over. I mouth, *stop it*. He frowns but nods and relaxes his stance. *Thank you.* He smiles. I look at Alex… "ANSWER ME!" I say, moving over to him.

"Nothing," Quincy whispers.

"Nothing at all," Alex says.

"Good." I point my accusing finger at Quincy and then at Alex. "Meghan, your mom wants you," I say, while motioning to the library. Quincy puts his hand over his heart. *Sorry*, I mouth. He nods.

Meghan walks over to the library door. She turns in the doorway and blows a kiss to and then waves at Quincy. Ugh, right in the stomach…feels like she just punched me right in the stomach. She steps inside. I sigh. "And you two," I start with another point. "Don't make me come back out here!" I grab the Crescent Moon Pendant and aim it at Quincy like a weapon. He nods. I aim at Alex. He does too.

I move back to the library door and push it open. "Wait," Alex says. I pause. I half-turn and Quincy returns to Alex…still on the stairs…six stairs up. He's still mad at Alex's cheap shot. "Sorry." I sigh in relief. "About all that crap I said. It wasn't for you…" Alex tilts his head in my direction. I duck behind the door. "It was for her." For me?

"Don't worry about me and Jamie," Quincy returns. My heart skipped a beat when he mentioned my name. "We're…"

"Not you and Jamie," Alex interrupts. "It was for Meghan. She…tends to fall for the wrong guy."

"What makes you so sure that I'm the wrong guy?" My jaw tenses…and tears fill my eyes instantly. Does he like her…?

"Should I start with the way your heart skipped a beat when you heard Jamie's voice," Alex poses. "…or with the fact that you went from fighting mad to cool as a cucumber with one question from her?" Quincy draws his lips into his mouth and nods. "She told me, you know? About everything with…you and your brother." Quincy walks down until he's directly in front of Alex. "That's not why I stopped you though."

"Then why…?" Quincy asks, still trying to hide some of his anger. I hold the Crescent Moon Pendant in both hands… he sighs and relaxes a little more.

"I wanted to know about that Rais-guy." I frown. Great, even Alex has a problem with him. It's not as if he tried to kill any of them. "What's Jamie's connection to him?"

"Did she tell you about the fight we got into with the dark witch and the higher order daemons?" Alex shakes his head. "Wow, she didn't tell you about that?" He does again. "Well, you do know that she was looking for her mom, right?"

"Yeah, she found her right after we gave her that crystal to hold on to."

"Well, her mom was mixed up in something bad. We had to rush in and save her and her mom from a dark witch and five daemons. Rais was one of the daemons."

"Rais is a daemon? That's weird because there was something so familiar about him."

"It's probably that whole all skinwalkers are kin thing."

"What are you talking about?"

"Rais, he's a skinwalker…like you." I swallow a lump. Alex is not a daemon… he can't be… I refuse to believe that. "You didn't know that?" Alex shakes his head. "Yeah, he does this weird wolf transformation…he has fur all around his neck, chest, and forearms and long claws and teeth."

"He's a wolf?" Quincy nods again. "I…"

"LIKE YOU WOULD KNOW!" Meghan shouts moving past me and back out into the vestibule. I move into the library just in time for Stephen to catch the door, pull it open and follow her. "DON'T FOLLOW ME!"

"I WOULDN'T HAVE TO FOLLOW YOU IF YOU DIDN'T KEEP WALKING AWAY FROM ME!"

"LEAVE ME ALONE!" She pulls the front door open.

"HARD TO DO WHEN YOU'RE MY RIDE!" Stephen follows her outside.

I look on with an agape mouth. Quincy catches me standing in the door. I gasp…spotting Tony on the stairs just above the landing. He's fuming. He looks down on his brother and then at me. He has the journal in his hand.

Anne steps out of the library and goes over to stand next to Alex. She whispers something to him, and my eyes go back to the top of the stairs, where Tony was. Quincy follows my line of sight before coming back to me. I frown and step back into the library.

"Hey," mom says. "I'm heading out."

"You didn't even bother taking your bag upstairs?"

"You knew I was leaving as soon as this whole thing was over with and you know why. It's important." I nod. "Come here, cranky pants." She opens her arms wide. I purse my lips and walk over to her. She wraps her arms around me. "I know everything's been crazy since this all started…" I nod and slip my arms under hers. "…and I know that…" She pauses. Her head bobs against mine. "…things have got your emotions all over the place." We separate. "But never forget that I'm your mother, I love you…and I'll do anything to protect you."

"Cause that's what mother's do," I recite the same thing she told me every night for five years straight after dad died. She nods and caresses my cheek then kisses me on the center of my forehead.

"Even misguided elf mothers who connive their way into a husband."

"Mom," I sigh and shove her shoulder. She laughs. "Be safe, okay? And tell Maria I said 'Hey,' thanks for her help, and I hope she finds Angela safe and sound." Mom nods and grabs her bag. She wheels it over to the door and steps out.

#####

Chapter 5: Spell

I sigh, wondering if Meghan and Stephen are still arguing. Before I can open the door, it pushes in on me. Quincy steps in and stares at me with serious eyes. I arch my eyebrows. "It's time," he says.

"Time? Time for what?"

"We're doing the spell now," Tony says, shoving past his brother. He moves to the center of the room before turning back to Quincy. The corners of Quincy's mouth turn down as he pushes the door closed behind him.

I point to the door. "What about Alex and…?"

"Everybody left," Quincy says. "Your mom took your car and headed to the airport." My car…? Right, dad's car…now my car. Like I can drive…okay, I can, but I still don't have my license. "Alex got a text and had to leave, and Meghan and Stephen went with him." He steps away from the door with a clenched jaw. "And I asked Anne to leave." He glances at me over his shoulder. "Quickly."

"What happened between you…and her…and my mom…?" His eyes go distant and he shakes his head. "Quincy…?"

"We're ready," Tony says. I march past Quincy, not forgetting that I'm a little mad at him for almost fighting my best friend and not telling me what's going on. Tony stands on the far side of the desk while Quincy and I stand on the door side. He places a large clay bowl on the desktop. "Alright," Tony starts. "We each have to put a drop of our blood into this bowl."

"Why?"

"It's a part of the spell."

"This sounds like blood magic…you know, dark magic…"

"It probably is," Quincy says.

"But," Tony jumps in. "The spell that binds each of us to you…spans your entire bloodline. We have to separate the three…the two of us from your line."

"Wait, will that…" I motion between them. "…separate you two."

"Our bond is our blood," Quincy explains, sounding clinical. It actually hurts my heart to hear either one of them talk about their family ties that way. I look at Tony…he sighs and looks off to the side. I mean, we're in their father's house…and… "Are you sure you want to do this?"

"If it's what you guys really want." Tony takes a letter opener from the desktop. He pricks his left pointer finger. He holds his finger over the bowl until a drop falls. He passes the letter opener to his brother. Quincy pricks his right pointer finger and repeats after his brother. I hold my right hand out, waiting for the letter opener. Quincy takes my wrist in his left hand…and pricks my pointer finger. I gasp and stare into his eyes. He moves my hand over the bowl…the drop trickles over my finger and down into the bowl.

He holds my finger up to his mouth. "Thank you…for this," he whispers. I nod. "Sano." My finger heals. Tony collects the bowl and marches around the table. Quincy lets go of my hand and places the letter opener on the desk.

"We need to form a triangle around the bowl," Tony says, standing between us. Quincy and I take appropriate positions. "Good. Now Jamie, repeat after me…" I nod and watch him carefully. "…caeruleo per spiritus grandis Aquilonis…" By the Great Blue Spirit of the North. "…Per spiritus Austri mag…" By the Great White Spirit of the South. "…Niger a malevolis occidentis…" By the Malevolent Black Spirit of the West. "…Benigna est, rufus erat, per spiritus ab oriente…" By the Benevolent Red Spirit of the East. "…Aurea, per caelum…" By the Golden Spirit in the Sky. "…In scelerisque spiritum super terram…" By the Russet Spirit of the Earth. "…Non opus auxilio decernimus…" I decree that I need no protection. "…confirmatum est cor meum. Mihi certum est. Fortitudo mea, et miserere mei…" My heart is strong. My mind is clear. My power is great. "…et de pueris meis libera. Cor. Corpus. Cave. Spiritus. Volutpat!" I free my servants. Servants? Heart. Body. Mind. Spirit. Release!

I recite the words just as he said them. "Repeat," he says as my magic swirls around us. I do. I peer into the bowl and…the three drops of blood pool together. "Repeat." I do and as I do, the blood starts to pull in three directions. But they said that… "Repeat." I do…and…

"Ugh," I groan, feeling my power drain away.

"Jamina?" Quincy says.

"Jamie, are you alright?" Tony asks.

"Yeah…but…" Something else swirls around us. It's not my magic…but it's powerful! How could something get through the barrier without us knowing about it? "…something's off. We should…" I feel weak suddenly. "…we should…"

"She's falling," Quincy says as everything spins around me and fades to black. "Jamina!" He sounds so far away.

"Jamie," Tony says, but it sounds like a distant whisper…and then laughter…a girl's laughter and…

#####

Chapter 6: Awakening

I moan. I must've passed out. I guess that spell drained me more than I thought. "Jamie?" Alex? I guess I should've said that aloud. My eyes flutter before opening.

"Alex?" I whisper as he leans into view. He nods. "What's going on? What are you doing here?"

"You don't even know where here is, Red," he jokes.

I frown and sit up. He moves back. An apartment...? The living room...long vertical blinds covering a window, a brown oval-shaped coffee table, and a chair with interlacing black, dark gray and light gray stitching that matches the couch on which I'm lying. The faintest hint of potpourri hangs in the air. The plain white walls...have no wards, spells, or protection sigils.

"Okay, you win. I have no clue where I am." Alex stares at me as if I might break any minute. "Where am I and how did I get here?"

"She's awake?" a voice calls from my left and the kitchen. The rectangular wall opening hints at a blurry, off-white refrigerator door that moves slightly. Where are my glasses?

"Yeah," Alex says. "I guess she just needed to get away from that house."

"What are you guys talking about? Why did you need to get me away from that house...? I mean, I kind of live there..." I bob my head unevenly. "...for now, at least." Ugh, there's a hitch in my back...feels like I slept on a brick...and my neck, tension knot the size of my fist. I groan while stretching both. "And why am I so stiff?"

A blur of blue and red topped off by blond hair jumps over my head and sits on the coffee table next to Alex. I frown, staring into his blue eyes...trying to place where I know him. "Kai?" I ask, while pointing at him. He nods. I look over his blue jacket over red hoodie. His swoop of blonde hair remains so perfect that it seems painted onto his head. "Nice job on the growing up. You're a little cutie."

"Thank ya," he breathes, biting into a huge slice of pizza. "You too..." He points at my chest with his slice. "...keep this up and you'll be as top heavy as your mom." I cover my chest with my arms as Alex smacks Kai across his arm. "What?" He bites the pizza again, and Alex gives him a *what do you mean what* open arm gesture.

I clear my throat. "Alex, what's going on?"

"Um," he starts and draws his lips into his mouth. He frowns...his eyebrows come together making that funny indention between his eyes.

"Oh, just say it," I whine, recognizing his face when he doesn't know how to say something…and being thankful that it hasn't changed since we were in the sandbox.

"Jamie…" Uh oh, serious tone. "What's the last thing you remember?"

"What do you mean?"

"What's the last thing you remember before waking up a minute ago?"

I shake my head and my mind goes over the party…and Rais…and mom…and… "Me and my mom talked to you guys about Meghan's glamour…and then…" I groan again, trying to clear my head. "…a spell? I was helping Quincy and Tony cast a spell."

"What kind of spell?" Kai asks, sounding serious this time.

My eyes dart between them. The corners of my mouth turn down. "You can tell us," Alex assures. I know I can…I just don't want to. "Please."

I nod. "Tony said he found a spell that could…break the curse. The spell was supposed to…stop them from loving me." I shiver.

"Is that even possible?" Kai asks. Alex looks at him and then me. "I mean spells that affect people's emotions…they're rare…and one that counteracts a curse at the same time?" Alex stares at him. "What? Every once in a while, I listen to Sora, because she actually says something useful."

"Right," I moan. "He's right. I didn't think it would work, but…they wanted it so bad and I…" I trail off. I can't…

"You still love them?" Alex supposes. I nod. "A lot of that going around."

"I guess, the spell…it felt wrong when it activated." I shake my head. "I knew I should've stopped but, I didn't…and it drained me. I passed out…and woke up here."

"Well, I don't know what happened with the spell," Alex starts again. "But…the Blackshears' party was three weeks ago."

"WHAT?"

Kai bobs his head. "We got back the day after that…because Alex got attacked by some ghouls or something. We've been here over two weeks."

I swallow deeply. It can't be…I mean, even if the spell drained me, it couldn't have knocked me out for three weeks, could it?

"Are you okay?" Alex poses. I shake my head. "I wish the answer to that was *yeah* because there's more." I groan and lean against the backrest; a few curly strands tickle the side of my face. I push my hair back, wishing I had a hair band to put it up in a ponytail. I motion for Alex to give it to me. He nods. "The brothers…Quincy and Tony have…um, have kind of lost it since whatever happened happened."

"What? Are they okay? They're not hurt, or anything are they?"

"Well, Tony's face is," Kai snickers. I frown.

"They've been attacking us," Alex admits. "It's weird…they seem weird…even for what I know about them."

They must have kept me asleep. That's why I was out for three weeks…not because of how much the spell drained me. It must have had the opposite effect. It made them hate me. I shiver…they hate me…no, they can't. If they hated me…they could've killed me at any time instead of keeping me asleep and…

"Jamie," Alex calls. I blink quickly, staring at him. "You okay?" I nod. "Better," he hums, even though I'm sure he knows I lied.

"So…how bad are they?" I ask, feeling weirdly guilty for having cast the stupid spell.

"They're keeping up the school thing," Kai says. "As far as I can tell they've been covering for you, too."

"Oh," I moan as Alex nods in agreement. I swallow another massive lump of guilt. They do still care about me. So, what happened during the spell…? Whatever that bad feeling was…it was real, and it's what's making them attack my friends.

"They still care about you," Alex says as if he can hear my thoughts. "Every time I said your name…they flinched…like they were hurt by hearing it."

I nod and instantly reach for the Crescent Moon Pendant…thankful that I still have it.

"That woman, Zoë," Alex starts again. "…told us to make sure you had that…it was hanging from your bedpost." I nod and look down at it. "Do you think maybe something's controlling them? Making them do this stuff?" he continues reading my mind.

"Don't know, don't care." I lift my eyes from the pendant. "I'm too busy being pissed at them to…" The doorbell rings interrupting me. Alex and Kai freeze. They look at each other.

"Is that…?" Alex poses as Kai takes a deep sniff. Alex tilts his head to the door and then leans in closer to Kai, who shrugs. Alex frowns and stands slowly. I focus on the pendant at the tips of my fingers.

"No," I sigh. "They're not even close to here." Alex looks at me as the doorbell rings again. "I…just know…okay?" I answer his unasked question. He arches his eyebrows. "We can sense each other through this pendant." Alex stares at it for a second as if…I want to say as if he knows who is behind it…but it's more as if it's calling to him. The ringing becomes forceful knocking. "Your mom, maybe?"

"At work and then checking on my grandma down in Georgia. Besides, she has a key."

"Your sister…?"

"Sora's still at school," Kai returns without looking. Alex swallows deeply.

"So...are we just gonna sit here staring at the door?" I ask. Alex looks at Kai and nods. He takes my glasses from the coffee table behind him and slips them over my ears, being careful to avoid snagging my hair. "Thanks," I breathe as they settle near the bridge of my nose.

He nods. They walk around the sofa, and I move to stand up, while adjusting my glasses. Alex holds his hand out to me in a halting way. I nod but perch on my knees and lean against the backrest so that I can see who it is.

Alex reaches the door and freezes. My eyebrows come together. He pulls the door open with one quick jerk and... "RAIS?" I call.

"Bunny!" he returns and vanishes. He reappears a step or two away from the sofa, as if he's unsure that I'm real. Kai and Alex are behind him in a second. I hold my hand up to Alex to stop him this time. Rais peers over his shoulder. "Well," he says with a casual sort of cool. "Look who went and got interesting." Alex frowns and tilts his head anxiously. "Good for you," he moans before bringing his attention back to me. "Where've you been, Bunny? I was worried about you."

"Oh, you know," I try to return with the same casualness. "Did a big spell...took a really long nap..." I push my mop of hair up on the side. "...woke up with killer bed head."

Rais steps closer. Alex practically growls. I glare at Alex with large eyes. "I see your friends didn't believe you when you told them that you trusted me," Rais says.

"How do you know that I said I trusted you?"

He points at the Crescent Moon Pendant...in my hands...again. I drop it and let it fall over my heart. "I can feel your faith in me through that." I swallow deeply. Rais takes another step. He's directly in front of me now...he lifts his left hand like he's going to caress my cheek. "I found that after not...sensing you for a while...I was worried about you, Bunny. More than I thought I would." He pauses just before his hand would've made contact and lowers it. He swallows deeply. "If not for that stupid barrier around their house, I would've come to check on you."

"I'm fine, Rais," I breathe. "Awww, you were worried?"

"Don't mock my feelings, Bunny!"

"I-I wasn't...I mean it. It's sweet...thank you."

He nods. "Well, I just wanted to make sure that you were okay...and since I'm intruding in your friend's home...your friend, whose adrenaline is building even now. I should go." He taps my hand, resting on the couch's backrest.

"Okay," I whisper. "Thank you for coming to check on me." He cups my right hand, draws it up to his mouth, and kisses the back. I smile. He lets go and turns toward the door. Alex glares at him. "Alex…let him go by."

"It's okay," Rais hums, staring at Alex. "He's interesting now…so…it's to be expected."

"Why am I interesting now?" Alex grumbles. "Last time you saw me, you couldn't have cared less about me."

"You're wrong," Rais replies. "I could've cared less…" He smiles. "…but now…you've awakened…you're like me."

"Is that true?" I ask. Rais nods. "Are skinwalkers…really daemons?" He turns those blue-gray marbles to me and smirks. "No," I moan, like a child hearing something they don't want to hear.

"I'm sorry, Bunny, but it's true," Rais says. "We…skinwalkers are daemons…or at least, our animal forms were daemons. We were cursed by the 2nd Fairy Queen to roam the earth in human form…until we…" He makes air quotes. "'…find ourselves.'" He bobs his head unevenly. "Who knew she meant literally?"

I shake my head. Rais stares at me. "If it means anything to you…" He glances at Alex. "…and you." He comes back to me. "Most fae don't know what to think of us anymore. We spent so many centuries…our ancestors…spent so many centuries living as normal humans." I sigh. "And labels only matter…if you let them…Bunny." I nod and scoff a silent laugh.

Rais slips his hands into his pockets and moves toward the door. "I'll keep an eye out for you, Bunny." He pulls the door open. "And I'll be in touch, cousin," he says to Alex…just to Alex. He vanishes. The door drifts closed behind him.

"He's gone," I whisper. Alex and Kai turn back to me with just as much confusion on their faces as I'm guessing I had when I woke up here. I motion toward the door. "How did things get so crappy that the guy who almost killed me last year is more worried about me than the two guys, who…?" I sigh. What if it DID work on them, and they were just keeping me alive for…?

Alex grabs my hand, probably noticing my bout of depression. "What do you want to do?"

I wipe under my eyes, just in case. "Well," I start…standing…and Alex is there to catch my arm…because of my wobbly legs. "Thanks." He nods. "First, I want to ward this house so that nobody else can just walk in without your permission." Alex nods again. "Second, I'm going to ask my oldest friend…if I can stay with him until my mom gets back to town."

"Bet," Alex says.

"Perfect timing, too," Kai says. "Your mom's going out of town so…"

"So," Alex picks up. "You can sleep in her room," he says, motioning toward the hallway. I nod. "Sora already kicked me out of my room." I laugh…until everything hits me, again…I try to fight of the tears welling in my eyes…over that stupid spell…and… Alex wraps me up. "You're okay…you're okay." I nod and put my arms under his. "You're okay."

"Yeah," I sigh, faking another laugh as we separate. At least, I managed not to cry. "Okay," I say taking a step back. "I should get started on those wards. Come here," I add, taking Alex's hand. I take him to the front door and open it.

"What are you…?"

"Shhhhh," I issue while placing his hand on the outside of the door. I make a circle around his hand. "Et oppilatæ claudatur a sanguine," I say and make another circle around his hand. "Now, no one can open your door except me…or a direct blood relation."

"What about me?" Kai asks.

"You're his first cousin. The only way you'd be more direct would be if you were his brother." Kai nods. "Same goes for your mom and Sora, too." Alex nods. "But…that means Gwen can't come and go either."

"No problem there," he lies.

"Don't be that guy, Alex," I say and step away from him.

"What guy?" He pushes the door closed.

"That guy who gets his feelings hurt and then acts like it's no big deal." He slips his hands into his pockets. "If you want to be the other guy…the guy who talks about how miserable his…" My head tilts to the left. "…ex-girlfriend…?" He nods. "…is making him…I'll be here to listen." I yawn. "I'm gonna call Zo' and see if she'll bring me some clothes." I pause. "She's okay, right? They didn't…"

"She's fine," Kai says. I nod and sigh in relief. "She let us into the house and led us to you."

"Good. I'm glad she's…" I yawn again. "…crap," I complain. Alex catches me, just as I wobble again.

"Are you okay? Should we take you to…?"

"No, I'm fine. I'm a little magic wiped." Alex lowers me onto the sofa. "Apparently, when they put me in suspended animation…I'm assuming since I don't have any IV punctures, and I'm not hungry…it was right after I did the spell." I touch my forehead. "I'm exhausted."

"Here," Alex says. "Dial Zoë's number." Is this a house phone? Where's his…? I try to ask…but my eyelids feel so freakin' heavy. I punch in her number and…

#####

Chapter 7: Grief

"Crap," I moan. "I fell asleep again." I sit up, look around the darkened room and check the sheets...and my clothes. Two boys, best friend or not, were here when I fell asleep so, I'm hoping...I breathe easy...same shirt, same pants...minus shoes. I nod and climb out of bed. I move slowly over to the door...that I can only make out thanks to the light coming from underneath. I open it.

Alex sits on the sofa, phone to his ear. His head is down, and he's caressing his temple with his other hand. "Yeah," he moans. "Okay. Talk soon...I love you too." He ends the call and tosses his phone on the coffee table.

"Hey, Alex thanks for..." He looks at me...and tears are streaming down his face. "...Alex? What's wrong?" I rush to his side and sit.

"That was my mom," he says with a weak voice. "The reason she hadn't heard from my grandma in a while..." He swallows deeply, and I can actually hear the dryness in his throat. "...is because my grandma's dead."

"Oh no," I sigh and put my arms around him. He remains perfectly still.

"It's stupid," he moans, while shaking his head. "I hardly even knew her, you know?" I nod, my forehead pressed against his temple. "I mean, she was just this old lady, who sent me Christmas and birthday presents..." He lifts his right hand to let it fall feebly to his leg again. "...who...always seemed to know..." He leans away and looks at me. "I started drawing because when I was five, she sent me my first sketchpad and some charcoal pencils. My mom was pissed at her...because I, of course, wrote all over the walls...but grandma...she just told ma to gimme time...I'd figure it out..." I nod.

"...a few years ago...when my dad died...she came to the funeral." He wipes his eyes. "I remember thinking she was sooooooo...weird...but in a good way, you know?" He sighs. "The Christmas after that...she sent me an easel...and some paint..." More tears fall from his eyes. "...it's like she just freakin' knew the whole time...like she knew me better than I did...and now...now she's gone too." He crumbles. I pull his head to my shoulder and he wraps one arm around my waist.

"It's okay, Alex...let it out..." He sobs openly...and I feel all the pain of everyone I've ever lost come rushing to the surface too...my dad...my grandma...even Alex's dad...and before I know it. I'm crying right along with him.

#####

Chapter 8: Approach

Dear Alex,

I sigh and stare at the two pathetic little words at the top of the email. *Dear Alex,* what…? What can I possibly say to him right now? I pull my knees up to my chest and wrap both arms around them. I stare at Kai's laptop…the little silver thing with way more RAMs and Gigs than mine could even pretend to have. "You're just trying to distract yourself, you lame wad," I say as a complaint.

Why wouldn't I? Alex has been gone for over two weeks already…I think I actually miss him more now than when he was still under my stupid memory spell. Probably because then, I could still see him at school…and I had my mom around…but she's still in New York trying to find a spell that will help her track down Meghan's cousin, Angela. I would actually answer her texts and calls with something besides, *Fine,* if I didn't think she'd drop the search for the missing witch to come and help me out of a mess that I got myself into. "And you're still trying to distract yourself," I say, while playing with the fingers on my left hand.

"Alex. Alex. Alex…what can I say to you?"

"You can tell him you love him," Kai says over my shoulder.

"Get out of here," I say with a whine and shove him away. I can't believe how nice he and Sora have been to me. They let me stay here…they brought me food…and they've acted like my eyes and ears while my strength came back.

Something in that spell held onto some of my magic. Little by little, it came back. I clench my right hand into a fist. "Extermino," I say and open my hand…a little candle-sized flame appears in the center of my palm.

"That is so cool," Kai says from the coffee table.

"Actually, it's kind of hot," Sora says in all her flannel and jean-covered, golden tanned skin with the blonde model vibe glory.

I laugh. "It's the first spell my mom taught me." I bob my head. "Successfully taught me. She tried a water spell first because most people try the harmless spells first." I shake my head and close my fist. "Aqua," I say and open my hand…I concentrate on generating water…moisture from the air pulls together into a small grape-sized bubble. I smile. "It didn't take.

"Next, she tried wind…" I close my hand around the water grape. "…ventulus." I open my hand slowly…swirling my fingers around the water, turning it into a tiny waterspout. It is a miniature version of the one Siemon almost used to drown me. I lift my eyes from it and look at Sora. She smirks and looks at Kai. He smiles outright, fascinated by the cyclone of water.

That spell took something out of me…but the aftereffect replaced it with something else…control. I don't even feel slightly drained from doing three spells back to back.

"We're headed to school," Sora says. "Are you sure you don't want to wait on…?"

"No," I say. "Today's the day…I need to go see my boys. I got this." She nods.

"They haven't been to school all week," Kai says. "We've been keeping an eye on Meghan, Gwen, and Stephen just in case."

"Don't know why we're watching that stupid, lying-ass kitsune's back," Sora says.

I close my hand over the cyclone. "Because, despite what she did…or how she acted…Alex still cares about her…and she did save his life." Sora sighs…I take that as a concession.

I open my hand and the water evaporates on its own. I look up again and their staring…again. "I'll be fine. Seriously. I'll catch a cab out to the estate, and I'll go and talk to them."

"Yeah," Sora says while turning toward the door. "I hope you talk a lightning bolt right up their asses. My insurance is through the roof because of my jeep." She pulls the front door open. Kai laughs, shakes his head, and follows her. He waves without looking back.

"Later," I say as the door closes behind them. I can't help wondering if they're being so nice to me because they think Alex and I are destined…as my mom used to say. Alex…I come back to the laptop screen. What am I going to say to him? I sigh. This might even be my last time to say anything to him…if Quincy and Tony are as bad as they say.

Alex's grandma left a will stating that she wanted to be buried next to Alex's grandfather down in Georgia. He stayed with his mom while she set up all the funeral arrangements, through the burial, of course, while she settled the estate…that turned out to be A LOT…and then trying to sell her cabin and her land…that also turned out to be A LOT. That was the last thing he told me…almost a week ago. He hasn't been on his instant messenger since then. I could call…or text…but what if he's in the middle of something important. My eyes flutter. As if possibly telling your best friend, since you were four, *good-bye* isn't important.

I lean forward like I'm going to type again…and nothing…I did say *like* I was going to type. What do you say to someone in this situation? ***Hey buddy, I know you're mourning your grandma, but just giving you a heads up…you may have to mourn me, too.*** I scoff. I'd probably say more than his ex…***I'm sorry for your loss.*** What the hell kind of crap is that? I mean, come on! That's what you say to someone that you barely know…not…I sigh. "You're distracting yourself again."

I place my hands on the keyboard:

Dear Alex,

I miss you, I love you, and I'm thinking of you.

Love,
Jamie

I press send and close the laptop. Smart. Keep it simple. I put my feet down and slip them into my boots. I stand and check my jeans and shirt. I guess I'm ready. I'm half-expecting a fight, so I should probably pull my hair up into a ponytail.

I move into the bathroom and stare at myself. My color's come back…and my hair is shinier. Still a bushy mop, but at least now, it's a shiny bushy mob of red curls. I pick up my hair band. I pull my hair back and let a few curly strands dangle around my face. I pull the bundle into a ponytail.

It's weird…I mean, it seems as if my magic rested during my forced hibernation, even though my body didn't. When it came back in full force, it, kind of, replenished my body, too. I feel stronger. That makes sense in away. My mom made sure that magic has always been a part of my life…my magic was a light that was always switched on. It got almost three weeks off. Now…I lift my eyes to the mirror again…the mirror covered in a sheet of ice.

I look next to the toothbrush cup…and there's the Crescent Moon Pendant. I took it off because I figured they could track me through it, but now, I'm going to them. I slip it over my head, maneuvering it around my ponytail puff. I feel them through it…as I always have.

I smirk and come back to the fully thawed mirror.

I hear a horn blare. I hurry out of the bathroom and grab my dark blue denim jacket from the back of the sofa. I slip my arms through it while hurrying over to the door. I step outside and pull the door closed behind me. The seal I made with Alex appears. No need for a key when you have a sealing spell. I hurry downstairs and over to the yellow taxi.

I file in, "Sorry for the wait." The driver nods causing his black Kangol to bob up and down. I guess those hats really are a trademark cabbie look. "1346 Guardian Trail," I say.

"I know that place…are you sure…?"

"Yes," I cut him off. "I know it's out in the boonies, and I know if you leave me out there, I might get stuck with no cell reception." He catches my eyes in the rearview mirror. "I'll be fine. Trust me." He nods and pulls away.

I grab the Crescent Moon Pendant...and play with it absently. I can't help wondering what went wrong. I mean, it seemed like a simple enough spell. It sounded like it had some Native American influence...the Red Spirit of the East...believed to be the benevolent spirit...the protector. You would pray for him to watch over and protect your family, friends, and your tribe.

Then there's the Shadow or Black Spirit of the West...he's basically death personified...you pray for him to strike down your enemies. Weird to hear both of their names called on in the same spell. It probably called on opposing forces to separate...to separate Quincy and Tony from how they feel about me. I never asked if it was supposed to separate me from how I felt about them. Because if that's what it was supposed to do... I look over the interior of the crescent. ...it didn't work.

"We're here," the driver says. I nod and reach for the door handle. "Uh, miss...I could...um...open the gate for you...maybe drive you up to...I hope, the house?" I open the door and laugh.

"No...thank you. How much?" He looks around at all the nothing past the gate and then the nothing stretching down the road in both directions. "I'll be fine. Really. My...boyfriend and his brother live here...they're what you'd call...a little bit reclusive.

"I'll say." He looks around the fence. "It'll be 13 bucks."

I grind my teeth, staring at the ten and five-dollar bills that Sora gave me. "Here," I say. "Keep it. I'm sorry the tip isn't better." He nods and heaves a heavy sigh. "Thanks for the ride," I say while sliding out of the taxi. I close the door and make my way over to the gate. I reach for it and pause. I turn and shoo him away. He waves and backs the taxi up...very slowly. He gets out into the street and pulls away just as slowly.

I push the heavy gate, and it swings open with a metallic groan and then whine. I extend my hand slowly past the threshold. Wow, Alex was right. They definitely strengthened the barrier, but compared to what mom can do, this is nothing. I'd destroy it, but I think I should go with stealth...at least, until I reach the house. I hold the Crescent Moon Pendant between my hands in front of my mouth. "Penetero. Pervagor. Praetego." I step forward with my hands still around the pendant in a praying fashion. As I move across the barrier, it feels more as if I'm diving into warm water. I pass through it with little more than the warm sensation.

"Dive in," I say, staring up the long gravel drive.

#####

Chapter 9: Resolve

I hurry up to the house pondering what I'm going to say to them…if I should attack first or wait. Along the way, I decide, re-evaluate, and come up with something completely different thirty times.

I reach the gravel-covered circle in front of the house. There's an old school, red mustang parked next to Tony's car. I guess Quincy finally got his car fixed. I walk past it, rubbing my left pointer finger from the hood to the trunk. I hate to admit it, but this is one sexy car.

I nod, take a deep breath, and stare at the front door. I've come and gone through this door dozens of times, but this is different. I walk over to it and lift my hand. I prepare to cast a fire spell and obliterate it…sigh…I lower my hand. I lift my hand to knock…sigh…I lower my hand. I lift my hand and place it against the door. The seal appears. I re-work its configuration like I did that one time out of anger, changing all the text to its opposite. Once I'm done, the door swings in on its own.

I step inside, half-expecting daemons to be swinging from the rafters. Nope, everything seems…normal. "I'm back!" I yell, trying to sound like a badass, but knowing I fell flat. I sounded more apprehensive than dangerous and that's because I am.

"Jamie?" Tony calls, stepping out of the library to my left. I turn to him as he walks toward me as if he doesn't believe I'm real.

"Jamina?" Quincy poses from the landing between the first and second floors. He steals a glance back up the stairs and comes back to me. He hurries down and rushes over at the same time Tony does.

"Whoa," I moan, while extending both hands to halt them. They do. "Not…one…step…closer." They frown and look at each other before coming back to me.

"What's wrong?" Quincy asks.

"Where've you been?" Tony questions.

I drop my hands weakly. "What do you mean where've I been? What have you two been up to since I was gone?" They frown and look at each other again. I point to Tony. "You…attacked Alex, his cousin, Kai, and Stephen!" Tony scowls. "You put Stephen in the hospital!"

I motion to Quincy. "And you tried to play Meghan, and you threatened Gwen!" His expression matches his brother's.

"You both nearly killed Gwen and Kai while they were trying to protect Alex! You know, Alex, my best friend from the sandbox, Alex!" Tony shakes his head and crosses his arms over his chest. Quincy slips his hands into his back pockets and looks down at the floor between us. "Oh, and don't let me forget…you placed ME in suspended animation!" They both look away from me, Tony peering to his right…Quincy looking to his left. "WHAT?"

"Jamina," Quincy says before lifting his head. "Yeah, we did those things…because you told us to."

"WHAT?"

Tony nods. "We only did everything we've done, because you asked us to."

"Why on God's green Earth would I ever ask you to attack my best friend…? Or, hurt Stephen and Meghan? Or put me…ME…into suspended animation?" Tony shrugs, being honest at least.

"We don't know," Quincy says. "I wanted to ask…but…" The corners of his mouth turn down. "…every time I tried to…nothing came out."

I shake my head. I tremble because I'm so angry right now!

"Besides," Tony says. "As far as the suspended animation…you were only down for a day." I glare at him as my mouth falls agape. I can't believe what I'm hearing. "You said your magic needed a recharge and…"

"Stop talking right now!" I say, extending my hand. "I was unconscious for three weeks…not one day…three weeks!"

"That's not possible," Quincy says. He scowls quizzically. He half-turns toward the stairs. "I was…just upstairs with you." My eyes dart to the stairs.

"You were what…?"

"Hey, Quincy," my voice calls from the second floor. "What happened?" she continues moving down to the landing…wearing my clothes…I gasp…and my face…but with straightened hair. "You said you heard something…holy crap…!!!" She stares at me as if I'm a ghost…or the devil himself. I scowl. Luckily for her, in this case, I might as well be the second one.

"WHO THE HELL ARE YOU?"

"I…I don't know what that thing is," she says, pointing at me. "But it's not me." She backs away slowly.

"Oh please, if you guys are going to fall for that damsel in distress crap…" They look at each other, then at me, and then back to fake me.

"SHE'S GOING TO KILL ME!" fake me screams.

They settle on me. "…I'm just going to have to kick both your asses!" Fake me smirks. "Oh, you're next, bitch!"

"Flamma," Quincy utters while extending his hand to me.

"Fulgur," Tony says almost at the same time.

"Expugnationis," I say, extending a hand toward each of them…with my pointer and middle fingers extended… Quincy's flames wrap around me…or my shield…Tony's lightning does the same. I quickly draw two tiny triangles on the perfect bubble surrounding me and add a pentagon on top of that.

Their magic covers the golden sphere before it draws the fire and lightning into it.

They look at me in shock. "Wait for it," I say. Quincy's fire whips out and knocks Tony through the library doors, causing them to explode into splinters. Tony's lightning throws Quincy against the wall behind him. He collides with it and falls to the floor. He twitches before falling unconscious.

I start to go to him…but my heart skips a beat thinking of Tony. I peer over my shoulder…he lies in the middle of the library floor. I used the most powerful shield spell I know and used a double reflexive configuration…the shield absorbed what they gave, tripled, and re-tripled it. I grasp the Crescent Moon Pendant. I inhale deeply. Both alive…both with steady, strong heartbeats.

I come back to the stairs. Fake me is gone. "Oh, now you wanna run!" I say, running after her. I reach the second floor. I look to the right and then the left. "You better not be in my room!" She steps out of the room at the end of the hall…out of Tony's room. "Wow, just when I thought seeing you with my face…and that stupid hair…made me as mad as I thought anything could."

She smirks. "Well, I guess I've done all I could do with this body."

"I've got some ideas about what to do with *that* body!" I say, while marching toward her.

"I wonder if they're as wonderful as the things that Quincy did to it." I stop…and swallow back the vomit that came up my throat at the thought of this…this thing touching Quincy. "Or should I tell you about the nights I spent with Tony."

"Liar!" I snarl. She smiles in a way that makes her face change…it's not quite my face anymore. It's paler…she's turning white. Her eyes seem lighter too. Even her hair seems to lose some of the red…becoming blacker…wavier. "Your make-up's running." She touches her face…and gasps.

She holds what looks like a huge diamond out to me. I shake my head. "Invitare lupus," she says in a voice that's not mine anymore. Mist flows out of the crystal and takes the shape of an ice wolf…about the size of a bear. It growls in an icy voice.

"Summoning magic, really? My mom always said that summoning magic is for people too weak to fight their own battles." She smirks…her pink lips turning paler. Her long straight-ish red hair…drawing up and turning darker still. "Last chance," I say.

"Attack!" she says in a nasally, whiny voice.

"You asked for it," I return as the wolf rushes toward me. I hold my hands out in front of me…first spell I ever learned. I inhale deeply and feel my magic flow around me…over me…through me. I make my thumbs and pointer fingers into a triangle in front of me. "Extermino." A fireball flies from the center of the triangle. It covers and vaporizes the ice wolf…and then takes its shape. The flaming wolf darts toward her and takes a deep bite out her left side. She yelps in pain as it knocks her out of the window behind her. She screams the whole way down.

I run down the hall and stare out of the window…all I see left is my flannel shirt still burning from where the fire wolf sank its teeth in. I sigh. Here I thought I didn't have a totem animal… "Wolf, it is," I mutter. "And if you know what's good for you, you won't come back!" I yell. I turn away from the broken window. "Now to deal with my boys."

#####

Chapter 10: Apologies

"I'm sorry, but I'm not sorry," I complain, sweeping up more library door splinters, which is surprisingly easy with the library's carpet. "You guys attacked me…*me* over her…that *thing* wearing my face."

"Doorknob," Quincy replies, while tossing it into the trashcan. He moves up beside me. "Gimme that!" He slips the dustpan out of my hand and kneels. I sweep some of the debris onto the little deep blue plastic pan. "We don't expect you to apologize…it was our fault."

"Sad, but true," Tony says, walking in with a large white garbage bag. "If we hadn't asked you to do that spell, none of THIS would've happened." He holds the bag up. "Swept up the glass inside, gathered up what was outside…and boarded up the window." He drops the bag in the trash with a broken glass rattle. "Did you have to knock her out the window…?"

"Did you have to try and hit me with a lightning bolt?" Tony purses his lips, points at me, and nods in concession. "Oh, come on!" I pause my sweeping efforts. "Don't tell me I knocked the fight outta you guys."

"We're…" Quincy says, emptying the dustpan.

"…repentant," Tony finishes. Quincy bobs his head in agreement. "If we had used stronger spells…we could've…"

"Died. That was the strongest shield spell I know, and I combined it with two reversing seals and two absorption seals. If you guys had used stronger spells, you'd probably be dead right now."

They both sigh and with almost the same expressions. "But you didn't…and that, in a weird way, means something to me." They stare in disbelief. "It means that even with ME telling you to kill ME…you couldn't. It means that whether it's REAL me, FAKE me, or even a picture of me…you guys couldn't…" I make a clicking noise in the corner of my mouth. "…pull the trigger. It's sweet in a way."

"Yes, it's sweet in a way," mom says. She walks into the library, dragging her bag behind her. She slips her shades off and hooks them on the front of her already low-cut shirt. "Just what storm ripped through here?"

"Hurricane Jamie," Tony says at the same time Quincy says, "Typhoon Jamina."

"You want some more? Because I could go another round…" Which is a lie…I couldn't use that shield spell again right now to save my life…even if it would literally save my life. "…I'll put you both through a wall this time."

"Stop!" mom says while waving her hands outward. "What happened here?" I swallow deeply…glance at Tony on my left and then Quincy on the other side of me. They both look like the cat got their tongues, so…

"We casted a spell from their dad's journal that was supposed to end their curse, or at least, the part of the curse that makes them love me. I passed out…a dark witch, I assume, wearing my face took over and made them put me in suspended animation that lasted three weeks. She…or he…then made them attack Alex and my friends repeatedly… none of them died… Alex and Kai broke into the house with Zoë's help and rescued me…I woke up…took another almost two weeks to recover after the big sleep…came back yesterday morning kicked their asses," I pause to motion to them. I come back to mom with my hands extended, palms down. "Sorry for saying asses…knocked the witch out of the second-floor window…but she/he/it got away with some weird diamond looking crystal from Tony's room."

Mom glares at Tony. He lifts his hands innocently. "First, I'm hearing about that part." Mom sighs.

"Come here," mom says. Tony steps forward. "Not you. I was talking to my daughter." I swallow a massive lump and step forward. She meets me halfway and wraps her arms around me. She sighs. "I'm just glad you're safe…and here…in my arms."

I gasp with the realization of what she means…they didn't find Angela…they couldn't track her or worse, they found her and she's… I put my arms under hers. "I'm sorry, mom." She nods against the top of my head. She lets go of me and wipes her eyes.

"I'm gonna go take a shower…and a nap." She points at Quincy and Tony. "Make them clean up this mess…alone and apologize to your friends." I nod.

"Hold on," Quincy says.

"She can't make us do anything," Tony replies.

"Yeah, she can," mom says turning toward the door and with humor in her voice. She stops next to her bag. She turns to us with her hand on top of it. "Because all three of you are different from when I left."

She cuts her eyes to Tony. "Hard to believe, but you love her a little less…which is a good thing." Tony purses his lips and looks down. She looks at Quincy. "You love her a little more…which might be a good thing, too." Quincy looks down, before looking to his brother, who returns his gaze. "And you," she says, looking at me. "You seem so much stronger…so much more yourself than when I left." I try not to smile and fail miserably. "You're beautiful, baby girl."

"Thanks, mom." She nods and walks out of the room.

"Awkward," Quincy says.

"Understatement," Tony adds.

"Not nearly as awkward as what's gonna happen in…" I look at the clock on the wall. "…five or ten minutes." They both frown and look at me. "Oh, I'd already started the apology train before mom even mentioned it."

Quincy nods and tries not to smile. Tony clenches his jaw…he hates apologizing…but he'll be alright. I wonder if we'll be alright though.

"Alex, Gwen, Stephen, Meghan, Kai, Sora, and even Gwen's brother are on their way here, so you two need to go and weaken the barrier around the estate." They nod. "Go!" I say, and they both disappear. Yep, they're in full make amends mode. Note to self: Do not take advantage of the boys…I sigh…because you still love them both very much.

"You sure sent them running," a voice that sounds like wind chimes hums.

"Twee?" A small blue orb floats down from the ceiling. "It is you!"

She bobs up and down in front of me. "Hello, my friend."

"Have you been here this whole time?"

"I've been here for over a month and a half." I frown and start shaping my mouth to ask *what*, when she makes a circle in front of me. "I came the night of the party…it was easier to get in through the barrier…I just barely beat your mom here." She floats down and lands at the top of the broom handle. "I wanted to wait 'til you were alone to talk to you…but the only times you were really alone were when you fell asleep that night and after they put you in suspended animation."

I shake my head. "No, no…it took me a little while to get out of that dress and all the other stuff Zoë and Shay did to me…for me," I say with a roll of my eyes. They didn't do it *to me*; they did it *for me*.

"Nuh-uh," Twee returns. "The tall one waited outside your door…he looked worried…and really, really sad."

"Quincy waited outside my door?"

"Yep," she returns. "You fell asleep before he left." I swallow deeply. "So," Twee says before I can comment. "Have you seen through the lie yet?"

I rub my forehead, before shaking it left to right. "Clearly, I need to have my glasses checked, because…no, I don't…I haven't…I…"

"You don't?" I arch my eyebrows as she pauses and floats off the broom handle. "Don't tell me you're…you're not in love with them, are you?"

"Twee," I say while looking away.

"Don't *Twee* me, Jamina Lynda Baggett," she replies managing to sound very motherly, despite her wind chime voice. "Uh oh," she hums. "That cute little skinwalker-daemonspawn of yours is here." She floats upward before I can respond to that. "We'll talk later." She hides herself among the black books with gold lettering along the spines behind the bar. I nod as her tiny blue light dims, causing her to become invisible.

Quincy and then Tony appear in front of me. They look around suspiciously. "Who were you just talking to?" Tony asks still checking the library. His magic flares. It causes mine to flow to counteract his and keep Twee concealed.

"My imaginary friend," I say, slamming the broom handle into his hand. I step between them.

"Where are you going?" Quincy asks with a gentler tone.

"My actual friend is here," I reply without looking back. "I'm going to meet him at the door." I half-turn in the doorway. "Apologies ready?" Quincy hooks his pockets with his thumbs. Tony nods as his grip on the broomstick tightens.

I smirk and move over to the front door as someone knocks. I open it to "Stephen? You're out of the hospital?"

"Yeah…thanks to Meghan, believe it or not. Plus, I was the only person who can touch the door without getting shocked." I nod and wrap one arm around him as he does the same. He steps inside, moving past me.

Alex immediately steps up behind him. I put both arms over his shoulders and hold onto him as though he were the last lifeboat on the Titanic. He puts his arms around the small of my back and holds me as if I'm his teddy bear, and he just woke up from a nightmare.

"How are you?"

"A little better…now," he answers, still with the sad ring to his voice. We part, but our arms remain around each other. "So, you kicked their asses yesterday?" I shake my head. "That must've been painful…for all three of you."

"Shhhh. We can talk about that later." He nods. "How's your mom holding up?"

"Same as always. Putting on a brave face for me."

I plaster on a weak smile; I'm guessing similar to the one his mom's been wearing. "That's what moms do," I say, remembering when I called out mom's fake smile…after dad. I lean forward and kiss him on the cheek. He nods, moves past me, and enters the library.

I turn back to the door to find Sora, waiting at the threshold. I frown because she doesn't seem to want to come inside. Kai waits patiently behind her.

Sora inhales deeply. "One thing before we come in," she whispers. "I trust you, Jamie." I nod. "That's pretty rare for me outside of my clan." Her eyes dart to the left. "I don't trust them…but if you tell me that we won't be attacked if we come in, I'll believe you."

"Careful. You sound like an Alpha, Sora." She smiles and brings it down to a smirk. "Only Alphas talk about their clans that way." She nods. "Please, come in," I say, motioning toward the library. She does and Kai follows her. Maybe I connect to all skinwalkers…or at least, the Garner Clan…that doesn't explain Rais though. I push the door closed. Even if he did call Alex 'cousin.'

"Hey," comes from a voice that reeks of pure boredom. I pull it open again. Meghan steps up to the threshold and pauses. "Jamie, I know our moms were besties in school and fell out over…" She rolls her eyes. "…you know who…but that doesn't have to be us. We don't have to repeat their mistake."

"It won't be, and we won't."

She steps past me and the kitsune with the strange blue aura walks up. His jet-black hair stands up in spikey little tufts on top of his head. His pale skin shows no hints of his Japanese heritage, even if it is flawless. His frost blue eyes seem to take in everything at once.

"You must be Gavin." His jaw tenses but he nods. "I'm Jamie. Please, come in." He hurries inside and away from me with a wary pace.

I turn back to… "Gwen." She moves closer, in full hat in hands mode, with her head bowed, and both hands on her thighs. I hold my hand up to stop her. "Best friend code demands that I have to kind of hate you until he's okay with everything and ready to move on."

She nods humbly. "Is he here?"

I nod. "Yeah, he and his mom just got in this morning."

"How is he…I mean, his obāsan and all…?"

"Ask him yourself." I motion toward the library. Her eyes dart in that direction and then go back to the floor. She fidgets involuntarily and…a strange red mark appears in the center of her forehead. "What…IS that?" I ask, slowly reaching for it.

"What?" It vanishes just as quickly as it appeared.

"Nothing…I guess." I point to the library again. She steps inside and pushes the door closed behind her.

We reach the library doorway…just in time to see Meghan draw back and slap Quincy. She hits him hard, too. She hits him like *mage-warrior elf, I can lift a car* hard. He falls to the floor and tumbles a bit. I want to go to him and make sure he's okay…but I don't…he deserves it, and Meghan deserves to vent.

Meghan plasters a huge smile across her face and puts her hands on her hips. "Apology accepted," she says in a snarl before storming out of the room, past Gwen and me. My eyes dart between Gwen and Alex, who's staring at her. Stay calm, Lex. Stay calm.

"Thanks?" Quincy says from the floor, still holding his jaw.

Tony releases a shoulder slumping sigh and approaches Alex. Sora and Kai step between the two. "Sora, Kai," Alex says at the same time that I do.

"Let him by," Alex continues. They separate. Tony steps forward. "Look," Alex interrupts him. "You don't need to apologize to me."

"Yes, he does," I say at the same time that Sora does.

"No, he doesn't," Alex snaps. "He made a mistake...I know since the day I met Gwen I've made about a thousand. We ALL have at one point or another..." I nod. Meghan comes back into the room.

"We...the ten of us in this room...we're all we've got..." Alex bobs his head unevenly. Quincy stands. "...plus, or minus parental support. The fact is...if we start holding grudges or asking for apologies for the mistakes we make...we're just gonna keep driving wedges between us...we're going to start...not trusting each other to watch each other's backs."

Sora nods at the same time that Quincy and Stephen do. Tony and Kai look down as though they're contemplating Alex's words. Gwen...Gwen can't seem to take her eyes off him though. I come back to him. This is who Alex really is. He's a peacemaker.

"I want you guys to know...all of you..." He pauses and looks at Gwen, who is still staring at him. "...no matter what...I've got your back...Hell or high water."

Gwen sighs and wobbles on her stiff legs. I put my hand on her shoulder. "I think we're good now," I say. She looks at me...and tears are streaming down her face. "Gwen, are you alright?"

"Yes, why?" she replies, sounding like she really is.

"You're crying."

"Am I?" she asks and checks her eyes as if she really didn't know.

Meghan hurries over to her side. "Come on, bestie," she says. "Let's get you cleaned up." Gwen nods absently, still bewildered by the tears, as Meghan wraps an arm around her and escorts her out. "Where's the nearest bathroom?"

"Top of the right-side stairs, go left and it'll be the first door on your right." Meghan nods and shuttles Gwen out of the room.

I stare and...I could swear that red mark on her forehead reappeared. Gwen's brother Gavin steps up beside me. He stares after her with glowing blue eyes. I frown. He looks at me as his eyes lose some of their fox magic light. He turns away and heads back into the library. He knows something about what's going on with Gwen, which means he probably knows something about why she ended things with Alex.

"Sorry, I had to get all deep on you guys," Alex says.

"I didn't know you had it in you," Stephen replies.

"Yeah, that was really good," Quincy says and offers him a fist bump that Alex reciprocates. Tony nods in agreement with his brother's sentiment.

Sora punches Alex on the arm causing him to take a few steps to his right. Alex laughs and then stares after Gwen and Meghan.

I wish I could do more for him…them really. Maybe, I can't do anything for them, but I can do something for us…something that needs to be done for someone I love.

"Alex," I say. "Can we talk a sec?"

He nods. I tip my head toward the foyer and move toward the stairs. He follows. I head to my room. He walks in behind me. I head over to the window.

"Close the door." He does. I focus on the door. "Absoluta silentium," I whisper, and the spell moves around the room, coating it…sealing it.

"What was that?" Alex asks.

"I casted a spell that stops people from being able to hear us outside of this room." He frowns and glances around the room. "It comes in handy when you live with two guys that can hear your hair growing."

"I guess so. So, what'd you want to talk to me about?"

"I know you said no apologies, but I'm going to anyway," I whisper. He opens his mouth, trying to stop me, and I extend my hand in a halting fashion. "Alex…you're my best friend, and I love you so much…and knowing that something I did put you and your family in danger…"

"You didn't know."

"It doesn't matter. I'm a…I'm a Witch of Light. I'm supposed to keep the balance, not mess it up. Not turn my would-be ex and his brother against someone that I care about." He shakes his head. "So…I'm sorry."

He nods and crosses over to me. I put my arms over his shoulders, and he puts his around my waist. "I miss you like," I whisper. "…always."

"Same." He rubs my back comfortingly. "So, what happens now?"

I arch my eyebrows inquisitively. "Alex if you're hitting on me with your ex and mine in the same house."

"No," he says with a laugh. I laugh, too. "I mean, what's going to happen between you…" He tips his head toward the door. "…and them."

"Nothing. I'm going to check on stuff with Rais."

"Jamie," he moans, while bowing his head.

"I know," I sigh and pat his back. "…but I…trust him. I don't know why, and I can't explain it, but I do." He looks away, and my head moves with him. "Plus…" He comes back to me. "…my mom's still looking into a way to safely destroy the crystal, so I'll probably be helping her."

He exhales audibly and then smirks. "Neither of those really answers what YOU'RE going to do about the brothers." I sigh and fidget, this time. "Jamie, I see the way you look at both of them, and the way they look at you."

"Kind of like how you look at Gwen." He nods. "Like you'd take a bullet for her."

"Yeah. Just like that."

#####

Chapter 11: Queen

"I'm alone," I say, returning to my room. "Tony's talking to my mom in the library, and Quincy went to the hardware store to get a new window and a set of doors." I look around the room and frown. I could've sworn I saw Twee fly out of the room as soon as Alex left, and my mom came back down. "Twee?"

"Close the door," she whispers. I sigh but do as she asks. "Now make sure no one can hear us…like you did with the skinwalker."

"Really?"

"Yes."

I sigh…again. "Absoluta silentium," I say with no energy. My magic coats the room, making it soundproof again. "Done."

"Good."

"Now can we cut out all of the cloak and dagger stuff so you can just tell me what you wanted to talk to me about?" Twee's little blue light appears at the top of the curtain. She floats down in front of me. I lift my right hand and allow her to perch on it.

"The Fairy Queen requests an audience with you."

"What?" I nearly choke over. "The Fairy Queen…? …wants to talk to me…?"

"Yes."

"Why? Why would your mother want to talk to me?"

"I don't know, but she wants to…she wanted me to request a meeting with you." I blink, much more than I probably should. I mean, mom raised me on stories of the fourth Fairy Queen and her 108 children. Now, she wants to meet me. "Or at least, she wanted me to request a meeting with you."

"So, she's not coming?"

"She's here."

"WHAT?" I nearly choke on again.

"There is no need for a formal introduction," a mature woman's voice calls out, seeming to come from everywhere at once. It startles me so much that I jump, causing Twee to fly away from my finger. I hear three distinct finger snaps, and three women appear in front of me. The tall woman in the center wears a long white, sleeveless dress with platinum colored hair cascading down her back and over each shoulder with two pointy ears parting it. She lifts ice blue eyes. Her skin seems to be glowing like the light of the moon, despite the fact that it's daytime.

To her right, stands the very definition of a blond bombshell…she looks like she fell out of the same tree that Meghan did and hit every ridiculously gorgeous branch on the way down. She's a little shorter than the woman in the center is, but every bit as beautiful. She has a series of intricate golden necklaces weaved into a pattern of vines and ivy leaves around the base of her neck. Her strapless dress holds firm to her body, and it is every bit as golden as her hair or the bling around her neck. Tiny white ruffles of silk with gold weaved throughout adorn her back. She glares at me with amber colored eyes and parts her crimson lips to sneer.

The tiny woman on the tall one's left wears a green peasant top with a ruffled deeper green skirt underneath. Her hair is chestnut colored and cut short, just below her pointy ears. She has a green band around her forehead that disappears into her hair. She stares at me with auburn eyes but smiles warmly…until she notices me staring and then she looks down, away, and anywhere else, except back at me.

"You should be bowing," the Golden Goddess says as a snarl. "You stand before the Fairy Queen." She motions to the woman in the center.

"No," I reply.

"NO," she says. "NO? YOU IMPUDENT LITTLE WORM…YOU…"

"HEY," I say back just as loud. "YOU'RE IN MY ROOM…IF ANYONE SHOULD BE BOWING IT SHOULD BE…"

"YOU EXPECT THE FAIRY QUEEN TO…"

"Enough," says the Fairy Queen, proving that her voice was the one that echoed throughout the room, because it does it again. Only this time it sounds like a sigh, and a soft breeze ruffles our clothing a little.

"Didn't know the acoustics were that good in here."

The Fairy Queen nods with a smile. "Please forgive, Stefana," she says motioning to Blondie on her right. "She is my seventh daughter and sworn protector." She stares at her daughter, but with warmth and affection. "A position that she takes very seriously."

"I noticed." Stefana glares at me before looking away.

"I would also like to introduce my fifty-second daughter, Ariella." Ariella's eyes dart over to me and then quickly fall back to the floor.

"Hi," she says in a mouse's squeak.

"Nice to meet you," I say. She smiles but doesn't come back to look at me.

"And you've already met…" The Fairy Queen pauses. "Twee?"

"Yes, mother…"

"Twee, what are you doing? Do not be ashamed of your human transformation."

"I'm not," Twee says like a child hiding behind her parent's leg but proclaiming to be brave. The Fairy Queen smirks and lifts her right hand slowly. She snaps her fingers…and Twee appears just as she did on the day that I met her…only much, much bigger. She's a little shorter than I am, but just as adorable as she was tiny and with wings. Her big brown chestnut colored eyes seem to sparkle over her adorably chubby cheeks. Her long black hair hangs down framing her face. She wobbles on her legs…before brushing off her powder blue dress and stretching her back. She looks at me and smiles. "Hi," she says in a voice that's less wind chime, but just as cute.

I put my arms around her. "Hey," I say close to her ear. She freezes for a second, not sure what to do. "I've wanted to do this from the moment I met you." She laughs and slips her arms around me.

"Ah," the Fairy Queen hums. "Fairies have been allies of Witches of the Light for generations…it's good to see that time has not diminished that as much as some feared." Her eyes dart over to Stefana. I giggle as Twee and I part. She remains by my side though. "As I was saying…you've already met my one hundred seventh daughter, Twelana."

"One hundred seventh?" Twee nods. "Man, the hand-me-downs you must've gotten." She covers her mouth and laughs. Ariella does too.

"Mother," Stefana says.

The Fairy Queen nods as her eyes drift closed slowly. "And of course, I am Queen Devi, 4th Fairy Queen and first daughter of Queen Sharon. McCabe Witch…"

"Baggett Witch," I correct her at the same time that Twee does.

"Apologies. Baggett Witch…as you may or may not know your mother came before me seeking a way to destroy a crystal." I nod. "Did she tell you that I refused her request?"

"No, she just said that you couldn't come up with a way to destroy it."

"Deceitful," Stefana say.

"Careful. You're talking about my mom."

The Fairy Queen glances at Stefana, who inhales deeply and takes a step back. "I refused your mother's request, because of the nature of that crystal's contents."

"Nature…? I don't get it. Alex told me that it held magical power drained from supernatural beings."

"Alex?" Ariella asks. "Oh yes, the daemon…"

"He's my best friend."

"I'm sure he's very nice…for a daemon," she says while taking a step back.

"So, what was REALLY in the crystal?"

"Power," the Fairy Queen returns. "The wielder of the crystal controls an inordinate amount of power." I nod. "Also, they control something infinitely more powerful than the magic drained from its victims. They control the very souls of those people."

"What? That's impossible."

"Are you calling my mother a liar, witch-kind?" Stefana says, finding new boldness.

"Of course not, fae-kind," I reply. "It's just a little hard to believe…"

"But I have heard tales that the kitsune near to the heart of this…daemon," the Fairy Queen says like an insult. "…this, Gwendolyn and her mate, Alex…confirmed this."

I nibble my lower lip. She's probably right. Gwen's an empath…so she probably felt their pain from the crystal…but still.

"I know this is a lot to take in," Queen Devi admits. "But that crystal has been the downfall of far too many supernatural beings. It has been used against fae and daemon alike."

"What about witches? Or vampires? Or wolves?"

"I sensed several vampires inside… but no wolves or witches."

A question springs to mind… in fact, it's the first question that I thought of when she first mentioned the crystal. "Queen Devi…why aren't you talking to my mom about this crystal? I mean, she's the one who brought it to you, and she's the one who still has it."

The Fairy Queen frowns, and her eyes seem to go distant. "Do not be offended." I frown this time. "The truth is…I do not trust your mother. She has been Claimed…and once Claimed always Claimed."

"I don't believe that. She made a deal with them, and they reneged on it. So, she quit."

"Foolish child!" Stefana says as if it's my name.

"Stefana!" Queen Devi says in a chiding way. Stefana scoffs and looks away. "My words will not make you see the truth…but you have sensed something in her yourself, yes? What once was harmonious and agreeable between you two, now seems fractured?" I cross my arms. She's right. I thought that it was just friction from my feelings toward Quincy and Tony. When you add to that, how she never told me about any of this.

"You see mother," Stefana interrupts my train of thought. "Even her progeny can see that there is something wrong with her."

"Stef," Twee says.

"I TOLD YOU! NEVER CALL ME THAT RIDICULOUS NAME, TWELANA!"

"AND I TOLD YOU, MY NAME IS TWEE!" Stefana walks toward Twee in a menacing way. Twee recoils…I move between them.

"Step aside, witch. This is fairy business…and more to the point, family business."

"Twee is my friend. I regard all my friends as family. If you want to get to her, you have to go through me." Twee clutches my arm.

"Nothing would make me happier, witch," Stefana says down at me. Geez, she's so effin' tall…in this form. "But my mother forbade me from putting you in your place."

"You're welcome to try." I taunt her, while pushing Twee behind me. Stefana places her right hand on her necklace. It glows softly and moves into her hand. She swings her arm outward, and the necklace acts like a whip, but maintains its glow.

"Stefana!" Queen Devi says in a warning tone.

"She's fine," I reply.

"Do you hear that, mother? The witch has signed her own death warrant." Stefana vanishes and reappears…behind me…I can still sense her whip, even though her presence escapes me which means…I duck as it swings over my head…narrowly missing Queen Devi, who doesn't flinch.

I aim my right palm at Stefana…as she brings the whip down toward me. "LEVITAS," I say without putting any magic behind it…suddenly, a hand wraps around my wrist…I look up, and it is Ariella…whose opposite arm has Stefana's whip wrapped around it.

"Mother said, *no*," she says in a sterner voice.

"I didn't put any magic behind my attack," I say.

"I know," Ariella says, while releasing me. Stefana gives the whip some slack, and it loosens on her sister's arm. She tugs it, and it recoils. Ariella's arm has burn marks wrapped around it, where the whip struck.

"Are you alright?"

"Yes," Ariella replies, focusing on her wrist. She sweeps her other hand over it. A green light surrounds her injured skin with a sound like a high-pitched whistle. The sound and light fade after a few seconds, and her wrist is healed.

"Wow."

Twee walks over to me. "Yes. Big sister Ariella is our strongest healer." Ariella blushes and returns to Queen Devi's side. Twee glares at Stefana. "Big sister Stefana," she says, speaking through a pout. "…is our strongest warrior…and biggest bully!"

"I heard you," Stefana says, replacing her necklace.

"Why do you have to be such a jerkface to your sister?" I ask.

"I have 105 other sisters…105 of them older than she is and only six older than I am…" She cuts vicious eyes to me. "…a part of my duty is to keep them in line, and Twelana, by far, is the most headstrong and the least obedient."

"105?" I motion to Stefana. "…106…" I look at Twee. "…107… Wait, that means you guys have a brother?"

"My youngest child," Queen Devi says with pride. "One day, he shall wed one of his sisters and create a new generation of fairies."

"Wed…his sister?" I moan, not able to hide my disgust.

"We're sisters in the sense that Queen Devi blessed us with life," Twee says into my ear. "Biologically we're no more siblings than you and Alex."

"Oh," I emit with a nod. "Gotcha."

"Baggett Witch," Queen Devi starts. "I have a request to ask of you. In return, I will owe you a boon…to be repaid upon your request."

"Okay. What's up?" Stefana shakes her head. "Get over yourself. If I'd put any magic into that spell, you'd be a baked potato right now."

"My request," Queen Devi says, bringing my attention back to her. "I want you to watch your mother…if she exhibits any behavior that seems out of the ordinary, report back to me."

"You want me to spy on my own mother?" She nods. "Okay, not saying that I will, but if I did, how would I…" I pause to get the inflection and the voice right. "…report back to you…?"

"I shall leave one of my daughters with you."

I glare at Stefana. "Not you." I put my arm around Twee and smile.

"I thought as much," Queen Devi replies. "That is not all though, young witch. I am not certain if you realize the severity of our situation. If Eden is allowed to return, it could be the end of life, as we know it. En Quosque has proven resilient in the past and clever in all their schemes and machinations. Therefore, I must place a terrible burden on you."

"Worse than saving the world?" I ask while glancing at Twee.

"More difficult perhaps," she returns. "If your mother's loyalty to her new master proves true…I must ask that you be the one to fell her."

"WHAT?"

"I know that it is a horrible thing that I ask of…"

"YOU HAVE NO IDEA…"

"But I do," she says. Stefana doesn't look angry for once…just sad. So do Twee and Ariella. "My mother, Sharon, was the fae, who separated Eden from his terrible power so many years ago… she never turned on Eden…she couldn't. His hold on her was too great. She forced me to bind her magic to my own. I uttered the wish, using her power…when it reflected back…it destroyed her."

"I'm sorry," I breathe. "I had no idea."

"Few outside of this room know this," she returns. "I only make this request of you, because in you, I see the same strength that I mustered so long ago." I sigh. "Strength like yours can change the world."

"Yeah, I'm so strong that I get weak knee'd over two boys."

Queen Devi smiles thoughtfully. "Being in love is nothing to be ashamed of…no matter the circumstance."

A knock comes from the door. I glance at it and come back to Queen Devi's delegation. "Stay. Um…shrink, please…but stay. I wanna hear more." Queen Devi bows her head as her eyes drift closed slowly. She snaps her fingers, and all four fairies return to their smaller forms. "Thank you…this shouldn't take long."

"We will stay as long as possible," Queen Devi returns. "Do not rush them, it may arouse suspicions." I nod and move over to the door. I look around for any sign of my visitors. I inhale deeply and yank the door open quickly.

#####

Chapter 12: Craftsmanship

"Hey," I say…to a shirtless Tony, standing in my doorway…being all shirtless and whatnot. "Wha…?" I try to manage words, but I can't seem to gather my wits…or tear my eyes away from the ab-tasticness standing in front of me.

"I just finished replacing the window," he explains, tilting his head toward that end of the hall. I nod and step out into the hall, while crossing my arms. "I noticed that your door was closed…" I purse my lips and continue nodding like an idiot. "…and you never do that…plus I wasn't able to hear anything coming from your room."

"So, you always listen at my bedroom door?" I ask, trying to distract him.

"No, that's…um…not what I meant," he says. "I was just…worried."

It's a little painful seeing him act this awkward. I turn toward the window. "You did a good job on the window." I move down the hall toward the construction project. "Did you get hot…and sweaty working on it?"

"Oh, I…um…didn't want to soil my shirt, and I forgot to put it back on when I finished." He hurries down the hall ahead of me. I hate his overly polite voice. Even though I told him I forgive him…and his brother, he's still being extra nice to me. He collects his shirt from his door handle and slides his arms into it. I nibble my lower lip as his chest juts out to get it over his shoulders. I hope the Fairy Queen doesn't think I'm making her wait for the sake of flirting…although, I'm trying to concentrate REALLY hard on NOT flirting…with my one and only ex-boyfriend, who just did the very manly task of replacing a window, frame and all.

He looks at me, and my eyes cut to the window. I pretend to survey his work. "Nice job. If I didn't know any better, I'd swear the window was never broken."

Tony nods. "Careful," he says, moving the warning hand toward me. "The paint's still wet."

"I would've never guessed you knew how to do this kind of stuff."

He bends over and collects his tool belt. He puts his arm through the loop it creates and hangs it over his right shoulder as he stands. "Yeah, I worked as a carpenter for a while when I was out in California." I nod and steal another glance at his abs still visible between the sides of his open shirt. I also notice that his bedroom door is open too. My first boyfriend, who sleeps down the hall from me, and I've never been in his room. I've slept in Quincy's bed…with him…but I've never been in Tony's room. He looks to his open doorway and then back to me…

"I was...just wondering..." I point. "...what did fake me steal from your room?" He frowns as he starts buttoning his shirt. I sigh. Just what I wanted to happen... He still doesn't answer. "It seemed like it made my mom pretty upset when she found out that it was taken. What was that crystal-thing?"

"Nothing." He moves toward his door. I catch his wrist as his other hand takes the handle.

"Tell me."

His eyes move away from me and back down the hall. "She...doesn't want me to..." He comes back to me, and I arch my eyebrows. "...she told me not to..."

"Tony."

He groans a sigh. "It was a Summoner's Stone." I frown and shake my head. "It's a special crystal that contains the blood of several summoners..." I shake my head again. "...it allows its user to summon any familiar that the summoners signed blood contracts with."

"Is that even possible?"

He nods. "The stone...the crystal...IS a containment spell. It keeps the blood as fresh and new as when it was in their veins."

I gasp. "That's...disgusting."

"Agreed. It's what your mom used to fight us when she first came back."

I scoff. "And here I thought she signed a bunch of summoning contracts." He shakes his head. "So, that crystal let her summon all those familiars...?" He nods. "...even that big fire man?" He nods again. "...and now *fake me* has it?" He nods again. "Why did you have it?"

"Your mom...wanted me to hold on to it for her...to protect it."

"Wow, really solid job on that." He bows his head. I groan and tilt my head back and to the left. "Geez man..." I shake my head and look at him. "...Tony will you let go of the guilt." He opens his mouth then decides against saying anything. "You apologized. You meant it. I accepted it. Now, can we just...go back to normal?"

"Normal is a relative term."

"Dude," I say as a complaint. He crosses his arms. I shove past him moving into his room. "I've never been in your room." He follows me inside. I look around at the...simple is an understatement...room. It literally has a bed, a desk, a nightstand, a dresser, and a bookshelf. They're all simplistic, woodgrain, and medium brown, including the head and footboard of his bed. Simple shear curtains with deep brown blackout curtains cover the windows.

"This is...very improper," he says.

"What part of our relationship has been proper?"

"Fair enough." I look around. Despite the boring décor, it all seems very him. It's not so much his personality as that it's all...

I turn to him. "You made all of this furniture yourself, didn't you?" He nods. I run my finger along his footboard. "Nice. You got skills…" I snicker. "…with wood."

"Thank you…although, I don't really understand how that's funny."

"Of course, you don't." I move toward the door.

"Wait." I stop in the doorway and turn back to him. He tosses his tool belt on the floor next to his desk. "Let me take you to dinner."

I shake my head. "Tony, we…"

"No, hear me out," he says, walking over to me. "As you've said before, I was your first boyfriend…your only boyfriend, and as such we never truly had the opportunity to date."

"Dude, your pillow talk is kind of lacking."

He smiles. "What I'm saying is…I'm not trying to win you back, I just want to give you a glimpse of what you…no, we missed out on." He stares at me for a moment. "Please."

"Okay." I sigh. "Tomorrow is Saturday…we can go out then…"

"I know a place, just off the square." I nod. "I will…talk with you more tomorrow…I have to go down and replace the library doors."

"Okay," I say, while stepping out of his room. I turn back to him and…and he runs into me. He wraps his arm around me to stop me from falling over. He pulls me closer. I adjust my glasses and…a swallow down a huge gulp. "Um, you forgot your tool belt," I say into his chest. He nods and slips his other hand behind my back. "T-Tony…" He tilts his head down toward me. "…we…shouldn't…" I tilt my head back, and my eyes drift closed as those familiar butterflies fill my stomach, my pulse races, and my heart skips a beat. I feel his lips press firmly against my…left cheek. My eyes drift open.

He releases me, and I almost fall…not because it was so sudden, even though that didn't help. My knees are a little weak. He retrieves his belt and then rejoins me in the hallway. He cups my chin and tilts my head upward.

"I…" he starts in a throaty, weighty…sexy…voice. "…am always so impertinent with you." His hand slips around to the side of my face. He holds his palm to my cheek, caressing my cheekbone with his thumb as his fingers tickle my ear. He presses his forehead against mine. "In a way, I'm glad that that spell didn't work on me." He lets go and disappears.

I wobble again. "Me too," I say and put my hand over the Crescent Moon Pendant. "Me too." I nibble my lower lip and hurry back to my room as I remember the Fairy Queen patiently waiting for me.

#####

Chapter 13: Normal

"So," mom says. "How long are you going to be with us?"

"As long as my mother requires it," Twee returns.

"Great," mom replies and looks up and down the highway. "Do you have to stay so…big?"

Twee nods. "Jamina didn't want it to seem like she was talking to herself or an imaginary friend…" She pauses to wink. "…so, I stayed in this form."

"You'd eat less if you were smaller," mom says as if buying food is the real issue. I think she knows that Queen Devi left Twee behind to help me spy on her. I never actually agreed to do it, but I did acknowledge that something seemed off about my mom.

"And what exactly are we doing here again?" Twee asks.

"WE aren't doing anything," mom says. "My daughter and I are going to cast the spell that will permit Quincy to leave town with me." I frown and look away.

"And why exactly is he leaving town with you?" Twee asks, sounding like the little bundle of adorableness that she appears to be.

"I'm going to see my friend, Nelfie, in New Orleans. She's a powerful voodoo priestess, who has some skill communicating with the dead." She looks at Twee. "I'm hoping that someone within the crystal has some insight on how to release them all from it safely."

"Right," Twee says. "And how does that explain why Quincy is going with you?"

"Because," I interrupt. "I didn't want her going alone…and she refused to let me go."

"And since I can't go," Tony says, startling all three of us. "My brother is the only choice remaining."

"Is that why you had me drive his car out here past the barrier?" I ask.

"Yep," Quincy replies for him, while leaning against mom's car…I mean, my car since mom bequeathed dad's car to me. "I haven't driven this thing in weeks…" He motions to it. "…even after I got it back. I wanted to drive it. Even if it's just to the airport." I nod.

Quincy stands and walks over to me. "You have the spell?" I nod. "Are you sure you can do this?"

"We'll be doing it together," mom interjects. I glance at her and nod.

He inhales deeply and nods, too. His eyes dart over to his brother. "You look like you've got something on your mind."

Tony scoffs. "What makes you two think that Nelfala LeBeau will be able…or, for that matter, willing to help? I'm sure she's not over that whole thing…from last time. Moreover, I mean, she's gotta be every bit of sixty-five now. Her aging magic can only keep her young for so long." Mom looks away this time. "For all you know, she could be dead already."

"She could be," Quincy says. "But we know that she's not following a certain wolf around anymore on the off chance he might fall in love with her."

"Wow, this sounds like yet another epically tragic tale from you guys' shared past," I say, motioning to Quincy, then Tony, and ending on my mom. All eyes turn to the ground and all mouths remain shut. "Just like normal." I look at Twee. "They never tell me anything." She nods.

"You mean like how you told us how and why Twee is here?" Quincy asks. I cross my arms and stare at him with cold eyes. "Sorry," he says. "I don't want us to part this way." I swallow down the anger that his pointing out my hypocrisy stirred up and nod. He wraps his arms around me. "I'll miss you."

"I'll miss you, too." He lets go and takes a step back. He taps the center of his chest and smiles. "No, I did not lie...I REALLY will miss you, you goof."

"What about me?" Twee asks, balancing on her toes in my borrowed sneakers. Who would've guessed that fairies normally don't wear shoes? Not me.

"Um, sure," Quincy says with an awkward smile and while rubbing the top of Twee's head. He looks at Tony. "Brother." Tony nods.

"Wow, don't get too emotional, you guys," I say as mom steps over to me.

"Now, you be a good girl."

"Aren't I always?"

"No." She laughs. I do, too. "Watch out for the town."

"D'uh."

"And help Alex as much as you can but recognize that you can't fight his battles for him."

"Coming from the woman who told me just last night, I should snatch him up since he and Gwen are broken up?"

She bobs her head unevenly. "I apologize for nothing," she says and hugs me. I hug her back. We part. "Ready?" I nod and slip the spell out of my back pocket. Mom moves up beside me and examines the spell.

"Shouldn't you know this already?" She laughs. "Okay," I say, lifting my eyes toward Quincy, holding the spell in my left hand and the Crescent Moon Pendant in my right.

"Don't you normally need a full moon for this spell?" he asks.

"That's with one McCabe witch," mom counters. "Now, you have two Baggett witches." I smile and nod. My smile fades quickly. I know it's for the best, despite what Queen Devi believes, but I don't want my mom to leave again so soon. I don't want Quincy to go with her either. Things might be awkward between the three of us right now, but Tony always seems…I don't know…different when Quincy's not around. It's as if his seals affect him less with Quincy here.

"Jamina," mom says. I blink and snap out of it. I moan a response. "Ready?" I nod. She takes a step back.

"Infractus vinculum," I read at the same time that mom recites it from memory. I clutch the Crescent Moon firmly. "…patefacio porta…solvo illa frater suum sarcina…" I look up, and a dim red dome seems to surround us…all of us…the entire town. "…suum abbas mos…exsisto laxo…" I continue as the weird shell becomes more visible. I can't help wondering if it's visible to everyone or just people with magic. "…tribuo lemma suum posterus… tribuo lemma suum licentia…" My eyes meet mom's, and she nods, while backing up. We repeat the incantation. Quincy turns and marches across the barrier fearlessly.

They reach the other side. Mom waves and moves around to the passenger side of Quincy's car.

He waves and slips his hand into the left pocket of his jacket. He removes his empty hand and points to me. I frown. He repeats the action, while pulling the driver's side door open. I put my left hand in my jacket pocket…and nothing. I reach into my right and find a folded slip of paper. Quincy starts his engine and pulls away quickly, kicking up a huge plume of dust.

I move over to my car and lean against it. "What's that?" Tony asks, staring at me, staring at Quincy's note. I shrug. He walks over. I lift my eyes to him. He stops and looks away.

I unfold the note. I pull my glasses down and read over them:

Jamina,

I miss you already. I know that sounds ridiculous and kind of selfish and kind of cliché, but it's true. At the same time, I recognize that you loved him first…so I think you should tell him. Tell him that you're still in love with him and that you're just a little confused right now.

I want you for myself. I've done a really good job of not admitting that out loud lately, but it's the truth. I do. He needs you though. You make him better…and I promise you, he'll make you better, too. Like he has for me. That's what he does…he's the hero. He makes everything better.

So, if you decide to do as I ask and make up with him while I'm away…I don't want you to feel guilty about that. I want you to be happy. Tony can make you happy. I know he can…cursed…blessed…or whatever.

I push my glasses back up and lift my eyes from the letter...my tear-filled eyes. "What's wrong?" Twee asks.

I shake my head. "Nothing." I sniff. "It's stupid." I crumple the note and shove it back into my pocket. I turn to Tony, who still looks put off, but less like an angry ex and more like a scolded puppy. "Come on. We have to get ready for our date."

"Date?" he asks. I nod.

"Yeah, well...my ex-boyfriend pointed out that we never went out, so…" He smiles and nods. I toss him the keys. "You drive."

He nods and beats me to the passenger door. He holds it open and pulls the seat forward. Twee dives into the back. He replaces the seat, and I take it. He closes the door behind me and walks around the front of the car at a nice, normal human pace.

I slip the note out of my pocket again and notice that there's writing on the outside too. I straighten it as much as possible.

I scoff into a laugh. "What?" Tony asks from the driver's seat.

"Nothing. I just remembered something stupid." He nods and starts the car. Okay. So, I'm going on a date with Tony. My first and only boyfriend...EVER. I sigh.

I feel Twee's tiny fingers on my right shoulder. I catch her reflection in the side view mirror. She mouths, 'You okay?' I nod and let my fingers play along the crumbled edges of the note. I roll my eyes at my own stupidity because I'm going on a peacemaking date with Tony...but now, thanks to this stupid note, I can't stop thinking about Quincy.

I look at Tony, who's looking at me. I smile and put my hand on my head to attempt controlling my hair...who am I kidding...one of my favorite things about my hair is its ability to resist the wind.

Tony's still staring, not paying any attention to the road. He's so stern, so formal, and so polite. He's everything that your grandmother would tell you you'd value later in life. Quincy's wild...he's unpredictable, and he keeps me guessing. No, that's not entirely true. I know exactly what he'll do…I pat the note in my pocket. He'll do just what he said he'll do…he'll do whatever it takes to make me happy…and how he does it is what surprises me every single time… I glance at Tony again guiltily. …like convincing me to go on a date with his brother.

"So, a date, huh?" I start. "We're going on a date?" Tony nods and slows the car to turn onto the driveway leading up to their house. "What brought this on unexpectedly? I mean, I didn't think to ask yesterday. I was still in shock from you asking…I guess."

"It was…," he starts, but pauses to sigh softly in that typical Tony, *why are you asking me this,* sort of way. He's overanalyzing, over-rationalizing, and just plain overthinking the whole thing. He wouldn't be him if he didn't. "…his idea," he finishes. He presses his lips into a line, while shifting the car into park. He climbs out and goes over to the huge gate.

"It was his idea…?"

I sigh and pat the note in my pocket again. Of course, it was Quincy's idea. I peer over the backseat at Twee. "What do you think?" She shrugs and arches her eyebrows. I would so clean her out if we were playing poker. "Come on, you have to think more than that."

"Well," she says, leaning forward. "If I had to say something, I would suggest that you be careful. The spell didn't work. Refuting their feelings didn't work before that. They love you still. You love them still." I sigh. Twee frowns and looks past me. "Where'd he go?"

"What?"

"Tony…where'd he go?" My heart thuds twice against my rib cage. I can honestly say no question has ever made me react that way.

#####

Chapter 14: Chicago

I face front and check the gate. It's still closed and there's no Tony in sight. I look left and then right quickly. My hand snaps to the Crescent Moon Pendant. He's… "…on the right!" I bark, while throwing my door open. "Twee, stay put! I mean it!" I don't even listen for a response. I just start running.

Soon, the car is out of sight as the stone fence curves to surround the property. I slow down enough to stop the pendant from bouncing and grab it with my left hand and adjust my glasses with my right. He's close. I move forward slowly. "Tony," I stage whisper. Nothing. "TONY!" A groan comes from the bushes ahead.

"Ventulus," I shout with a flick of my right hand. A gust of wind parts the shrubs and… "GET OFF HIM!" I yell at the four tiny creatures wrestling with and snapping at Tony with sharp teeth.

"Stay back," Tony says and then punches one of them in the…I guess, "face" since that's where its teeth are.

"Shut up," I yell back at Tony's lunacy. These things are nightmares. The little, glossy white creatures have heads the size of the rest of their bodies with big hands and feet. Their little dagger-like teeth are almost as big as their bony little fingers.

"Flamma," I spit and throw a fireball at the one holding Tony's right shoulder down. I hit it and knock it to the ground, but it didn't burn. Weird, I hear skittering behind me. I turn to find six more of the little nasty things sneaking up on me. "Crap."

"Lightning," Tony says between gritted teeth. I glance at him over my shoulder. "You have to hit them with more force…hard enough to break their skin…it's like really thick porcelain."

"I got this." My eyes drift closed. I draw a seven-sided seal with a square inside with my left hand pointing toward the sky…disruption plus strength. I focus my magic, and I can already hear the sky rumbling. I open my eyes as the six little terrors rush me. I point at them with my right hand and stretch my left toward the sky. "Levitas," I say, and the air crackles with electricity. An ozone smell cuts through the air as lightning rushes down my left hand and then past my right hand. It crushes all six of them at once. I spin on my heel and aim just above Tony. He's fast…he manages to lay flat and let the continuing surge hit the other two. I sigh as the magic subsides.

"You're lucky I was here," I say as he sits up.

His knife zips by my head and thunks against something behind me. "You missed one," he says as I spot his huge knife sticking out of another one's head. I nod. A C-sharp whips by both of us, tossing my hair…not as wind resistant as I thought. A porcelain crack sounds. I look past Tony and see another of these little monsters crumbling to pieces with a skittering, sort of hiss.

I look behind me. "You missed one, too," Twee says.

"I thought I told you to stay in the car." Twee puts her arms behind her back and digs the toe of her right shoe…my right shoe…into the ground. I run over to her and put my arms around her. "I'm so glad you're just as hardheaded as me." She sighs and slips her arms under mine. Tony walks by and pulls his knife out of the last one's head. "What are these things?"

"Ghouls," he says, while standing. I look into the hole that his knife made and…

"…it's hollow!" He nods and replaces his knife. "I've never seen ghouls like these."

"I have," Twee and Tony say at the same time. They look at each other. "Chicago, nine years ago," Tony continues.

"Same."

"You were both…in Chicago…nine years ago?"

"Guess so," they say at the same time again.

"Super," I spit and leave my lips protruding after the R. "Great. Great. Great."

"Don't be weird about this," Tony says with a frown.

"Why would I be weird?" I return hearing my voice go up to a nasally pitch at the end. "I mean…it's just another one of those random coincidences that you'll dismiss as nothing and not tell me about for whatever cockamamie reason you've cooked up in that old man head of yours." I turn and stomp off.

He appears in front of me. "I was there on the hunt for a vampire coven that was causing too much commotion. That's how I met Shay. She was about to be vampire chow, and I saved her life," he explains quickly. "…but not before she was bitten. I cared for her for several days to make sure she didn't change…she didn't because of her siren blood. After that, I tracked down the rest of the coven and slaughtered them all with the help of a wolf named Nathan Francois. Nathan and I parted ways over a dispute."

"Dispute?"

"They fought over Shay," Twee says.

"So, you did know him before you came here?" She nibbles her lower lip and nods.

"But," Tony interjects. "I'd never seen her before, and fairies are notorious watchers." He glances over his shoulder. She flashes a big fake smile and waves. "In fact," he continues. "It's normal for the Fairy Queen to send someone to watch over troublesome situations."

"I know that," I say with my arms crossing over my stomach. "You fought…over Shay?" He swallows a massive lump. "She was what…sixteen at the time…?"

"Eleven," he whispers.

"ELEVEN?" His eyes lower, and he cuts them to the right. "You two fought over an eleven-year-old girl…? What kind of pervs are you and this wolf?"

"They didn't fight over her…exactly," Twee says. "They fought over what to do with her…since the vampire coven killed the rest of her family before Tony could save them." I look at him. He seems…sad. "She wanted to go with them…and fight monsters like them…the wolf insisted that it was too dangerous, and she would end up getting killed. Tony said that she had the right to choose her own path…"

"…no matter what end it led her to," he says in a low voice.

"Normally, I'd agree," I say. "But she was eleven years old. Clearly, she was infatu…" He tenses. "…or is it…" Twee shakes her head and looks away. "…Shay's still in love with you!" He lifts cold eyes to meet mine. "That's what Mitchell was hinting at…that she…and you…" I frown, step back, and shake my head. "…and you knew, didn't you? This whole time!"

"She never came out and said it…but I suspected," he admits.

"And you," I add with a growl directed at Twee. "You knew too…didn't you?" She opens her mouth to respond, and then it snaps shut. She swallows deeply. "Ugh!" I groan and turn away from them.

"Where are you going?" Tony asks.

"Away from the two of you!"

"But," Twee adds.

"I've been talking to her," I say, snapping back to them. I point at Tony. "…about you! She's talked me down off more than a few ledges about my feelings for you…and she…" I shake my head. "…I'm so pissed at the two of you right now that I could scream…seriously!" I storm off. A tiny blue orb of light drifts past me. "TWEE," I complain. "GO AWAY!" She floats off.

I kick a rock out of my path. I can't believe they let me torture her like that. I smack myself on the forehead. I can't believe I didn't see it sooner. A ridiculously hot girl like her…following around some nearly two-hundred-year old guy… "…of course, it's because she's completely and totally in love with him."

"For what it worth," Twee says in her wind chime voice. "He's never led her on. He made his feelings toward her perfectly clear from the start."

"Is that supposed to make me feel better?"

"Does it?"

"Of course not. She's kind of awesome and…the guy who she loves is in love with me, and she never took that out on me."

"That's normal."

"HOW IS THAT NORMAL?"

The tiny blue light hovers in front of my nose. "It's normal…to sacrifice your happiness to make someone that you love happy."

I shove my hands deep into my jacket pockets and encounter Quincy's note. I sigh. "Normal is stupid."

#####

Chapter 15: Venom

"So," Quincy starts, dragging it out for way longer than its two letters. "Can you say something without sounding like you have a mouthful of venom?"

"I can't believe you're taking up for him!" I take the cell from my left ear and move it to my right.

"Swing and a miss."

"He should've told me!"

"Strike two."

"She's been with him since she was eleven…"

"Strike three and you are outta there!" I sigh. "Sure, she's been with him since she was eleven…by choice. And you said it yourself; even Twee admitted that he was upfront with her from the start."

"Yeah, but…"

"And you can't help who loves you." I groan. "I mean, I'm sure if you could, you'd stop people from loving you."

I sniff. "Okay, so do you want me to be pissed at you now?"

"I was kidding."

"Why would you even joke about that?"

"Can you see your face right now?" I take my cell away, tap the speakerphone and switch on the front-facing camera.

"Yeah."

He laughs. "That's why."

I make my lips into an asterisk to stop from laughing. "I hate you," I say with a little bit of a giggle.

"No, you don't," he says in that deep, breathy way that makes my heart skip a beat. "Just like you don't hate him. In fact, you're not even mad at him…"

"Yes, I am."

"Ow."

"Sorry." I imagine him wincing in pain and holding his chest over the whopper I just told.

"It's okay. Just go to him and let him explain his feelings. I know you feel bad for Shay, and I know you feel like you're stealing the affection she deserves, but that's not your fault, and it's not his either."

"I know," I say in the form of a whine and play with the inner thigh stitching of my jeans. I glance at my toes peeking out from under my right knee. "How can you be so cool about all of this?" I ask, hearing my voice drop seriously. "I mean, you're…you know…you and Shay are in the same…you know…"

"Because," he says with that deep, sexy bass in his voice that causes me to nibble my lower lip and boing one of my curls involuntarily. I stop the second I realize I'm doing it…of course…well, not THE second. "It's because I'm in the same boat that I can be…cool about it." I sigh and stare at my phone glad that he can't see me right now.

"Did you like the dress?"

"Huh?" I respond while swiping at the tears pooling in my eyes.

"The dress…? Did you like it?"

"Yeah, it was nice…"

"Was nice? So, it's not nice anymore…? What did you do? Set it on fire?"

"No," I laugh. "It's just…"

"Wait until after your conversation with him to decide on whether or not you're going to cancel your date."

"How did you know…?"

He laughs. "Speak soon. I think we've got a line on Nelfie, so we shouldn't be down here too long."

I smile. "Good."

He makes a positive noise in response. "Later."

"Bye," I say and end the call.

I put my phone down and look around my room. There's the scorch mark that I left on the headboard when I *removed* that stasis seal. I uncross my legs and throw them over the edge of the bed.

I tug on dad's Braves t-shirt. I never knew what he ever saw in Atlanta's team. He said something about an epic pennant run when he was a kid, but I don't know. I pull my door open, and the soundproofing spell shatters. I smirk. I am getting too good at that spell.

"Twee?" I step out into the hall. She took the room closest to the other bathroom down on Quincy's end of the hall, since mom moved to the bedroom across from me to let Mitchell have the one next to me. Shay took the one next to… I sigh. Maybe I should move into the one next to Twee…or maybe, the one on the first floor.

"Twee?" I repeat moving over to her door. "Hey, I'm here to say sorry…for yelling at you…it wasn't your fault." I frown. "Twee?" I wonder where she went. I wish I could say that it's not like her to wander off, but that's pretty much all she's ever done.

I move over to the stairs and hurry down. "Twee?" I reach the bottom and round the banister heading toward the kitchen, her second favorite spot in the house besides my room. The Crescent Moon Pendant taps near my heart and… "Ugh," I complain. I lift it by the necklace. "Why are you so cold?" I ask as if it would or could answer. I frown. "And where is Tony?" I place the tiny C shaped ice cube in my left hand and concentrate. He's in the library, but why does he feel… I hurry over to the doors and throw them both open. Tony is face down in the middle of the floor with a stack of books beside him.

"TONY!" I yell and rush over to his side. I turn him over onto his back. He's not burned or cut or scratched or anything. His skin is as pale as a sheet of paper, and some of his veins appear blue underneath. I open his eye, and the white seems darker…as if a thin film of something transparently black covers it. "Tony? Come on, Tony! Wake up! WAKE UP!"

I cradle his head in my arms and balance his shoulders on my legs. "Sano," I say, and nothing happens. "Libero," I spit and still nothing. "Cor-"

"Stop," Twee chimes before I can finish. She snaps her fingers and appears in human form on Tony's left.

"What's wrong with him? Why won't any of my healing spells work?"

"I know this," she says, tracing the dark blue vein running up his arm. I arch my eyebrows impatiently waiting. "It's venom…ghoul's venom. Those creatures are cesspools of germs and bacteria." She hums, and her eyes drift closed. "It's affecting his human half."

I frown. "I can use the Way of Healing spell." She shakes her head. "Wh-what about the Prayer of Heaven's Light?"

"No. The poison has progressed too far…his human side is dying."

"How did this happen?" I look around. "We were around those things…and we're okay."

"They have to bite you to pass along their venom."

"Bite?" I shake my head and start feverishly searching…my hands clumsily move along his body…looking for… "HERE," I snap, finding what feels like dried blood on his right side. I try to slide him off my legs. "Help me." Twee grabs his shoulder and pulls. I draw my legs out, and we lay him flat on his back. I rip his shirt up the side… "No," I moan at the sight of a bite mark on his oblique. There's very little blood, but the entire area of and around the bite, looks like a gigantic bruise, and his veins appear the same color leading away from the wound. "Why didn't he say anything?"

"We can ask him after we save him."

"But you said…"

"I know." She frowns and stands. "That kitsune with the strange blue aura. Ghouls like those attacked your friend…the daemon…Alex. He was able to heal him…maybe he can help Tony."

"Do you think he will?"

"Never know until you ask," she sighs and snaps her fingers. She vanishes. "I'll see if I can find him."

I nod as tears stream down my face. I lean over Tony and tuck my hair back behind my ears as best I can. "Don't die. Don't die," I chant and rock back and forth on my knees. He groans. "Tony?" He yells out in pain, and his arm flails out…his hand hits my knee…taking all my breath away and making my eyes flash red for a second…and knocks me to the floor. "Ugh."

"Jamie?" He gasps. "Jamie, where are you?" His voice sounds pained and desperate. "Jamie, I can't see you…why is it so dark?"

"Stop moving," I say. He cringes and rolls over onto his side. He moans in pain again. "I'm coming to you." I get up on my knees. The second the left one touches the floor I know it's bruised if not worse. It's throbbing like a raw nerve, but I ignore it and move over to him. I put my hand in his.

He cradles it in both of his and then moves his entire body so that it seemingly, miraculously wraps around my arm. His breathing is irregular, and his eyes search frantically. "Where are we? Why's it so dark?"

"It's not," I say, trying to keep my voice even. "It's…" I nearly choke. "…it's your eyes…something's wrong with your eyes…because of the ghoul venom."

"Venom…? Right," he says. "My father's book…I researched the ghouls…deadly toxin…" He groans and grits his teeth. "…if I were human…I'd have been dead a long time ago…" He groans again. "…instead of writhing in agony still."

"Don't talk like that! You're gonna be fine."

He shakes his head. "Gaaaaaaaaaahhhhhhhhhh," he yells out, clutching at my arm desperately, but still trying not to hurt me.

My resolve crumbles. "Tony, I'm sorry."

"For…?"

"I should've told you…I…the spell never worked on me either. I was still in love with you…denying your love didn't work either…I've still felt the exact same way toward you this whole time."

He laughs humorlessly. It's less of a laugh and more of repeated gasp. "So, I have to die to get you to admit your feelings for me?"

"You can't die. Okay? You can't…because that's why I never told either of you…" I sniff as more tears and…other stuff run down my face. "…it's why I never chose either of you…because I was scared. I was so scared that if I picked one, I would lose the other and then lose both of you…for my…"

He reaches up and caresses my face. "For your family," he gasps.

"Yeah. So, see…you can't die…I didn't pick because I didn't want to lose either of you…I can't have…WE can't have gone through all that heartbreak for nothing."

He nods, and his eyes close lazily. "Book…," he says, while moving his arm.

"What…?"

"Red book…gold trim…black…glossy…letters…" I look at the three books around him on the floor.

"Got it," I say while collecting the one near his head. "Diocles of Carystus…?"

"The other…one…" I grab the book closest to me…that I didn't notice like a goof. "…page…1-3-5…" I put it on the floor between us and quickly search until I find circled in red…

"…asclepias curassavica…the bloodflower?" He swallows a dry lump and nods. "How am I…?" He lifts his right hand with his pointer finger out…his middle finger about a quarter bent and his ring and pinky fingers about half bent…his hand looks like my mom's when she… "…memory spell?" He nods. I lean forward until his hand touches my forehead. I wonder if he taught mom this or if she taught him. I close my eyes.

I'm running at night…dim moonlight falls on everything… Wait, was that thought his or mine? I run across…what is this a stone cylinder. It has a grate on top. I smell fresh water. It's a well. I nod and search through the waist high grass until…I see several dozen bright orange flowers with deep red sepals just above bright green stems. "Bloodflowers," I sigh. I open my eyes. "I know where they are."

"Just…need…one…and rest…" He stretches his opposite arm out. "…desk."

"It's a cure, right?" He nods and purses his dry, cracked lips. "Okay. Okay, I'll go get the bloodflower. Save your strength, okay? Don't die," I say while standing. "Don't die!"

I run out of the library and up the stairs. I slip my feet into my boots without tying them, and I slide into my jacket. I check the pocket, happy that I did get the keys back from him.

I run back downstairs and stop in the foyer. I peer at him lying perfectly still. I shudder. "Tony?" His eyes drift open lazily, and he tilts his head in my direction. "I'll be right back, okay?"

I run out the door and over to my car. I jump in, start it up, and throw it into gear. I back up and then rip down the drive as fast as my dad's old car will carry me. I turn right onto the street and floor it. I hope I don't get pulled over…I can drive, but I still don't have a license yet.

#####

Chapter 16: Unexpected

I reach the southeastern edge of town…that I thought was all trees. My mom told me that our family used to own land out here. I sigh and pull onto the side of this tree-lined road. I park and yank the keys out. I jump out and run into the woods. I follow Tony's memories as surely, as if they were mine. Unfortunately, I don't move as fast as he does, and I don't see as well in the dark. The sun's almost down too.

Before long, I reach a clearing…with several smaller pine trees growing around it. I walk forward through the waist-high grass with tiny saplings growing out of it randomly.

"Ow. Damn it." I stubbed my toe on…on…a stone…no, it's too rectangular to be a normal stone, and it looks like weathered concrete…and there's another one leading up from it…it's stairs…two stairs…Tony's memories pass through my mind again. The house…black…ashen wood…sun-bleached and rotting…a small house. The porch was just beyond these stairs, which means that…I turn to the right and start walking. The well was… My hands touch the rim of the stone cylinder. I smell fresh water past the rusted metal grate.

I turn left because the flowers were… "Wow." A sea of orange petals with deep red sepals sways gently in the breeze. They are already in bloom despite the fact that it's still late March. Now that I think about it, the grass is up to my waist, and it's green. Everything around here is. It feels warmer here, too. Like I could take off my jacket.

"It's said," a familiar voice says. Rais walks toward me wearing a white button-up shirt and jeans. He hooks the belt loops of his pants. "…that this entire area was blessed by a shaman and his daughter." He looks around at the overgrown property. "Anything planted in the earth here…will grow, regardless of what time of year it is." He comes back to me and starts walking toward me. "This land is immune to snow and even the bitterest cold."

"Stop." I extend my hand, palm out. He does. "What are you doing here, Rais?"

"I told you, Bunny." He takes another step.

"Don't come any closer." He swallows deeply and stares at me. If I didn't know any better, I would swear he was hurt. "Answer the question first."

"I sensed you outside of the barrier…and…" He bobs his head unevenly. "I wanted to see you, Bunny."

"And that's the only reason you're here?"

He moves his right hand over his chest. "Cross my heart…" He makes the appropriate motion. "…and hope to die…" He holds his hand up toward the sky. "…stick a wrought iron needle in my eye." I nod and lower my hand. "Why are YOU out here, Bunny?"

"I need…an um…" He looks past me.

"Are those…Bloodflowers?" I nod. "Those are rare in this part of the country…and to have so many."

"All I need is one." He nods this time. "Are you okay? You seem off."

"Speak for yourself, Bunny."

I decide to drop all pretense. "Tony was attacked by a pack of ghouls." I turn and move over to the tiny Orange-Red Sea. I pluck the nearest flower. "One of them bit him…and instead of telling me about it…"

"He hid it from you?" he asks from over my shoulder. I nod and turn to face him. "I would never keep anything from you." He stares into my eyes, and I take in the gray blue of his.

I twirl the flower in his face. "Good, then tell me the other reason that you're here."

He smiles. He lifts his hands as if the flower is a gun, and I'm mugging him. "Ah, you got me." He holds both of his pointer fingers up in a wait a minute way.

"I don't have a minute. I have to get back."

"Just…," he breaks off while renewing the gesture. He vanishes and reappears holding someone under his arms.

"Who is that? What DID you do?"

"No idea who this is," he replies. He drops him in the grass. "…who he was."

"Was? As in…? Rais, you didn't?"

"He was watching you, Bunny." I look at the dark-haired figure laying in the grass. "He stalked you from the estate as best I could tell and then followed you out here. He looked like he was about to attack you, and I…admittedly, could've responded better…but I thought he might hurt you and…" He bobs his head from side to side. "…and I kind of lost it."

"Rais, you can't…"

"I know, I know, Bunny. Only the Blackshear Brothers for you."

I show him the flower again. "I have to get back."

He takes my hand…flower and all…holds it up to his mouth and kisses it. "I know. I'll take care of our mysterious friend. I'm sorry I disappointed you, Bunny." I nod and pull my hand out of his. His head bows forward as I step past him, heading back to the car…or, at least, that was the plan. So, why am I stopping with Tony's life on the line?

"I'm not disappointed," I say without turning to look at him. I glance over my shoulder, and he does the same. "Just…I want you to be careful, Rais. They killed Liz for losing my mom…what would they do to you for killing one of theirs." He marches over to me and tips my head up with the side of his right pointer finger on my chin…like Quincy would…

"I don't care about that, Bunny," he says. "I care about you." He takes my hand with the bloodflower again. "You have gotten under my skin…" He peers at the flower, and then his eyes come back to meet mine. "…and there is no cure for me." I sigh as tears well in my eyes. He's like Shay too…in love with someone that's in love with someone else.

"I…"

"I know." He pats my hand. "Go. Save him."

"Thank you," I say, turn, and run through the woods as fast as I can. Rais is following me. I don't know how I know…that's not true…the Crescent Moon Pendant tells me.

I reach the car much faster than I reached the clearing. I climb inside and start it. I glance at the woods again before making a huge circle across the street. I turn back toward the estate, and I don't feel Rais behind me anymore. He must have stayed behind to take care of that guy. Can't think about any of that now. I have to get back. I rip through town, thankful that clearly this is a low traffic time for Edenton, in terms of other cars and law enforcement.

I turn back onto the gravel driveway leading up to the estate and every crunch of gravel under the tires seems to bring my mind back to Tony's repeated groans on the library floor…I push the gas pedal to the floor. I swing around the circle at the front of the house, and I don't bother parking or turning off the car. I slam the gearshift into park and climb out. I run over to the door and burst through it. I turn to the library and…

"G-Gavin?" I ask the leather jacket kneeling over Tony.

"So good of you to join us," he says without looking at me. A blue light erupts from the other side of him.

"What are you doing?" I run around him to find him covering Tony in blue flames. "YOU CAN'T." I move to stop him.

"No," human-sized Twee says catching me around my waist. "He's helping. Don't stop him."

"Twee? He's…he's what?"

"Helping," Gavin says with a strained voice. "My fox magic is the only thing keeping his human half alive and coincidentally, if his human half dies then his daemon or fae or whatever side goes with it." He peers at me over his shoulder. "So, you might want to let me concentrate."

"Sorry," I say, tossing my mess of curls out of my face.

"He agreed to do whatever he could since similar ghouls are what brought him back to town," Twee says. I nod. "Where've you been?"

"I had to get this." I hold the flower up and move toward the desk. "Pass me that open book on the floor." Twee grabs it with both hands and hurries over to me. I grab the big stone bowl and pestle from the edge of the table. I place the bloodflower inside and grind it up. "Open it to page 135." Twee does and lays it out in front of me. I read over each ingredient carefully and apply the recommended amount. "I need sage," I say to Twee, and she darts out of the room.

"You're bossy now that your boyfriend's life is in danger," Gavin says.

"He's my ex-boyfriend and trust me…I'd be just as bossy if your life was on the line." I lift my eyes to him. His glowing blue eyes meet mine. The corners of his mouth turn down, and he makes a face that tells me he's impressed by my resolve.

I go back to the book. "Crap." I groan, looking at the last ingredient from the spell.

"What?"

"Last part…I need blood from his wound…"

"A little squeamish?"

"Try a lot."

"Lose your lunch, or lose your ex?" I take a deep breath before swallowing a knot in my throat. I nod and march over to Tony.

"Just keep up the kitsune life support, okay?"

"Yes, ma'am," Gavin responds. I reach behind Tony's back and catch the loop of his knife. I pull until it comes free. "Holy crap, that's a big knife."

I nod. "Yeah. I need you to switch sides with me." Gavin nods, rises to his feet, and steps over Tony all while maintaining a constant stream of blue flames. "Thanks." He nods again and kneels at the same time that I do. I move Tony's arm, grit my teeth, and…jam the knife into his side. It sinks in with a sort of glurp and thunk.

"Aagh-ha," he yells out and clenches his teeth.

"Sorry," I whisper into his ear. He relaxes, but only a little. I pull the knife out, stand, and try to hold it as level as possibly while hurrying back over to the bowl.

Twee comes back to the desk and offers me the sage. "You are so strong," she says. I shake my head and flick the tip of the knife over the bowl, dumping a few droplets of dark red blood into it.

"Trust me, underneath I'm all bubbly guts and frayed nerves."

"Can't tell from where I'm standing," Twee replies. I take the sage from her and add a dash. I mix the paste up a bit more and evenly distribute the tiny brownish-gray leaves. "What now?" Twee asks. I collect the bowl and hurry back to Tony's side.

"Now, I have to apply some of this directly to the wound…" I gather some at the tips of my middle, pointer, and ring fingers on my right hand. I smear some over the tiny jagged teeth marks there. I smooth it out. "…and…I have to put some under his tongue." Twee moves up to his head and opens his mouth. "Thanks." She nods as I place my pointer and middle fingers under his tongue and spread some of the paste around.

"And now?" Twee asks.

"We wait."

"We won't have to wait long," Gavin says. "I can already feel him getting stronger." He tilts his head to the left. "Plus, look at his wound." I check it, and the darkened veins and bruising slowly melt away.

I sigh as Gavin stops his kitsune life-support. "Thank you, Gavin."

He nods. "It's like my sister's little skinwalker said, we're all we've got." I nod. He looks at Twee. "But it looks like ten…has become eleven." Twee flashes a huge smile. My eyes drift back down to Tony, as color returns to his cheeks little by little.

#####

Chapter 17: Candlelight

"Jamie?"

I moan some response and inhale deeply. I feel warm and just…happy. I open my eyes slowly. I feel a hand on my right hand…on Tony's chest. I look up at him. "Hey," I say with a groggy, Elmer Fudd voice. "You're awake?"

"Yeah, I'm feeling much better…" He frowns. "…but I do have a question. Why are we lying on the library floor covered by a blanket and who changed my shirt?"

"Don't forget the pillow," I say while covering my mouth with my newly freed right hand. He laughs. "This is…where we found you…and since Gavin didn't want to carry you up to your bed…" I sit up. He props himself up on his elbows. His clean, black shirt hangs open just enough to show his dog tags. I didn't know he still had any of them, let alone wore them. "…so, I decided to make you a palette on the floor and…" I shrug. "…I didn't want you to wake up alone." I draw my lips into my mouth and fail to suppress a shiver. "I thought I'd lost you."

"I imagine. I'm glad you were able to figure it out."

"It was pretty easy; you left everything right where you said."

"Where I said?" he asks with a frown.

"Yeah, you told me which book…which page…" He stares at me blankly. "…and you don't remember any of it?" He shakes his head slowly. "None of it at all?" Head shake.

"I had a strange fever dream about you…" He tilts his head to the left. "…that I wish I hadn't just mentioned to you." I laugh. He does, too. "You saved me."

"You've done it for me a few times." He nods. "So, you really don't remember ANY of the things we talked about?"

"No. Sorry." I draw my lips into my mouth and nibble the bottom one. "Why? Was it something important?"

Only that I'm still in love with you, something that your brother already knows. "No." He nods. "I…should…" …stop staring at your chest… "…head up to bed."

He inhales deeply, but nods again…never losing eye contact with me. He looks at me as if he wants to tell me that he loves me. He stares at me as if a kiss could save his life just as surely as the potion, I mixed up did. He watches my every breath as if he wants to own me, but more than that, he wants to be owned by me. He would be fine if I destroyed every part of him as long as I held every tiny fragment of him dear. It's a little overwhelming how much he loves me…and worst yet, Quincy loves me just as much… I feel a twinge in my chest. …and I love them just as much.

"Right, bed," he says and nods.

"Ugh," I utter as a complaint, rising to my feet. My left knee twinges. It starts throbbing again…it is killing me.

"What's wrong?" I freeze, thinking about how it was injured. I didn't even feel it while running through the forest.

"I'm fine." I grit my teeth and finish standing. "See…?" I cringe, and I feel like I'm going to topple over from the pain.

"That…is NOT fine," he says moving closer to my legs. "Let me see." I hobble away. He tugs up on my pajama leg.

"No, it's…I must've banged it when I tripped over a branch in the woods. I'll be fine." He stands in a blur and sweeps me off my feet in another. "Hey!" I whine as he cradles me close to his heart. He moves over to the sofa and lays me down. "I said I'm…" He issues me a quiet finger that does just that. He pulls the pajama leg up above my knee and reveals the huge purple and dark blue bruise covering my left knee and part of my thigh. "Sssssssss," I emit while looking it over.

"That," he says in the stern Tony disapproving fashion. "…is not fine." He motions to it. "Why didn't you tell me about this?"

"You're one to talk." He looks down and places his hand on the bruise…I wince and groan from the dull ache doubled by his touch. "Ow."

"Sano," he whispers, and the bruise drains away, and my skin returns to normal…if a little dry. I inhale deeply. "I'm a lot sturdier than you are."

"You didn't see you lying on the floor," I whisper, trying not to cry about the image in my head. He nods. "But I can't be mad at you for not telling me…I did the same thing…" I frown and wonder if one of his fever dreams included my confession. "…just now, with my knee," I lie.

"Pride is a dangerous sin."

"All of them are." I drape my legs over the edge of the sofa. He drapes his left arm over my thigh and positions himself so that he's kneeling directly in front of me…between my legs. I try to stop my heart from skipping a beat…and then two more after that one. He looks like he's about to pounce. I just hope I don't look like I intend to let him.

"Why is it so dark in here?"

I scan the room. "I…" I swallow deeply. "I tried the light switch, but the bulb blew…and I didn't know where to get a ladder so…I found all these candles and…"

"…and lit them, before you lay beside me on the floor?" he says while sweeping a few curls behind my left ear. I nod. "And," he starts again, inspecting my dark blue tank top and blue-on-green plaid pajama bottoms. "You changed into pajamas."

"Yes."

"You can understand how I could misconstrue this as being a bit romantic, right?"

"Candles? Blanket? Pretty girl lying beside you in her PJs? Pfft, how could any of that be romantic?"

He caresses my left cheekbone, draining all the humor out of me…another skipped heartbeat…my eyes meet his. He can hear them…he can hear every thud of my heart and right now, it's pounding away. I can't do anything to slow it down. I swallow a nervous lump as he tilts my head back gently, bringing my lips closer to him…to his. He leans forward, and my eyes close slowly. "Uh oh," I hum as he pulls me in…

"Sorry." He presses his forehead against mine. "Ugh, it's just…" He taps the sofa with his right hand. "…when I get this close to you…I could swear I almost feel how much you love me." My eyes snap open and meet his that are still closed. "It makes me happy, but then I have to remind myself that you don't feel the same way about me." I resist the urge to put my arms over his shoulders. He leans back and opens his eyes. "Right?"

"Right." He nods. He takes his arms from both sides of me. He sits back. "I should…" I point up. "…bed." I stand awkwardly and maneuver past him just as awkwardly. I hurry over to the door, left hand on the Crescent Moon Pendant and right hand over my mouth.

"Thank you." I pause in the doorway and half-turn to face him. "For saving my life." I force a smile and tilt my head forward.

I hurry up the stairs and to my room. I contemplate leaving my door open…but I close it and lean against it. I tilt my head upward until the top of my head touches the door. I feel dizzy. If he hadn't stopped…I would've kissed him…I would've kissed him a lot. I run both hands over my hair and go back until I hit my ponytail. Focus on the fact that you're glad he's alive. Remember that. "I'm just glad he's alive," I say aloud.

A knock comes from the door. My eyes bulge. If he came for round two, I might be the one pouncing. I step back and pull the door open to… "Twee?"

She yawns and rubs her right eye sleepily while standing in her oversized pale blue PJs. "Hey," she whispers, sounding like Elmer Fudd. I snicker thinking about how I just sounded like that. "Are you alright? I heard you slam your door."

I did? "No, no…I'm fine. I just…Tony's awake, and he's fine so I decided to…why are you looking at me like that, Twee?" She lowers her left eyebrow slightly. "Twee?"

"Say that again."

"Twee?"

"Not my name…his name."

"Tony."

"You almost kissed him," she says with a hiss, between clenched teeth.

"No?" Her mouth falls open, and she cants her head to the right. "Maybe." She frowns. "Okay, so yeah…but…"

"But nothing…you wanted to."

"How could you possibly know that?" I growl while pulling her into my room. I close the door behind me. "Absoluta silentium." The room seals off. "Okay, tell me. How do you know that? You just woke up."

"I can sense emotions connected to sounds." I arch my eyebrows. "Lust, if you must know."

"Oh. I didn't know that." I moan in a much deeper voice and move over to the bed clutching the Crescent Moon Pendant in both hands. I climb on top and cross my legs under me while playing with the pendant.

"I can't imagine," Twee says, climbing onto the bed next to me. "I can't imagine feeling the way that you do about him…about both of them." I arch my eyebrows and let them fall. "And the fact that you're still resisting both…"

"I didn't." I let the pendant fall. "I didn't resist him…he resisted me. He stopped the kiss at the last second."

"How can he do that?"

"How can I sense them through this?" I whisper while motioning to the pendant. "How can Quincy tell when I'm lying because of a pain in his heart? How can Tony feel the emotions that I've been denying?" Twee shrugs.

I look across the room and spot the dress Quincy bought for me, hanging on my closet door. I stare at the intricate sunflower pattern cutout of the lacey top and the fringe around the bottom. The sleeves have a similar pattern but are silkier and nearly transparent. He even bought hunter green shoes that match the dress perfectly. I sigh and climb off the bed.

"What are you…?"

"Help me with my hair," I say while claiming the dress. "I want to have it so that it all kind of hangs over my…" I pause to think. "…left shoulder." She nods and moves over to me. She stands behind me, undoes my ponytail, and then gathers up my hair as I slip off my pajama bottoms.

"Um, Jamie…what are you doing?"

"We had a date," I reply while stepping into the dress. "And I don't intend to let my stubbornness or even infectious ghoul bites stop that." I work to get my tank top off while holding the dress against my chest with my right hand. I toss the tank to the side and slip my arms through each sleeve gently, hoping…no praying, that I don't rip them. My hair falls neatly over my left shoulder as I smooth the awkward, bunching places in the dress. "Zip me up."

"You do realize that it's three-thirty in the morning," she explains, but complies.

"Yep," I reply while slipping my foot into one tall heel and then the other. "That's what will make it special for him." I turn to her and cup her hands in both of mine. "Will you make us a picnic lunch?"

"But," she says and breaks off. I arch my eyebrows. "…but he's…" I begin to pout. "…and you're…" I make my lower lip tremble. "Ugh, you are as annoying as my sister Mary-Elizabeth…" I frown. "…she's my 13th sister, but she acts like she's younger than I am." She turns on her heel. "It'll be ready in five minutes."

"Thank you." She opens the door and marches out of the room.

I grab my purse, of all things that mom brought back with her from Georgia, and hurry to the bathroom. I look at my pale cheeks, exposing the slight pattern of freckles on each of my cheekbones and going across the bridge of my nose. I apply powder and try to remember the feeling of it sweeping across my face when Zoë and Shay made me up. My reflection has guilty eyes. "A friend date…it's just…a friend date." I nod…crap, I can't even convince myself of that.

I finish by applying a bit of brown lipstick, a few shades darker than my skin tone that Zoë swears works for me. My head tilts, and I part my lips. Does it really work though? Maybe, he won't notice. He is a boy…a nearly two-hundred-year old boy, but still a boy.

I check the random curls hanging over my forehead…I nearly gasp…my huge forehead… I close my eyes and shake my head. He loves you…billboard forehead and all. I nod, shove everything back into the purse, and turn away from the mirror.

I walk out of the bathroom and toss my purse on my bed. I pause. Should I grab my glasses? I shake my head subtly and carefully hurry over to and then down the stairs. I try to keep my steps as quiet as possible and not fall at the same time. I reach the foyer without incident. The pendant tells me he's still in the library with the doors closed. I frown, but I decide I don't care how much noise I make at this point. I stride with a fair amount of stair-descending confidence over to the doors and throw them open. And he's blurry from here…but I can tell he has his back to me, while standing at the desk. He replaced the light overhead and blew out all the candles.

I step inside and flick the switch behind the door on my right. He looks up, as if the fixture is malfunctioning. I point at the candelabra holding three white candlesticks on top of the desk. "Extermino," I whisper, and they all light at the same time. He glances at them, before turning to me. He closes the book in his hands with a puzzled expression on his face. "We had a date." I walk toward him. "It wasn't your fault that a random ghoul attack spoiled it."

Tony places the book on the desk and approaches me. "It's a little sad that random ghoul attack ranks as more mundane than date in this house." I smile. "But it's late…and…"

"…and…I want you to take me on a picnic…" He opens his mouth to respond. I place my right pointer over his mouth. "I know it's late…and cold out…but I know…and you know a place where it's always warm." He smiles.

"We don't…have any food…"

"Now, you do," Twee says from the doorway. She places the huge picnic basket on the floor, smiles, and heads for the stairs. I motion toward the door.

Tony smirks, bows his head, and nods. He fastens all the buttons of his shirt, except the top one and then runs his fingers through his hair, pushing it all away from his face. I hadn't noticed how long it's gotten.

"Come on," he says. "We'll take my car."

I nod. He grabs the basket along the way, and I follow him outside. He holds the door open for me like always and then places the basket in the back. He raises the top, before climbing in. He starts the car and pulls away. I shiver. It's colder outside than I thought. He reaches over and pulls me to him. He's warm…and as a result, I nestle in next to him. Ugh, it's bad enough that his skin's warm, why does he have to smell so good, too?

He parks the car along the same roadside where I parked mine earlier. He helps me out of the car and then passes me the basket. "Hold onto this," he suggests before sweeping my legs out from under me again. He rushes through the woods effortlessly and with practically no light, moon or otherwise. His natural warmth seems to extend out in front of him, shielding me from the cold still.

We reach the clearing, and he carries me over to the well. He sits me on top of it. "Stay here for a second." I nod, and he vanishes. I look around the open space only slightly more visible than the woods, because of darkness and glasseslessness. I lean back and smell the fresh water below the metal grate.

Tony reappears with a rolled-up blanket under his right arm. He tosses it on top of a large patch of waist-high grass…and it just kind of sits on top of it. I open my mouth to take a jab… "Wait for it." He clasps his hands, pressing his palms together and intertwining his fingers. "Unda," he says and concentrates. The blanket slowly lowers to the ground.

"You pushed the water in the grass down to make it lay flat." He smiles and walks over. I put the basket in my lap as he takes me in his arms again. We move to the blanket. He kneels and sets me down.

I start unpacking the lunch Twee made. Inside the basket are four sandwiches, two pickle spears, two bags of potato chips (low fat, low sodium, of course, because Tony's such a health nut), two bottled waters, two snack cakes (also, low fat, Tony can have mine), and… "…a candle?" He frowns as I place the candle and its single candleholder down on the blanket. "Ex-ter-mi-no," I say, and the little candle ignites.

Tony smiles. The glow of the candlelight makes him look like an angel, glowing in tones of bright amber and gold. "What?" he asks. I shake my head. "You're staring."

"Hold still." He frowns but complies. I crawl over to him and wrap my arms around him. I lean away…and stare into his eyes. "I may not be able to say that I'm IN love with you…but never doubt that I love you so much…and I always will, okay?" He nods. I lean in to kiss him…but redirect and kiss him on his right cheek. I squeeze him as hard as I can as his arms wrap around my waist.

"I'll always love you too, Jamie." I sigh, and a tear falls from my left eye. Even if I tell you, I've been lying to you this whole time?

#####

Chapter 18: Dawn

I feel warm sunlight on my cheek. I inhale deeply, and my eyes flutter open. "Tony?" I purr before reaching out for him, and…all I get is blanket. I lift my head. "Tony?"

"He went walkies," Rais says. I sit up and find him, perched on the edge of the well…dark jeans over a white button up rolled up to his elbows…the shirt's top three buttons are undone. His hair hangs over his ears, a few strands border his face, and some hang over his forehead, casting a dark shadow over his eyes. His elbows rest on the tops of his thighs, and his hands dangle between his knees, prominently displaying his wolf's head ring. He looks as if he's about to pounce.

"What are you doing here, Rais?" I ask out of shock. I look around. "If he comes back, and you're here…"

"He won't be back for a while."

I frown and move up to my knees. "What did you do?" I rise to my bare feet and shake out my mess of hair.

"Me?" He motions to himself. I nod with a clenched jaw. "Nothing. He heard a noise, went to check it out…and then went running as quick as lightening through the woods after…something." He points at me. "You look amazing when you're sleeping, by the way…" He looks me over more thoroughly. I fidget nervously holding my right arm in my left. "…you look even more amazing with the sun shining through that fiery hair of yours, Bunny."

I move my hair back and over to the left. It tickles the base of my neck…so, long…even when it's not brushed out. Focus, Jamie. "You should leave, Rais," I say, pointing down. "You can't just keep popping up every time I leave the…"

"Fairies are watching you, Bunny."

"Wh-what?"

Rais hops down from the well and slowly moves toward me. "I said…the fairies…they're watching you, and I wanted to know why."

I swallow deeply. "I don't know why."

He nods, draws his lips into his mouth, and looks away. "You don't have to lie to me, Bunny." He comes back and stares into my eyes with those gunmetal blue marbles of his. I shake my head. "I promised I'd never keep anything from you." He points out and to his left. "That's more than either of them has ever promised. Tell me I'm wrong."

"You're wrong," I snap. He takes a half step back and glares at me…viscerally.

"That...wasn't a lie." My breathing speeds up because I'm seething over his assumption. He clenches his jaw, inhales deeply, and takes a step forward. I step back. "I would never hurt you, Bunny. You know that."

"But you don't trust me?"

"No, YOU don't trust me...I heard your heart...it skips a beat when you lie...and you just did when you told me you don't know why the fairies are watching you."

"I know why one fairy is watching me, and that's because she's my friend."

"Twelana?"

I frown. "How do you know that name?" He smirks. "Don't try to be cute. Answer the question."

"I talked to her. She spotted me...outside of the Blackshear's estate and...she tried to stop me." He rubs his right ear. "Her sound attack thing is a bitch, by the way."

"Language."

"Yes, ma'am," he returns with a faux salute. "She's rooting for me."

"Rooting for you?" He collects my right hand and holds it up near his mouth. He nods and places his forehead against the back of my hand. I try to pull it away. "Let go," I say in a weak voice.

"What do you want from me, Bunny?"

"I don't want anything from you, Rais."

"Liar," he moans and drops down to one knee in front of me, still holding my hand up to his forehead. If I didn't know any better, I would swear that he's about to propose.

"When you figure out what it is that you want from me..." He lifts his eyes, and I look down into them. He trembles...it was subtle, but I felt it. He's serious. All this time, I honestly just thought that Rais was flirting with me. On my side, sure, but all the rest...I thought he was just one big flirt. "...say the word and I'll be it..." It never dawned on me that maybe, he might be like the wolves or the vampires...wolves with their scent bonding thing or how vampires fall in love at first sight. I shake my head. "...your friend, your lover, like a brother to you...your mate..." He kisses the back of my hand. "...name it and I'll be it."

I sigh. "You should go," I say as the Crescent Moon Pendant tells me that Tony is coming back. He stands, caresses the left side of my face, and then holds his palm firm to it. He stares into my eyes still.

"Fine, I'll take this for now."

"Take what...?" He leans in, and I push against his chest, trying to stop him from kissing me...on my cheek...I frown. His lips are softer than I imagined they'd be. He smells like wild flowers, and the dust when it starts to rain…and eager passion…or at least, what I imagine eager passion would smell like.

I draw my lips into my mouth and push against his chest with both of my closed fists. He moves back. "I thought you were going to try and kiss me."

"Only when you want me to, Bunny." I nod. He stares at me. "You really are beautiful; you know that…? And the fact that you're very pretty…" He smiles warmly. "…only adds to that." He releases me and steps back. "Hopefully, I'll see you again soon, Bunny." He vanishes.

"Bye," I whisper. He called me *beautiful* and then said that I was *pretty* too. I frown. What did he mean by that?

"You're awake," Tony says, behind me. I turn and nod, still not quite ready to form words after my exchange with Rais. "Good morning," he says and slips his arms around me. I hesitate but lean into him. My head rests on his collarbone, and I put my hands on his firm, muscular arms. "You're trembling. Are you cold?"

"No. Just ready to go…" I nod against his chest. "…home."

"Fair enough." He releases me, and I take a step back. I gather my shoes by the heels in my left hand and reach for the basket with the right. "What's with that expression on your face?" I shake my head, and my nose tweaks. "Fine," he says. He's angry, and I heard a bit of my old sparring partner somewhere in that one word.

I stand up and glare at him. "What?" He frowns and looks away. "No, if you have something on your mind, please don't hold your tongue on my account."

"Fine," he says again. "You are the one who demands honesty and openness from me at all times, but you are keeping things from me. I don't know how I know or even if they're big, heart-rending things or tiny, inconsequential things…but I know that you are keeping things from me…and it confounds me to no end that you insist on doing it."

I watch careful as that old fire returns to his eyes. His shoulders move up and down quickly with his accelerated breathing, and I have to fight not to stare at his chest…his eyes are a close second, so I look there. He's so hot right now.

"I only keep things from you," I start. "…because I don't know how you'll react to them…"

"Same." His jaw clenches, and he moves closer. I might be insane, but I can actually feel the heat, building between us.

"…no, you keep secrets because you're ashamed…and you're afraid…you're afraid of how I'll react to them toward you. I keep secrets because I don't know what you're going to do in your reaction to them." He takes a step back. He never backs off until I prove him wrong. I groan. I hope he's not still in making amends mode. "Whatever," I say like complaint and shove him to one side so that I can reach the basket.

"I can't help wanting you, okay?"

"Yes, you can. I manage just…" I look at him…or more accurately, I look at the Avarice Seal on his right forearm glowing bright red and the Wrath seal on his left, glowing with the same intensity. I drop my shoes and the basket at the same time. "…Tony," I say, extending my hand to him in what I hope is a calming manner. He stares at me with furious eyes. "Tony, it's okay. I'm right here. There's no one else around…" I nod unevenly. "…I'm yours, okay? There's no one else here to claim me." He moves closer and wraps his arms around me again. "S-see…" I stutter with my hands on his chest. "…yours…all yours…"

"Mine."

"No, she's not."

My eyes bulge. "No," I weep as Tony releases me and instantly places himself between Rais and me.

"Let her go," Rais demands. Tony growls.

"Rais don't," I say between clenched teeth.

"I told you, I would protect you, Bunny," he returns. "And as long as those things on his arms are glowing, you're in danger."

"He…draws…strength from them. He gets stronger by drawing on their power and…"

Tony wraps his arms around me and lifts me off my feet, while turning his back on Rais. "MINE!" he says. "She's all mine and you can't have her, dog!"

"Tony, calm down…Rais isn't going to…" I fall… "…ugh…" …on my butt. I turn to the side and rub it…probably bruised. I lift myself up onto my knees. Rais flies through the air. He rights himself, twists, and manages to land on his feet. He rips his shirt off, and his skin explodes with black fur as his claws extend. He roars, exposing all four of his sharp canines.

Tony walks toward him, holding a lightning bolt in his left hand. It builds a brighter, more intense charge with every step. "Stop," I yell. Rais's red eyes dart to me and go back to Tony instantly. Tony has no intention of stopping.

"Fine," I say, running toward the space between them. "I'll stop you." They run toward each other. I lift my left hand toward Tony. "Expugnationis," I say, while drawing a square in mid-air with my pointer and middle fingers. I look at Rais and hold my right hand out to him. "Cohibeo." I draw a triangle with my pointer and middle fingers there. Tony collides with the spherical shield that I placed around him. Rais falls to the ground with his arms bound behind his back. I can almost see the invisible shackles on his wrists.

"Now," I say, slowing to a walking pace…and trying to ignore the pain of stepping on a rock just now. "Are you both willing to listen to me or do I have to get rough?"

Tony throws his lightning bolt against the shield. I wince from the intense spike in pain, but the shield…and I…hold. Rais stands and slowly moves his arms from behind his back as he did with my shield when I fought him months ago. He knows that its design gives it the ability to throw back at him what he gives it, so he's taking his time. I can feel the binding shatter. He throws his arms up denoting his freedom and then moves toward me while lowering them slowly. Tony growls and punches the shield. I wince again…that one I actually felt in my chest.

"FINE. Rough, it is." I extend my left hand toward Tony. I draw a triangle in mid-air, and then form a square around that…reflection and strength.

I turn my attention back toward Rais. "Diverbero," I snarl while creating a square and then a seven-sided figure around it. He slams into the ground as if there's a large weight on his back. He lifts hurt, pained eyes as the redness melts away from his pupils and the darkness changes to whites.

"I…," I start, motioning to myself, hand landing on the Crescent Moon Pendant. "…am NOT a possession! I am Jamina-Lynda Baggett! I am a Witch of Light, and I have had ENOUGH of this crap from the both of you, okay?"

I turn to Rais. "Rais, when I release you…leave! I don't need your protection! If you want to keep watching my back, fine! I can't stop you from doing that…but clearly, I'm not the same helpless girl that you, yourself, nearly killed six months ago!" He purses his lips and nods.

"AND YOU!" I turn to Tony. "We could've had a nice morning…but no, you had to be overprotective and go chasing something through the woods which, by the way, was really stupid, because you left me here asleep and defenseless!" Tony bows his head with his left hand resting on the shield.

"When I release you…long after Rais is gone…you're going to gather up the blanket, the basket, and my shoes, and then you're going to carry me back to your car, and you're going to take me home! Yeah?" He nods.

"Okay." I sigh and snap my fingers on my right hand. Rais, normal, human-looking Rais, stands. He stares at me as if he were a puppy that someone squirted with a water gun. He swallows deeply, sighs, and then darts off to my right. I stare after him and frown.

I come back to Tony. "Show me your arms." He holds his forearms out, showing me that his seals are dark again. I snap the fingers on my left hand,

and his shield dissipates. He walks toward me. I hold up my hand to halt him. "Basket. Blanket. Shoes." He stops and nods.

He gathers the blanket up and folds it neatly. He places it inside the nearly empty basket and my shoes on top of the blanket. He looks at me…with the same expression that Rais did. I give him the *come here* finger. He walks over and bends as if he's going to sweep me off my feet. I wrap my arms around him before he can. "I hate what those things do to you," I say.

He puts his left hand on the small of my back. "I'm sorry. I thought I had finally gotten a handle on them."

I look up at him. "They're sins based on emotions. Your emotions. You're not supposed to *handle* them; you're supposed to learn how to process them." He nods again. "Take me home…I wanna sleep in my bed." I reach down and take the basket from him. He lifts me effortlessly. I put my right arm over his shoulder and then cradle the basket in my lap. I can't help feeling a little guilty. I feel like I'm leading both him and Rais on, but if that's true…then aren't I leading Quincy on, too?

#####

Chapter 19: Trust

Tony quickly carries me out of the woods and places me in the front seat of his car. He places the basket in the backseat and climbs behind the wheel. He starts the car and reaches for the shifter. I catch his hand. "What were you chasing through the woods?"

"It's not important."

"Tony."

"Vampire," he says, while shifting into drive.

"What?"

"It was just before sunrise. I heard him before I saw him. I sniffed him out, and I chased him off." He swings the car around. "I checked the area for any more of them, despite popular theory," he says with a glance in my direction. "...and then I picked up his scent again and tried to track him down."

"Did you?"

"No," he says while shaking his head. "He must've found someplace to hide just before dawn..."

"But you were tracking his scent, right?" He nods. "Then how did he...?"

"...he ran out of town." We zip through the square. "I couldn't follow." He hits the steering wheel. "The rest of the time I spent going around the border making sure that he didn't double back." I nod. "Was Rais there before I came back?" I frown. "You didn't seem all that surprised when he came out."

I ponder lying, but with all my talk about honesty, I decide to say, "Yeah" in the form of a sigh. Tony purses his lips and looks out the side window. I can even see the muscles in his neck tense up. "Are you mad?"

"Nope. I'm as happy as a clam."

"I don't think clams lead the happy-go-lucky lives that people think they do." He glares at me. That was dumb. "I should've told you."

"Yes, you should've." He frowns. "What did he want?" I shake my head. He stops just before turning onto the estate's driveway. He shifts the car into park, leaving us in the middle of the empty road and leans back on his seat. He stares at me. "Jamie, what did he want?"

"He pledged himself to me," I admit in a whisper.

"HE WHAT?"

"He..." I break off, already feeling like I'm on thin ice here. "...he told me that he was mine...and that I could have him..." Tony squeezes the steering wheel so much that it groans under his grip. "...I could have him in...whatever capacity I wanted."

"What is that supposed to mean?"

"He said it can mean whatever I want it to…friend, protector…" I swallow deeply. "…lover…"

"So, that's what it is?" I frown. "You want to sleep with him, don't you? Is that what it is?" He glares at me. "You want to be his little whore?" My hand makes contact with his face before I even realize what I'm doing.

"Don't you…EVER…talk to me like that again, Anthony Blackshear! Do you understand me?" He scowls and seethes with anger. It's okay. I'm doing the same. I throw my door open.

"Where are you…?"

I climb out and slam it behind me. "AWAY FROM YOU!" I start walking down the road with no clear idea where I would even go and no shoes to help me get there. I just know that I have to get away from him before I do or say something that I can't take back. I have to get away, because being around him right now makes me feel nauseated and dizzy…and-and…hurt…it really, really hurt. I clutch my stomach and try to hold back the bile I feel welling up in me. A few tears roll away at the thought…the very thought that he believed that I would…

"Jamie?"

"Stay away from me!" I shout without looking at him.

"Jamie, I can't…"

I turn to face him. "Have I once…ONCE asked what you or Quincy was doing with 'fake me' while I was unconscious? Huh?" He looks down and slips his hands into his pockets. "No. Because I trust you…I trust you enough to believe that on some level, in some way, despite the fact that that…that thing was wearing my face…you would know the difference…that YOU wouldn't do anything that would hurt me." I sigh and shake my head as more tears fall. "Why can't you trust me the same way?"

He sighs, and his shoulders slump. I motion between us. "We…had an amazing night last night…and I thought…for one shining, beautiful moment…I thought you and I were getting back to being good…" I shake my head. "…but you're only happy when things are bad. When it's all gloom and doom and misery. I can't live like that Tony. I can't…and I won't." I turn… "Just…just leave me alone, okay? Go away." …and resume walking.

"Where will you go?"

"I can stay with Alex or Meghan for a few days until my mom gets back." He catches my left hand on a backswing. "Let go." He doesn't. I turn. "Let…go…"

"I can't." I try to pull away. "I'll do better. I promise…just…just don't leave." He caresses my left cheek with the back of his right hand. I move away from his touch. "I…I couldn't sleep a wink last night…because I lay there beside you, and I thought…this amazing woman wants me to be a part of her life. Even if I'm not her mate…her love…I should accept her invitation to be a part of her life graciously." He holds my left hand up near his heart and places both of his hands around it. "I wanted so very much to see you at dawn…the sunlight shining through your hair…tiny rays of light beaming against your skin…" He swallows deeply. "…I can be…I can be what you need me to be."

He nods. "Jamie, I am…sorry for every stupid thing that I've ever said to you…but I can't guarantee that I won't say more stupid things to you." He shakes his head. "I am totally and completely in love with you…and because of that…my heart will always make me a clumsy, blithering idiot around you." He caresses my hand with both of his. "But I will set my feelings aside…to be the friend that you need me to be. Just don't go. Please let me be your friend."

I laugh humorlessly and another…this time happy…tear rolls down my cheek. "You dummy. You don't let someone be your friend…they just are." I tilt my head down and kiss his hands on mine. "And you ARE…my friend…" …that I'm in love with too… "…just act like it, okay?" He nods, smiles, and wraps his arms around me. I put my arms under his. "I love you, you big idiot."

"I love you, too, Jamie."

#####

Chapter 20: Seal

"Hi." I pause to read her nametag. "Emily," I finish. "Um, is Gwen working today?"

"No," the girl with the caramel complexion and cinnamon colored hair with eyes to match answers. "She has the day off. Can I help you with anything?"

"Oh, yeah. I'll have a medium mocha latte with whipped cream and a hot chocolate with cinnamon…" Eek, did I say that because of her ridiculously gorgeous hair or what? "…and whipped cream on that, too."

Emily nods and rings me up. "That'll be…six-eighty-five." I nod and pass her a ten. She gathers my change, and I hold up my hand letting her know to keep it. She frowns. "You sure?" I nod. "Thanks. I'll bring your order out to you," she says while depositing the money into the small glass jar next to the register.

I nod and turn back to the brown table near the center of the shop with its tiny black chairs with woodgrain brown seats.

Twee smiles as I make my way back to her. "So," she says. "Can we talk now?" I nod and sit. "You've been acting weird lately."

"Weird? What do you mean?"

"Well, what's going on with you and Tony? You guys have barely said three words to each other in the last couple of days." I instantly feel a pain in the pit of my stomach. I try to remember if that's right, but it is. Tony and I haven't said anything to each other in days. He gives me a ride home after school and then he disappears for hours.

Twee puts her elbow on the table and rests her chin on top of her hand. "In fact, you guys haven't said much to each other since…that late night picnic." I sigh. "Did something happen? Did you guys…?" She moves her free hand in an awkward circle. I shake my head subtly, letting her know I don't know what she's trying to say. She arches her eyebrows. "…you know? Did you guys, you know?"

She's asking if I hooked up with…I gasp. "What…? No." I push my glasses up. "What is with everybody thinking that…? Do I really seem like that kind of girl?"

"Well, when I first met you, I'd say 'no,'" she admits. "But now…"

"But now…WHAT?"

"Here you go," Emily says, placing our drinks on the table.

"Thanks."

"Enjoy." She walks away.

I slide the hot chocolate over to Twee and try to smile. As soon as Emily returns to the counter, I come back to Twee. "No, Tony and I have not done anything."

"Are you mad at me?" I sip my latte. I don't answer; too busy trying not to let the feeling of rage subside.

"No," I grumble, which isn't fair. I mean, before I met Quincy and Tony, I never even thought of doing…anything with anybody…no one in particular anyway. I nibble my bottom lip. That was before I nearly ripped Tony's clothes off…my head slumps down to the tabletop…and then started undressing myself…in my bedroom…in his house.

"I'm sorry," Twee says in a soothing voice, while stroking my hair. "I am, okay?"

"Why are you apologizing to her?" Stefana says.

My head snaps up as she takes the seat across from me with her back to the counter. She wears a deep red silky top that's just sheer enough to show the tiny camisole underneath it. She has one gold necklace with a pendant that looks like a sword with fairy wings as the guard. Her golden hair falls down her back and across her shoulders in long waves. Her golden eyes dart to me as she puts her elbow on the table and rests her chin on her right hand.

"Private conversation," I groan, adjusting my glasses. She makes a disinterested noise and rolls her eyes. She glances at the counter. "What are you even doing here, Stefana? I told your mother that Twee would be…"

"Insufficient to keep a proper watch over you."

"Stef!" Twee shakes her head.

"I told you never to call me that!"

"So, it's true," I cut in. They look at me. "The fairies…plural…have been watching me." Stefana nods. I look at Twee. "And you knew?" She looks away. "We're supposed to be friends, Twee." I turn back to her sister. "Why? Why are the fairies watching me?"

"I don't have to answer to you."

"You do if you don't want me to knock you off that high horse you've put yourself on."

"Jamie," Twee says. I glare at her, and she sits back with a defeated expression. "I'm sorry," she says in her fairy voice.

"Don't apologize to this human."

"Not human," I say. "Reigning Witch of Light," I over-exaggerate my position. "And don't you forget it." Stefana's eyes narrow.

Emily moves over to Stefana's side. "Hey, sorry for the wait. Blame the barista who decided he wanted to no-call, no-show for his shift today."

"It's quite alright, Emily," Stefana says without even looking. "I'd like a coffee…black with a flavor shot of cinnamon."

"Coming right up." Emily hurries back to the counter as two more people walk up.

"Why have you fairies been watching me?" Stefana doesn't answer. She looks at me as if I'm something smaller than I am. She looks at me like a cat facing something smaller, not as an adversary, but more like something hardly worth her notice.

"Mother told us to…"

"TWELANA!" Stefana says.

"…she's my friend," Twee says back.

"Why would your mother tell you to watch me? I thought she was suspicious of my mom." Stefana's top lip turns up at the corner. "Come on, Stefana. The can's open…the worms are everywhere. You might as well fess up."

"What a vulgar metaphor."

"It's not that she doesn't trust you," Twee says. Stefana crosses her arms, clearly not happy with this turn of events. "She was worried about you." I frown. "She knew that your mom is…was En Quosque. She was worried that…since you're even stronger than your mom, that they might come for you next."

I sigh. "I thought of that, too. I might be stronger than my mom…but she's a lot more in control of her magic…and she knows way more than I do…and-and…she's more experienced…"

"You weave seals in mid-air," Stefana grumbles this time.

"So…what does that…?"

"No, witch…white…dark or any other kind has EVER been able to weave signs in mid-air and make them apply to their magic," Stefana says begrudgingly.

"So, I can apply seals…"

"No," Twee says. Her voice echoes like a chiming sort of whine. "Not only do you apply seals, but each of the seals has a meaning for you." She draws a hexagon on the table with her right pointer finger. "Touch it." I scoff, but I do it. Twee collects the sugar from the center of the table and pours it into the hexagon…the sugar instantly moves to the inside edges of the finger drawn shape…including the random bits that fell just outside. "Draw."

She draws a square next to the tiny sugar hexagon. She removes the cinnamon stick from her hot chocolate and places it in the square. She tips her head to it, and I tap the space with my right pointer finger. Stefana collects the cinnamon stick in a blur and stabs the tabletop with it. She removes her hand, and the stick stands up…no, it's not standing up. She drove it into the table. "Strength," Twee says.

"How is that possible?"

"You tell us," Stefana says.

I shrug. "I know you don't know," Twee says, glancing at her sister. "It comes naturally to you. You weave the seals as if they're second nature to you. It's like they've been driven into you with priest-like devotion to the point that your magic doesn't understand how these shapes could mean anything else. It's like your mind instantly fills in the blanks for you."

I stare at the cinnamon stick standing up from the table. I focus on it…close my right eye and use both pointers to draw a small, seven-sided shape around it. When I finish, the cinnamon stick crumbles into cinnamon powder. I gasp.

"Disruption," Stefana says.

"That's not possible."

"And yet, you just did it," Stefana says.

Emily places Stefana's coffee down next to her. "Here you go…uh oh, did someone spill some cinnamon?" she asks while moving over to Stefana's left to wipe it up.

Stefana leans in closer to Emily, who's almost leaning over her. She inhales deeply. I frown, and my eyes dart to Twee. She shakes her head, while staring at her sister.

"How much do I owe?" Stefana asks as Emily wipes the last of the reddish-brown powder away.

"Um," Emily hums. "That's a buck-fifty."

"Here you go," Stefana says while passing Emily a twenty…making sure that her hand brushes Emily's as she passes her the bill. "You can keep the change if you bring me one of those delicious looking scones, gorgeous." Emily smiles…and blushes…before taking the twenty with a nod. She returns to the counter.

"Gorgeous?"

"Stefana likes girls," Twee says.

"I'm not ashamed of that fact." Stefana leans back with a blasé sort of confidence. "It's how our mother made me. I'm proud of it." She glances at Emily, who is removing a cinnamon scone from the display case. "And that is one gorgeous human." She comes back to the table. "Unlike present company, who I don't find appealing in the slightest."

"It's okay. You don't really do anything for me either." I motion to my chest. "You've got a lot more boob than I prefer on guys I date." Twee snickers. Stefana glares.

"So, your mom was worried about me…*turning to the dark side*. Why didn't she just tell me?" Twee and Stefana look away from the table…in different directions. I nod. "She wanted to see what choice I would make. If I would make the same one that my mom made."

"Yes." Stefana turns less than usual cold eyes on me. "She doesn't know you well enough to trust you." I nod. "You can't blame mother. She trusted your mother…and look how well that turned out."

"I'm not my mother."

"No one's saying you are," Twee says.

"You should've had faith in me, Twee. I'm your friend. Alex would never doubt me like this. I'm not asking for that level of loyalty, but you could at least give me the benefit of the doubt."

"Here you go," Emily says, placing Stefana's scone on a saucer next to her. "I…warmed it up for you." Emily's flirting. Stefana stares at her and smiles. "Um…your receipt's underneath." Emily's free hand falls on Stefana's shoulder. "Let me know if…*you* need anything else." Stefana nods, and Emily backs away before returning to the counter.

Stefana immediately slips her bill out from under the scone. She stares at it for a moment, smirks, glances at Emily, and then folds the receipt. She puts it in her pocket. Twee and I stare at her. "Phone number," she says with great satisfaction. I arch my eyebrows and glance at Emily before coming back to Stefana. She glares at me. "So, what are you going to do with this information, White Witch?"

"I don't care who you like…"

"Not that!" She bites her scone and purrs with delight at the taste. I hate to admit it, but it smells amazing. I want one now. Stefana looks at me and arches an eyebrow.

"Oh." She did just ask me a question, didn't she? I shrug. "Nothing." She frowns. "Twee's still my friend…your mother was just worried about me…and you just reconfirmed that I'm awesome, so…" Twee giggles. I wrap my arm around her and give her a squeeze.

"Why can't you two take all of this more seriously?"

"My thought exactly," Tony says over my shoulder.

I gasp. "Tony? When did you…?"

"He's been here for most of the conversation," Stefana says and sips her coffee. I frown and look at the Crescent Moon Pendant…dangling in mid-air. I sigh. I guess I have to be touching it for it to tell me where they are. "What's the matter faux-fae…?" Stefana stares at Tony with just her eyes. "No faith in your little White Witch since her tryst with the daemon in the woods?"

"Stef!" Twee says between clenched teeth. "I told you that in confidence." Stefana continues sipping her coffee nonchalantly.

Tony steps forward, and Stefana rises to her feet. I jump to mine and put a hand on his chest. "Not in public." Tony doesn't look at me. His eyes wander to the rest of the coffee shop, but never land on me.

"I mean, didn't she protect him from you?" Stefana's taking jabs. I glare at her. "Oh, please tell me if anything I've said has been untrue."

I turn back to Tony, and he still refuses to look at me. He backs away and turns toward the door. I come back to Stefana. She smirks, sits down, and sips her coffee again. She is a warrior…but she doesn't just cut with her whip or a sword…her tongue is just as vicious. She knows how to push people's buttons, and for Tony, next to Quincy, I'm the biggest button he has.

"You suck," I say in the form of a snarl before moving to the exit.

#####

Chapter 21: Faith

"Tony." I spot him at the corner. He stops, and his head bows forward. "You know that I wasn't protecting Rais from you…I was just trying to stop you two from fighting."

"That's what I don't get," he says, turning to face me. "I know that he said he was on your side and that you believed him for…whatever reason…but what has he done?" Tony shakes his head. "What has he done to earn this blind faith in him? Has he protected you? Has he helped you in anyway? Or has he just shown up randomly trying to place some wolf-right on you?"

"Well, he didn't pee on my leg if that's what you mean." He scoffs and turns away. "Stop walking away from me!"

"I'm not…walking away from you…I'm just walking away…"

"…from me." I grab his arm. He turns back to me with an exasperated sigh. "Let me ask you this. What did you do?" He frowns. "What did Quincy do for that matter?" I throw my arms out to my sides. "Nothing. Neither of you did anything for me before I showed up on your doorstep asking for help…I put that kind of blind faith in the two of you. Was I wrong to do that?"

"That was different." He purses his lips and shakes his head. I sigh. "I worry about you, Jamie."

"I know. I worry about you too, but I've never doubted that your heart was in the right place…" I shake my head. "…even if it leads your brain into weird places." He nods with a bit of a smirk.

"We need to talk," Rais says…behind me. I gasp and turn to him. He stares at me with a stern expression. He lifts his eyes from me to Tony. "Now."

"I can't right now," I reply. "I'm with…"

"I mean, all of us," Rais says. I glance at Tony. He frowns, and we both come back to Rais. He tips his head toward the side of the building. He steps past us, rounds the corner, and moves away from the square. I look to Tony. He shakes his head. I take his hand and pull him along behind me. We follow Rais down the block and to the chain coffee place on the next block.

"Welcome to Jumpin' Bean!" the entire staff chimes as we walk through the aluminum siding looking door. That was super creepy. The whole thing looks so new aged, techno nightmare. The coffee smells over cooked and not a thing in the pastry counter looks even remotely appetizing.

"Come on," Rais says, walking over to the counter.

"How can I help you?" the overly perky blond says behind the counter.

"Coffee," Rais says. He motions to Tony. "…coffee…" He moves on to me. "…I'm guessing…caramel latte…" I nod unevenly. "…all mediums."

"We don't have medium, sir," she returns. "We only have…"

"The middle size," Rais cuts her off abruptly. She sighs and rings him up.

"You didn't have to be rude." He frowns while the crew behind her preps our order. He gives her a twenty and places the change in the tin can next to the register. He passes our drinks along, motions to one of the silver-on-red booths near the back, and we move to it. I sit, and Tony slides in next to me. Rais sits opposite us. I put my drink on the linoleum-feeling tabletop.

"I know you didn't just bring us here for the terrible coffee," Tony says.

"And you'd be right." Rais stares down at his cup. He looks…sad…and tired.

"Are you okay?"

He looks at me briefly and nods. "How's the search going?" he asks.

I frown. "What se-?"

"Not well," Tony replies before I can finish my question. I glare at Tony, as Rais starts pouring sugar and creamer into his coffee. "How did you know…?"

"Because ever since our little…skirmish…I haven't been allowed back in," Rais says and sips his coffee. Tony does too…but black. Bleh, I moan to myself while draping my tongue out of my mouth. "I've been searching for it myself." Rais puts his paper cup down and taps his fingers on the table unevenly. "You know it's the center, right?" Tony nods and sips his coffee.

"What are you guys talking about?"

Tony sighs and puts his hands on the table around his coffee. "I've…been searching for the building that we fought…" He lifts his eyes to Rais and immediately comes back to me. "…them in. See, the first time that Quincy and I found it…we only found it…"

"Because of my clan's pendant," Rais says. Tony tilts his head back and eyes Rais like the opponent he perceives him to be.

"Guys, not helping the detail impaired redhead at the…" I rub my fingertips together. "…ugh, sticky table. Why are you searching for it?" I look at Rais. "And why aren't you able to find it?" I shake my head. "My mom found it without trying."

"She's one of the eight. I'm a vassal…was a vassal of Liz's…I was only granted permission to enter while she was alive." I nod.

"So, I'd have to be granted permission to enter it?"

Rais nods. "It's the most powerful…and somehow…simplistic glamour I've ever seen," Rais says. "If you're one of the eight…you wouldn't even see the glamour…you'd only see the building…" He motions away from himself with a downward sweep of his hand. "…but to anyone else…damn near impossible to see through it."

"That's why," I say. They look at me. "I remember thinking that I'd never seen that building before my mom pulled up to it...and this is Edenton. Edenton's too small not to know exactly where everything is."

"Exactly," Rais says. "So, they hid it in plain sight...but they hid it well."

"They've been hiding it for at least two hundred years," Tony says. His hands clench into fists. "My brother searched for the last seal the entire time he was here..." He looks at me. "...and whenever I'd come back...we'd resume the search together."

"It's the last seal?" They nod. "It's the one that would...kill everyone in Edenton to restore Eden's mind?" They nod again.

"Supernaturals wouldn't be affected," Rais says. "Call it a benefit of being in the know." He takes his coffee and stands. Tony glares at him. "If I find anything, I'll let you know."

"Good," Tony says.

"Not you." He looks at me. "You." I sigh and nod. "Also, the fairies are acting strange."

"What do you mean?" Tony asks. Rais's jaw tenses, and he looks away from the table.

"Rais?" He returns to us. "Thank you for telling me about them watching me...Twee admitted it."

He nods. "You can trust her. The little blue fairy is different from her sisters..." His eyes narrow. "...with any luck, she'll be the next queen."

"But Twee's the youngest..."

Rais nods. "And the next Fairy King is younger than she is so..."

"What did you mean, they're acting strange?" Tony asks.

Rais shakes his head. "Don't trust any of the others, especially not the Queen." I swallow deeply. "The new fae of En Quosque...is a fairy. A powerful one at that. I heard the first thing she did when she joined was laid claim to Morten, Devon, and one other higher order daemon." He shakes his head. "Fae hate daemons...so if she's recruiting daemons first...that means she hates her own kind more than the daemons."

"That's depressing."

He nods. "You're welcome for the coffee," he says to Tony and walks away.

I feel the vibration of Tony's right foot tapping against the floor. "He's better informed than I thought," he says as a complaint. "Did you believe him?"

I nod.

He doesn't even look at me, but I know he knows. He nods, too. "Faith?" I take his right hand in both of mine and lean my head against his shoulder.

"Faith."

####

Chapter 22: Course

"Okay," I whisper to Tony and Twee across the aisle. "I'm a little worried." I steal a glance at Mrs. Pritchard to make sure that she's not paying us any attention. "Forgive me…but I don't have over a hundred siblings…and my single relation doesn't come and go every twenty years or so." Twee smirks, and Tony gets that irritated look on his face. "I'm worried about them." I shake my head. "We haven't heard from them in over a week."

"Ms. Baggett, Mr. Blackshear," Mrs. Pritchard says in that horrible nasally voice of hers. She pulls down on her rectangular glasses and tilts that salt and pepper bun back to see us. "Would the two of you and Ms. Fairchild like to stay after school for detention?"

"No, ma'am."

"No," Tony says.

"No, thank you," Twee chirps.

"Then do be quiet and pay attention." I nod, and she resumes talking about…snails or something.

I sigh and tap my pen on my notebook. I still see Tony out of the corner of my eye. He mutters something to himself. He finishes and touches his forehead with right middle and pointer fingers. His eyes drift closed. He stretches out to me.

I extend my left hand to him. Our corresponding fingers meet. He motions to his forehead. I bow my head and touch my forehead. My eyes drift closed slowly. It's a twist on the standard memory spell. He put a string of thoughts into a sort of package of memories.

"I hate to admit it," he says. "I miss him…them and I'm worried about them too…you're beautiful…" My nose twitches. I don't think he meant to include that one. "…I've been calling Quincy…yes, I've been calling him…even though he's the only thing standing between us and because of that I'd like to punch him in the face…" Another errant thought.

"…no worries though. I have a few friends down in New Orleans…" I scowl, because this thought even has visual images like picture attachments…lots and lots of pictures…all his *friends* are women. Every single one of them is a witch, true enough, but they're ALL women, gorgeous women. He seems to hold onto the image of three women in particular…a tall woman with chestnut brown hair, a shorter woman with darker brown hair, and a woman with medium brown hair and purple tips. He has a special sort of affection toward miss purple tips with her big brown eyes and all her chestiness. I groan aloud, and my eyes dart over to Tony. He takes notes like a diligent student, and I drag my nails across my desktop…rather than hitting him.

"He's not mine. He's not mine. He's not mine," I say to myself like a mantra. I hear a soft, sly whistle. I glance at Twee. She arches her eyebrows. I shake my head subtly. I sigh and play with the Crescent Moon around my neck…thinking of Quincy. I wonder how many witches he has in his past. I sigh.

The bell rings, and we file out of class. "So, these friends…" I start when Tony walks out into the hall with Twee behind him. "…are they…" I shake my head. "…girls or are they guys? A little of both?"

Tony laughs humorlessly and shakes his head. "Careful, Jamie. You almost sound jealous."

I scoff. "I…do not sound jealous." Yes, I did because I am. "I was just asking a simple question about your past. I mean, you are pretty old so…"

"You guys aren't going to fight again, are you?" We both turn to Twee walking behind us. "Because this sounds like another fight."

"We're not going to fight," Tony says.

"Yeah. I mean, Tony has a past…Quincy has a past…I'm sure even you have a past Twee…"

She purses her lips and shakes her head. "Not really…I'm only 15 years old."

"You're 15," I pose…too loudly.

Twee immediately shushes me. "I may look like I'm 17…"

"No, you look like you're 15," Tony interrupts.

"…LIKE I was saying," Twee continues. "I may look 17, but I've looked like this since I was 5…most fairies mature in 5 or 6 years."

"I did not know that." She nods. I turn back to Tony. "Now, back to these witches…" He and Twee groan. He walks toward the parking lot, and Twee follows him. "What? I just wanted to know if you'd heard anything from them."

Tony opens the passenger door of his car and holds the backseat for Twee. She climbs in, and he releases it. The seat falls back with a springy thunk. I step between him and the open door. "Seriously though, these witches…?"

Tony sighs, and his head bows forward. "I called one of my friends…outside of the Quarter first…she said that she would take a few other witches from her coven down to check it out. That was three days ago…I haven't heard back from her yet." He tips his head toward me and taps his right finger on his open door. "Good?" I nod and fall into the front seat. He closes the door behind me and moves quickly to the driver seat.

"Do you think they're in trouble?" I ask while Tony zips through town. "My mom and Quincy and all the radio silence…?"

"I don't know. My brother's a lot things but weak isn't one of them and then there's your mom." I nod. He turns onto Guardian Trail heading back toward the house. "Besides the witch who I called for help is…" He peers out the front window. "…standing directly in front of my car." I turn to the front as he steps on the brakes.

A beautiful, chesty woman with purple tips stands in front of us with her hand extended toward us to halt us. She's one of the three women I saw from his memory spell. I feel magic swirl up around her; her black jacket and long pale blue dress blow back behind her. Her magic makes contact, and the car screeches to a stop causing us to lunge forward and Twee to bump into my seat.

"You okay?"

"Yeah," she squeaks, holding her forehead. I adjust my glasses and return to the front.

"Hey, my handsome man," purple-tips says while lowering her hand. Her voice sounds sweeter than sugar dipped in honey. She smirks and bats her eyes in a flirty way. "Did you miss me?" I groan. "Better question," she says with one arched eyebrow. "Did you lose something?"

I frown and look at Tony. He frowns, shifts the car into park, and steps out. He blurs over to her and stares down at her with that same dangerous scowl. She stares right back up at him. He smiles and wraps his arms around her. She puts her arms around him and laughs as he lifts her off the ground. "I loves my snuggles," she says with a lot of giggles.

"And I'd love to hold onto my lunch," I say with my arms crossing over my stomach.

"It's really him," the woman says, moving the hair away from her face. "Take it down." The space behind them ripples and then shatters, revealing a red jeep with a hard top parked diagonally across the road. The front doors open, and the other two women that I saw in his memories climb out. The shorter one with dark brown hair done up in big baby doll curls and alabaster skin smirks before barely parting her deep red lips. She's as chesty as the snuggler is.

The taller one pushes glasses up on her slender nose and smiles. Her shoulder length chestnut hair hangs straight around her adorable face. She arches one perfectly manicured eyebrow and takes in Tony and the snuggler thoughtfully.

"Tony," Twee says, standing on the backseat. "Who are they?"

"Sorry. Jamie," he says tipping his head to me. "…Twee…" He lowers the snuggler to her feet. She smiles at me…and I want to punch her in her gorgeous face. "…this is Sara." He said her name as if it were something delicate. He gives her another quick squeeze. "…and two members of her coven…" He motions to princess pouty lips. "…Amie…with an I-E…" He half-turns to the tall, leggy one. "…and Rebecca."

"Hey," Rebecca says with a bob of her head.

"Hi," Amie says with a soft voice.

"Ladies, that's Twelana in the backseat. Call her Twee." He looks at me. "And this is Jamie."

"Oh, you were right, Tony," Sara says, stepping closer to the car. She puts both hands on the hood and stares at me. "She is stunning." I frown. Tony smirks, looks down and moistens his lips with his tongue.

"Okay," I say. "This is all very…cute or whatever…but why are you three here and what about him losing something?"

"Yeah, we found the hot one," Amie says. Rebecca glares at Amie over the hood of the car. Amie shrugs. "What? Tony's cute and all…but he doesn't quite have the do-ability that Quincy does."

"Quincy? Did you find him? Where is he?" I ask, making all three questions sound like one, while ignoring her cringe worthy 'do-ability' comment.

"See for yourself," Rebecca says, motioning to the car.

I move to climb out. "Not here," Tony says, putting a stay put hand out to me. "Let's get up to the house…" I frown and start to argue. "…if he could get out of the jeep on his own…hearing your voice, he'd already have his arms around you." I swallow deeply and nod. "Let's get up to the house." I sit back down, and Twee does the same.

Tony turns to the fence and mutters a quick spell. The barrier flashes over in bright orange, and their jeep flashes in the same color. Sara winks at him before taking the seat behind Amie. Tony reappears in the seat next to me. He shifts the car into drive.

"Sara?" I say, while pointing at the jeep.

"Is a friend." He smirks. "Jamie…are you…are you jealous?"

Yes. "What? Pfft, no. It's just…you guys seem REALLY close."

"She's…" He nods unevenly while pulling through the gate. He glances at me. "…she's my best friend." I frown. "Just friends."

"No. I figured…it's just…" I laugh. "You have a best friend?"

"I know, right?" Twee says from the backseat. I nod.

"Can we focus on the fact that they found my brother…made no mention of your mother, and the fact that my brother's unconscious?"

I nod.

#####

Chapter 23: Betrayal

Tony parks, and they park next to us. Amie pops the rear gate, and Tony is already out, pulling it open. He sighs and collects his brother. He throws a very unconscious Quincy over his shoulder and disappears before my heart can start pounding. I hurry into the house, and Twee follows.

I twist and turn in the vestibule debating which way they went. I grab the Crescent Moon Pendant and turn toward the library. I run inside just in time to see Tony lay his brother down on the sofa. "Quincy?" I say, kneeling next to him. "Is he?"

"He'll be fine," Sara says, striding confidently into the library past Twee. "When we found him, he was spelled. We released the spell, and now he's just sleeping off the effects." I sigh and nod. I frown when another thought occurs to me. "Don't worry," Sara reassures. "He'll be fine."

"I'm not worried," I say while rubbing Quincy's arm. "Not about him anyway." I nod and look at Sara's contemplative face. "You…only found him, right?" She nods. "Any sign of a struggle?" She purses her lips and shakes her head. I look at Tony, who's staring at me with a frown. "I'm more worried about who spelled him and why." I shake my head. "I can only think of one person who could get close enough to Quincy to spell him without a fight…" I shrug. "…besides me."

"Who?" Sara asks.

"Her mom," Twee sighs, and her shoulders slump.

"You can't," Amie starts sounding annoyed. "…seriously think a White Witch would…"

"We can…and she already has," I interrupt. I turn to Twee. She frowns and fidgets awkwardly. "Go…let Stefana know that she was right…about my mom anyway."

"She was hoping she was wrong," Twee says and lifts her right hand. "She really did…I can tell." Twee snaps her fingers and vanishes into a tiny pale blue light. "I'm sorry." She flies out of the library. I bow my head. "Jamie…"

I lift my head and spot Twee floating in the doorway. "I thought you were going to…"

"…you're my friend," she says. "I'm your friend…and as your friend, I feel I should tell you that a third fairy was left to watch you." I frown. "She's here. Now. Watching you." Twee sighs and bobs up and down. "I'm gonna go."

She floats out of the door. "Twee." She pauses. "You are my friend. Thank you for telling me." She bobs again and floats away.

I turn back to the interior of the library. "ALRIGHT! WHOEVER YOU ARE, GET OUT HERE! NOW! YOU DON'T WANT ME TO FIND YOU!" A tiny, green light floats down from the chandelier and moves between Sara and me. "Who are you?"

"It's me," a soft voice says. A finger snap sounds, and Ariella appears in front of me. She taps her pointer fingers together and stares at the ground. I sigh. "Sorry." She lifts her eyes to me only to have them dart back to the floor. "Mom…I mean, the Fairy Queen asked that I stay to aid Stefana the 7th and Twelana the 107th. I had no choice, really."

"I don't care," I say. "If you're going to be hanging around, make yourself known." She shivers. "I'm not mad; I'm just saying…I don't care if you guys watch me, because I don't have anything to hide."

"I had to report your meeting with the Daemon in the woods." I swallow a knot. "Both times…" I sigh.

Tony growls from the desk. "Both times?" he barks.

"Ariella," I say, placing both my hands on her shoulders and ignoring Tony entirely. "If you want to make things square with me…" I turn to my left and stare at Quincy. She follows my gaze. "…do you think you could do anything to help him come around faster?" She comes back to me. "It would really help me out, and it'd give you something else to report back to your mom…I mean, the Fairy Queen."

Ariella smiles and nods. She rushes over to Quincy's side and kneels next to him. She puts her left hand over his eyes. "Ah," she hums. "A hibernation spell…whoever lifted it was more concerned about its strength than its effects."

Sara steps forward. "What?"

"Sorry," Ariella says, before returning to Quincy. "He just needs a little boost." She reaches into a small brownish-green pouch nestled on her hip. "Unlike a suspended animation spell…" She glances at me. "…like the kind they put you in…" She comes back to Quincy, while taking a maple leaf and placing another leaf against it. "…a hibernation spell still lets you feel the effects of aging, hunger, and everything else on your body."

She looks at me again. "Also, unlike a suspended animation spell, it has to be held in place…sustained. It takes a lot of magic to maintain that kind of constant grip on someone rather than just the one shot of suspending them." I nod. She rubs the leaves together. They glow softly with her green magic and that whistling sound fills the room. "Whoever did this to him didn't plan to keep him under for very long but didn't want him at full strength when he came out of it." She places the leaves over his eyes. The glowing green moves from the leaves down his face and absorbs into his body.

"You're really chatty when you're explaining things," I say.

"Sorry," she says, falling back into her humble tone.

"You should explain things all the time. You sound confident when you do."

She smiles and takes the leaf away from Quincy's face. "That should do it…he should be coming to…about…" Quincy's eyes flutter. "…now."

"Wow," Sara says. "She's good."

"I'm adept at spirit and healing magic…" Ariella stands. "…heal the mind to heal the body," she says in a very bookish way.

I smile with a nod and claim Quincy's right hand. "Hey, are you okay?"

He opens his eyes, and they find me instantly. "Ugh, what happened? I feel like I drank too much and then let someone tap dance on my head." I play with each of his fingers until he wraps them around mine. He sits up in a blur and wraps me in his arms. "Jamina…I'm sorry…I'm so, so sorry…"

"I already know," I say into his ear. I slip my arms around his in return. "She did it to you, didn't she?" We separate, and he stares into my eyes. He nods. "So, she's still with En Quosque, and she caught you off guard?"

"Not exactly," he says. He lets me go. He turns so that he can put his feet on the floor, and I just want to hold him until he gets his bearings. He groans again, and I'm already there holding his arm. "We…we found Nelfala…just like I told you."

"You found Nelfie?" Tony asks, stepping closer.

Quincy nods. "Not just Nelfie…guess who else was paying a visit to the French Quarter at the same time we were." I glance at Tony, and he frowns. "Nathan Francois…"

I frown, recognizing the name, but not from where and knowing that Tony would. He growls. "What…was HE doing there?"

Quincy shakes his head. "Not sure…says his names, Dumont now." Quincy nods. "It's weird though…he had a newbie vampire with him that your mom…" He pauses to look at me. "…she seemed to recognize." I frown. He touches his forehead. "I can't shake the feeling that she reminded me of your friend Meghan, too." I nod.

"So," I say. "What's so weird about a Quarter Witch, being with a vampire? Vampires and witches work together all the time."

"Nathan's not a witch," Tony says in a grumble. I turn to him, and he seems actively pissed. He crosses his arms, and I can see his Avarice and Wrath Seals burning bright. He inhales deeply when his eyes meet mine. He releases his breath, and the seals' glow fade. "He's a wolf."

"Oh, that is weird," I say. From what I know about wolves and vampires, they are mortal enemies…like Aldiens and daemons, or like fae and daemons, or like vampires and daemons…wow, everybody hates daemons, right?

"I'm sorry," Amie says from the bar...where she's making some alcoholic beverage float out of its container. "What does any of this have to do with tall, dark, and gorgeous being betrayed and left unconscious?"

I glower at her.

"What?"

"Rude," Rebecca says in her direction with her arms crossed over her stomach. Amie shrugs and forces the alcohol back into its bottle.

"She's right," Quincy says. "I only mentioned them because Nelfie mentioned them... 'Two blasts from the past in one night,' she said." He scowls. "I should've known better...she used to follow Nate around like a lost puppy...hoping that he'd fall for her." He looks at me. "It's the only way I met a Quarter Witch...not being able to leave town and all." I nod.

He sighs, and his shoulders slump. "Anyway. Nelfie confirmed what your mother always suspected. Nelfie traded half her magical power away for an extended life." I frown. What kind of life could she have with half her magic? It'd be like trying to throw away half your soul and thinking...I shake my head...I don't even want to think about the rest of that statement.

"She also confirmed something else. The reason that the Fairy Queen refused to destroy the crystal, like Daphne asked her to, it also contains the souls of its victims." The coven witches all gasp. Ariella twitches like a pin pricked her. Tony clenches both his hands into fists.

"So, it's true."

"You knew?"

I stare into Quincy's eyes and nod. "The Fairy Queen told me...I asked Alex about it, and he said that Gwen's mom managed to escape, by using her portion of the crystal to help Gwen and Gavin beat their uncle."

"Wow," Rebecca says. "That's amazing." I sigh.

"Well, Nelfie seemed convinced that she could release the souls from the crystal. Release the souls...their power goes with them and no more power..." He nods. "...no crystal." He wrings his hands. I slip mine between, and he looks at me. I nod, and he does too.

"Nelfie said she needed time to prepare. With her magic halved, she needed to rely more on the potions and sigils than on her actual magic. Daphne and I went looking for Nate...Daphne said that it was important that we confirm the vampire with him was who she thought she was. We found signs of a fight at the boat yard...some vampire blood...some daemon blood...but apparently, Nate and the newbie walked away from the scuffle. I tracked them. They left New Orleans after they left the docks...didn't even go back to the hotel for their things.

"Anyway, Nelfie called. She was ready…in more ways than one. We went to her magic shop, and she wasn't alone. She had three daemons with her." Tony growls again. "I recognized two of them." Quincy looks at me.

"Rais?"

He shakes his head. "No. His…other two friends…"

"Morten," I say. "The one with the horns and the big hammer and Devon the fire guy?"

"That's them," Quincy says. "There was a girl with them too…I didn't get a good look at her, because as soon as I walked in, I almost got a hammer to the face." He runs his left hand through his hair, pushing it away from his face. "I was losing…bad…and Daphne stayed back. I figured, waiting to land a final blow or at least, trying to see what Nelfie would do." He pauses and looks down.

"I thought about you," he says into his chest, before his eyes dart over to me. "…my…Lust Seal kicked in…because I wanted to keep my promise to you…to end this." He nods. "I started kicking their butts…until…I heard Daphne start a spell…" He frowns. "…and Nelfie joined in. Next thing I know, I'm waking up here." He cranes his neck. "No, wait…" He looks at Sara. "…I saw your face in my dreams…telling me to 'snap out of it.'"

"You're welcome." Quincy laughs humorlessly.

"So, mom…Nelfie…and the crystal…" I sigh. "…Ariella, did you get all that?"

She looks at me with sad, reluctant eyes and nods. She lifts her left hand, preparing to snap her fingers. I nod. She follows through and vanishes into a tiny green light. The light fades, and she's gone.

"Wow," Amie says from the bar, where now she has a brown liquor and a clear one swirling around each other in a yin-yang pattern. "Fairies, wolves, and vampires…"

"Oh my G-"

"Rebecca," Sara says, cutting off her sisters' argument. "Do you think you can do anything to help Quincy regain his equilibrium?" Rebecca nods and steps forward. "Tony," Sara continues. "Do you think you could go get our bags out of the car?" Tony frowns. "Amie, be a lamb and go upstairs and pick out three of the unoccupied rooms for us."

Amie smirks and tosses Tony the keys to the jeep with one hand, while replacing the alcohol with the other. She hurries out of the library.

"What are you up to?" Tony asks, stepping closer to Sara.

She smiles at him and traces the line of his jaw with her fingernail. "Oh, you know I hate it when you clench your jaw like that, darlin'." I frown. Tony seems to find less humor in her statement than I did. "Relax. You're clearly into something big, and I want to stay and help you out."

"What about Gordon?" He looks at Rebecca, who holds both of her hands on either side of Quincy's temples. "Or Drew?" He comes back to Sara. "What about Jessica and Stephanie?"

"They'll be fine for a couple of days without us," Sara says. "Besides…" Her eyes dart over to me. "…how often do you get to brag about meeting an actual McCabe Witch?"

Tony lifts a right pointer-finger to Sara in a warning manner. "Sar…?"

"Yeah, yeah," she returns, while shooing him. "Bags. Jeep. Now." Tony sighs and stalks out of the room.

"How's that?" Rebecca asks, looking up at Quincy from her crouched position.

"Better," he says. "I don't feel dizzy anymore. Thanks."

Rebecca nods and stands.

"So," Sara starts, turning to me.

"Later," I say, helping Quincy to his feet. "He needs some food and then some rest."

"Okay. Go. Take care of your man."

"He's not my…oh forget it." Quincy drapes his arm over my shoulders, and I help him…as much as I can against all his muscles.

"Jamina," Quincy whispers as we step out of the library.

"What?"

"That vampire girl…bothers me."

"Not the whole…my mom betrayed you thing."

He shakes his head. "Maybe you know her, too. Her name is Angela."

"ANGELA?" He nods. I frown. It couldn't be. "And she reminded you of Meghan?" He nods again. He takes his arm off my shoulders and balances himself on the stairs' banister.

"What?" I shake my head. "No. Tell me what."

"I think she might be…"

"Ahem," Tony says walking through the front door. He drops three VERY large bags by the door. "This place is not a hotel."

"They're your friends," Quincy says. "Plus, why don't you complain about what's really bothering you?" Tony trembles…but it's not with rage. It's with sadness. He looks like he could cry at any minute. "You know what this means, right?"

"What, what means?" I ask.

"I know what it means," Tony says as if I wasn't even here.

"What does it mean?" I whine.

Quincy stares at me and releases an exasperated sigh. "It means that your mother's all in with En Quosque."

My eyes move over to Tony. "From here on out," he says, trying to stifle that emotion shaking his voice. "She is our enemy, Jamie."

I shiver, because now I know why Tony was so upset. If the Fairy Queen is right, I may have to kill my own mom.

#####

Chapter 24: Trip

"We shouldn't be doing this," Tony says.

"It'll be fine," I say and lean against his arm.

"It won't be fine, and this is stupid!" I frown and lean away, as he glares at me. "I can't believe I let you talk me into going along with this class trip…I have two seals…once we cross the border, I'm going to burn."

"First of all, have a little faith in me, because and second of all, I'm starting to understand how my magic works in conjunction with the pendant and your seals. Remember, I kept both you and Quincy from burning at the border…that basically boiled down to two seals, so…"

"I still think it's too risky to try on a hunch of yours…"

"Do you want me to let you burn?"

He sighs, and his shoulders slump. "I trust you, okay? And I believe you when you say you can do this, but I just don't think it's the best time to leave."

"I know." I lift my head. "I just can't deal, right now…okay?" He nods.

"We're approaching the border," he says, staring out of the bus's front window. I nod, wrap his left arm up in my right, and then put both of my hands around the Crescent Moon Pendant in a praying position. I hum as I feel that familiar vibration flow through me and out from it. "We are at the border…" I hear the tension in his voice and ignore it. He holds his breath too. "And…" Still not breathing. "…and…" Breathe, damn it. "…we're through." I sigh and realize I held my breath too. He laughs as I rest my head on his shoulder.

"I'm going to take a nap."

"You earned it. I'll wake you when we reach Elizabeth City."

"Okay," I say…more like a moan and close my eyes.

"Jamie…"

"…I just closed my eyes!"

"…we're here." I open my eyes…and wipe a bit of drool away from my chin…and his sleeve.

"Sorry." He laughs and slips my glasses back on. I look around still feeling groggy.

"Mr. Puckett went over the itinerary while you were…" He clears his throat.

"If you say anything besides, 'napping,' 'sleeping,' or 'dozing,' I may brain you." He laughs again. I smile. I know it's an act. He puts on a brave, humor-filled face for me. He knows how much mom going over to the dark side hurt me. It hurt me so bad that I haven't even been able to talk to Alex about it. Then again, Alex has problems of his own.

"...nodding," Tony says. I stare at him. "You forgot to mention, nodding, which is what I was going to say." I nod to confirm my approval of his nodding comment. "We're going to do a walking tour of Elizabeth City State University from 9:00 to 10:30am, the harbor district from 10:45 to noon, and we'll be eating lunch there." I nod and fail to fight off a yawn. "After lunch, we'll go to historic downtown Elizabeth City where we'll be..." I stare out the window with my left hand under my chin. "...are you listening?"

"Not really," I say. I look at his adorably scowling face. "Sorry, it's just...this is all a distraction really. Trying not to think about any of it, you know?" He nods. "I doubt if I'll even go to ECSU."

"Then why are we...?"

"Because I signed up for this trip at the beginning of the school year...before...everything..." I gaze into his eyes. "...even before you." He nods.

We file off the bus with the other students. Twee still hasn't come back...Alex backed out of this trip, which freed up a spot for Tony. Kai and Gwen didn't even bother signing up because they came too late in the year, although had they been interested, they could've taken Alex's spot. I sigh.

Our tour guide takes us all around ECSU's campus...it's beautiful...the campus overlooks the water, it has a lot of green spaces, and nice clean, tech heavy buildings. I sigh again. I've been doing that a lot lately.

It would've been nice to go here after I graduate. College just doesn't seem to be in the cards for my family line. My dad didn't go...my mom didn't...none of my ancestors who got the witch gene did. They were too busy preparing to save the world to bother with college. Sometimes, I get why Gwen originally came to the States, why she wanted to be 'normal.' A nice, normal, boring life seems...appealing sometimes.

I sigh and toss my fry down into my basket. "Fish and chips," Tony says while holding one of the soggy 'chips' between his pointer and thumb. He tosses it down into the basket.

"You don't like it?" He shakes his head and smacks his hands together, trying to clear the excess and excessive salt. "I told you we could've gone to one of the fancier places if you wanted."

He smirks. "No, this is fine. You wanted this so..."

"So, what I say goes...?"

He sighs. "I don't know what you want from me right now, Jamie."

"Neither do I."

He frowns and springs to his feet. He collects his basket. "Done with that?" I nod. He takes my basket and moves away from the table. I sit back and sigh. It started as such a nice trip. My mood killed all that though. Who can blame me? Between the Fairy Queen, my En Quosque mom, no future beyond being the next big bad Witch of Light... I turn to Tony, standing near the trashcan with a couple of college girls (which I can tell by their colorful ECSU sweatshirts) chatting him up. ...my smoking hot, highly cerebral ex and his equally smoking hot, muscly brother, I've got a lot on my plate...

"...basket," I murmur, picking at some of the salt left on the table. I fall back into my chair again. The Crescent Moon Pendant taps my heart. I frown. "Rais?" I gasp. My eyes swell, and I instantly turn to Tony. Good. He didn't hear me over the...okay, enough sluts! Leave him alone! You saw that he was with me! Geez!

I turn back to face front and spot Rais standing outside. I sit up and steal another glance at Tony. I come back, and Rais points at me. He motions to himself and makes a talking puppet hand sign. I nod. He does too and steps away.

"Come on," Tony says. "We're loading up again."

I stand. "Are you sure you don't want to stay here, spend a little more time with your fan club?" He glances at the girls, who all offer him finger-wiggling waves. I shove my hands deep into my jacket pockets.

He comes back to me with the corners of his mouth turned down. "You do realize that you're the only fan I want, right?"

"Not as good a line as you might've thought it was," I say, while pushing past him. I wiggly-finger wave at the girls as we exit. They glare at me. We quickly file onto the bus and fall back into our seats. Tony doesn't bother trying to talk to me. He knows me well enough to know when I'm in a mood.

We're unloaded again in the center of the historic district...historic if you don't count the chain coffee shop just off the square.

"Jamie," Tony says, tugging on my left arm. I turn to face him. "You know they were just trying to talk me into attending ECSU when I graduate and that I tried to confer that I have no plans to come here."

"Fine. Whatever. Okay. We have a free hour, and I want some coffee."

"Okay. Let's go get some..."

"No," I cut him off. "I want coffee, and I want you to go away."

He scowls. "Just because I was talking to some other girls?"

"No. This isn't about them. I just..." I groan. "...I just need a beat, okay? I like your company...but you're just a constant reminder of everything I'm trying to distract myself from today." He huffs and turns without another word. "Tony...?" He doesn't respond. I grumble to myself. Great. That was exactly how you wanted to put that to make him feel even more like crap than he has of late.

I make my way to the coffee shop and just as I figured, Rais is already inside at a seat near the window. He waves me over. I sit across from him, and he slides a coffee over to me.

"It's black," he explains.

"Thanks," I say with a nod. I remove the lid and start dumping a mountain of sugar into it. "So, what'd you need to talk to me about?"

"I didn't say I needed to talk to you about anything." I replace the lid and arch my eyebrows. "I just wanted to talk to you, Bunny," he says with a smirk. My lips make an asterisk, and if he weren't providing the distraction I really needed, I'd be super pissed at him.

"So," he says with a casual demeanor. He removes his lid and places it closer to the window. "I noticed how distracted you looked with soldier boy." His eyes look over my face thoughtfully. "You didn't even seem to notice when those three girls started flirting with him." I frown, and I feel my left eye twitch. "You know you can tell me anything, right?" I lean forward and put my hands together under the table. I nod, peering up at him with just my eyes. "Despite your best efforts, you still love them both, don't you?"

"I don't get it," I say, wringing my hands under the table. I put my forehead down on the table…pushing my glasses against my closed eyes…if he were either one of them, they'd put their hands on me in some way to comfort me. Not Rais though.

Is he that different from them? I lift my head, and he's staring at me with an awkward expression, his mouth hanging agape. I lift my head more, and he has his hand just above my head, as if he were going to pat it. I sigh. I guess he's not that different.

"Sorry," he says in a growl, letting a little of the wolf out.

"It's okay." I take a napkin from the silver dispenser and wipe my smudged glasses. "Girl on the verge of crying…" I put my glasses back on and then sip my coffee. "…you were going to console me. It's a natural response…you're human…well…" I bob my head unevenly as he pours a mountain of sugar into his coffee. "…human-ish…" He laughs.

"So," he starts again stirring his coffee. I lift my eyes to his slowly. "You're in the impossible situation."

"It's been called that." I shake my head. "Impossible would be a nice step down though," I explain. He smirks and sips his coffee. "You're the only person I know who puts more cream and sugar in their coffee than me."

He lifts the coffee back up to his mouth sans lid. "And you're deflecting," he says before taking another drink.

I sigh…again. "It's insane. It's not impossible. It's insane. I live with them, but I have to keep my distance from them. I love them both but can't have either of them. I can't stand to lose either of them, but I can't stand picking one of them for the fear of how much it'll hurt the other one…and for me…."

He laughs. I groan again and run my hands over my hair. "I haven't had anyone to talk to about it either. I mean, I can't say anything to either of them. My mom is…" I shake my head again because I so do not want to go there. "…Twee's MIA, and Zoë's still visiting family in Georgia so…I have to admit, it's driving me a little crazy, and I might be freaking out a little bit."

"Only a little…?" Rais asks, putting his cup down.

"Yes, in the totally and completely sense…" He laughs again. "…and the worst part is they won't let up…and it's only gotten worse since Quincy got back, and this whole thing with my m-" I cut myself off…don't…because if you do, you'll cry, and you don't want to cry. He arches one eyebrow. "Never mind. It's just that…every time I turn around there they are, staring at me, comforting me…" I cover my face with my left hand. "…almost kissing me."

"Well, you know," Rais says with that crazy cool manner of his. He drapes his hand over the top of his cup, showing off the large platinum wolf's head ring on his middle finger. He lifts his coffee. He points at me over the top, "You could always go with your third option."

"Oh, you'd like that, wouldn't you?"

"Oh, yeah…I REALLY would."

"Not what I meant," I say with a laugh. I down the last of my coffee. "I mean, you know it'd irk Tony to no end, and I know that you both kind of hate each other, and the only reason you haven't torn each other apart is because of the cute redhead sitting across from you."

"True." I smirk. "Especially the cute redhead part."

"So, flirty," I say as a complaint, but really, I'm flirting back. Why am I flirting back? "I…should head back," I say and even I'm suspicious of my motives, given the way I said it. He nods. I stand. "Thanks…for the coffee…and the distraction…and the talking part. I needed it."

"Anytime on all three," he says, before sipping his coffee with no sign of chalance. I nod, wave, and step away from the table. Why did I wave? I must've looked like such a goober. Better question, why am I flirting with Rais? Am I really trying to distract myself, or do I actually feel something for him?

#####

Chapter 25: Rooftop

I walk out of the coffee shop and head toward the end of the block. I look around. I know I should find Tony…and apologize. I look down at the pendant. I know how I can find him quickly. Why don't I want to?

Wait, where am I? I don't recognize the random buildings on this block, or the block behind me. Where did I walk to, and how do I get back to the historic district? I purse my lips and turn quickly. I stop, and the Crescent Moon Pendant thuds against my heart again. I smirk. "Rais," I say, while tuning to face him. "You know, some people might consider this stalking."

He grins. "Come with me." I frown and shake my head. "Hey, remember…I was told to look after you, so I wouldn't do anything to hurt you." He steps closer and peers down at me with those gunmetal blue eyes. "And besides, you already know…I'd…never do anything to hurt you."

"Where are we going?" I ask with just as much flirt as I'm receiving, if not a little more. He looks at a four-story redbrick building behind me. "Some moldy old building…? Big pass on that one."

"Wrong. Some moldy old building's rooftop," he says, while taking my hand. "Come on." He runs at a nice, normal human pace, pulling me along behind him. We reach the side of the building, and I look up at the fire escape.

"Now, what?" He wraps his arms around me. "Hey…"

"Hold on," he says. I frown. "Hold…on…" I put my arms over his shoulders. He bends his knees. He straightens them and propels us upward. We rocket through the air, cresting over the top of the building, and come to a stop on the edge. I pant as he loosens his grip on me. I adjust my rattled glasses and look over the edge of the building at the spot where we were just standing.

"Wow." He laughs, and it's warm and infectious. It makes me laugh. I stare into his eyes.

"What?" he asks, getting that I'm reading something there. I shake my head. He steps off the ledge and walks across the rooftop. I follow. "Come on. Spill, doll face," he adds while turning back to me. I mouth 'doll face?' "I tried something new, Bunny."

I nod. "Wow," I say, taking in the breathtaking view of the water from this height. The deep blue ocean seems to go on forever, only stopping to meet pale blue sky at the horizon, turning gray at that point.

"Yeah, yeah. Go ahead and tell me."

"Alright. I was just trying to think of a word that describes you."

"Amazing…Astonishing…Awesome…"

"Words that don't start with an A…?"

"Oh, this is just before I move on to the Bs and the Cs and so forth and so on." I laugh. "What did you come up with?"

"Trouble. That pretty much describes you."

"Ouch. I'm trouble?"

"No," I say. "Not you so much as…the best way to describe you…" He frowns. "I don't even mean it in a bad way, Rais. I just mean that a guy like you gets girls into trouble…you make them want to try things they've never tried…to do things they've never done before…"

"Like what?"

I close the distance between us. Dive in. "Like this," I say, before perching on the balls of my feet and…and…I kiss him. He wraps his arms around my waist, pulls my top lips between both of his and…and…

"What's wrong?" he asks as soon as our lips part, due to a lack of response from mine. I draw my lips into my mouth and shake my head. "You didn't like it?"

"No, no…it was a good kiss, it's just…"

"You didn't feel anything?" he asks. I shake my head slowly. "Not like with them…?"

I shake my head again. "This is so stupid…"

"No, it's because you're in love with someone else."

"Two someone elses. Well, at least, my magic didn't warn me about you." His eyebrows tweak. "There was this guy once, and the second he touched me, I knew something was off with him…and I didn't get that feeling from you."

"Like this you mean," he says and caresses my left cheek, surprising me.

"He didn't even get that far. He took my hand and put his other hand on my hip…we were dancing…at a dance, and I just knew, you know?"

"So…" He collects my left hand in his right and puts his left on my hip. "Like this?"

"Yeah, except it looks weird now, because we're not dancing, and there's no music playing." He nods, takes his hand from my hip, and slips it inside his jacket. He pulls out his phone, searches through it…and music starts to play. It's soft and romantic. He replaces the phone and then reclaims my hip.

"What're you doing there, Rais?"

"Providing a distraction," he says with so much flirt that I can't help going along with it. I put my free hand on his shoulder. We dance.

"Nice." He smiles. "Trouble."

"What'd I do now?"

"Just making a girl try something new…like dancing on a rooftop."

"Well, if this is new to you…" His voice takes on a throaty, semi-raspy charm. "I have a whole world that I could show you, if you'd let me, Bunny."

I inhale deeply. He stares into my eyes and…his don't phase over to his wolf side, but still…there's something there. It's ravenous and lustful…it's desire. He wants me, and for the first time, since the day I met him, I'm actually a little nervous around Rais…but not for the same reason as the day we met.

"Ahem," comes from the top of the fire escape. Rais and I stop dancing and turn to find Tony sitting on the ledge. He stands. "I'm sorry," he says in a way that tells me, he's not sorry. "I feel like I'm interrupting something here." Rais lets go of me and takes a step back.

"Nope," Rais says, slipping his right hand into his pants pocket and his left into his jacket. The music stops. "We were just…talking."

"Talking…?" Tony steps forward. He's angry. I move between them. "What were you talking about?"

"Things," I say, feeling a pang of anger myself.

"Bunny?" I look over my shoulder at Rais. "Your head might be confused and feels like it's being torn apart…but your heart will sort it out for you."

"When…?"

He shrugs. "I can't say…but I know how strong you are…all of this is just another obstacle in your way."

I nod.

"What were you doing up here?" Tony asks between clenched teeth. "You weren't just talking."

"Yes, we were talking…and dancing."

Tony purses his lips and nods. "You were dancing with…" He cuts off abruptly and looks around. I turn, and Rais is gone. "What was that that he mentioned about your heart?" I shake my head. Tony steps closer. He looks down at me with his stern, penetrating stare. "Was it…about me?"

"Maybe." He nods and leans forward. My eyes dart to his lips and then back to his eyes. He gets close enough to kiss me, and I put my hands on his chest. "You should know that I kissed Rais." Tony takes a step back. He stares at me as if I just tried to stab him…in the heart.

"You what…?" I swallow a large lump of guilt and to a smaller degree shame. I try to repeat it, but it gets stuck in my throat. "You kissed…him?" he asks, but it's more as if he stumbles over it while pointing after Rais. I nod. "Why is it that every time you stop me from kissing you, it's to tell me that you kissed someone else?" He huffs again and steps away again…only to come right back. He points one trembling finger toward where Rais stood. "You chose him…over us…" He points at himself, seething with rage. "…over me?"

"No! I didn't choose anyone!"

"But you kissed him?"

"Yes. I kissed him."

"Or did he kiss you?" he asks with murder in his eyes. Oddly enough, I never knew what that expression meant until right now.

"No. I…kissed…him." Tony's hand sweeps across his mouth, and he steps away. He walks toward the fire escape. "Hey," I say and run after him. I catch his arm at the edge. He jerks away. "Stop it!" He glares at me. "We kissed, okay…? But that's all we did."

"That's all?" I nod. "And what if I hadn't shown up? Would there have been more to this story?" I gasp and before I know it, I slap him, which surprisingly didn't help with his building rage. Then again, mine is kind of on the rise thanks to his accusation, but still…

"I'm sorry. I shouldn't have hit you…but you should know me better than that."

"I thought I did."

"It didn't mean anything to me…I didn't feel anything from it…I just did it to see if…it would be different…if I would feel different." He stares at me with bewilderment. "And it did…it felt different…because I didn't feel the same thing I felt when I kissed you…because…" I half-turn away from him as my anger transforms into a frantic panic…my thoughts and words fumbling over each other. My stomach twists into a knot. I run my trembling fingers over my hair and turn away with a groan from the tension headache I'm getting.

"Because…?"

I come back. "Because I don't love him…" I sigh. I have to be honest with him. I shove him in the chest with my left hand. "…I love you, stupid. I'm in love with you." I shake my head with tears welling in my eyes. "No matter how much I try to fight it or struggle against it…I love you, okay?"

"More than okay," he breathes, wrapping his arms around me.

"No," I moan. "It's not okay…it's…it's…"

"What…?"

I want to kiss him. Before I can stop him, he kisses me. It all comes back to me. My heart flutters just before it skips a beat, I feel butterflies in my stomach, and my knees feel like they could buckle at any minute. We part, and I breathe heavily. "It's not," I say with a weak tremble to my voice. He nods and presses his forehead against mine. "I still love Quincy, too." I push him back, and he lets me. "And that's why kissing anyone…isn't right. I should be figuring out how to break the curse, because clearly it's not broken."

Tony frowns and looks down. "Now," I continue. "Get me off this roof before we get left behind…" I sweep both my cheeks trying to clear my tears away. "…or I fall and break my neck."

He nods, steps over to me, and wraps his arms around my waist. He tilts us over the side, and we fall for about a second before coming to a stop. I open my eyes and take a step back. I try to fix my discombobulated glasses because my hair is immovable.

Tony steps forward and cups my face. I stare into his eyes with something behind them that I don't recognize…it's not anger, or fear…but an uneasiness.

"First of all," he says in his stern tone. "You should've told me that the spell and whatever else you tried didn't work on you." I nod. "I've been going mad thinking that you could let go of how we felt about each other that easily." I swallow yet another massive lump of guilt. "Second…" He pauses long enough to move in kissably close to my lips. All the air rushes out of me as my mouth opens a bit. My eyes dart down to his lips only to come back to meet his eyes. "…you let me decide what's fair for me. Clear?"

I nod absently, yielding to the intensity of his words and his penetrating gaze.

He nods. "We should get back to the bus." He steps away, and I almost fall. I was actually hoping that he'd kiss me then. I mean, you don't just say something that intense and not finish with a…

"Oh, and one more thing," he says. He wraps me up and kisses me again. I fall into this kiss. He puts his hands on the small of my back, and I lean back. He pulls at my lower lip before his tongue sweeps across it with the softest caress. I moan in pleasure before I can stop myself.

We part, and I can't seem to catch my breath. I stare at him hungrily. If I didn't want him so much right now, I might actually be upset that we're making out in an alley. "Now, we can go." I nod, still not ready to form actual words yet.

He takes my hand and pulls me toward the street. The second we round the corner, I trip over someone's foot. Tony catches me and stops me from stumbling forward. He stands me up and glares after the woman in the black leather jacket and skinny jeans.

I straighten my glasses. "YOU COULD SAY SORRY!" I yell after her.

"Don't." I look at Tony. "Daemon," he says with a hushed voice.

"Daemon?" He nods. "Then shouldn't we…"

He puts his hand behind my back and ushers me back toward downtown. "We should get back to the bus…it's almost 2:15." I scowl and stare after the woman. "She's tomorrow's problem, okay?"

I stop resisting and walk with him, conceding that he's right. He offers his left arm. I hook it with my right. "What I said earlier, about you being a reminder…you know, about stuff," I say. He looks at me. "I didn't mean it…and I'm so-"

"Are you going to apologize about something you said out of frustration, and that I've already forgotten about?" I frown. "Now, who's stupid?" I let him go and shove him with both hands. He laughs. He comes back and drapes his arm over my shoulders. "I love you too, Jamie."

"I know…but there's still OUR problem."

"That's tomorrow's problem, too." He pulls me closer, and I lean my head against his shoulder as we step up to the bus's doorway. I stare back in the direction of the skinny jean-rocking daemon. Whoever she was, I hope she's not a huge problem…tomorrow.

#####

Chapter 26: Confusion

I toss the ECSU booklet to the side with a sigh. I push my hair back from my face while tracing one of the stitched lines of my comforter. "Normal life," I say aloud. I never thought I would want it, but the deeper into this whole En Quosque thing I get, the more I want one. I want my mom back. I want to have a boyfriend…one boyfriend and fall in love with him…and just him. I want to go to college and grow up with a few normal, non-magical friends like Zoë.

A knock comes from my door…my open door. I don't bother looking or even reaching for the Crescent Moon Pendant. "Come in, Tony."

He steps inside, looks at me, and then does a quick scan of the room. He spots and bends to pick up the booklet. He draws his lips into his mouth, as he looks it over. "This…still bothers you, doesn't it?"

I shake my head.

"You don't have to lie to me, Jamie."

"What's up?" I ask, trying to deflect.

"Right." He puts the booklet down on the bottom of my bed. "Sara, Rebecca, and Amie are out back. They wanted to talk to you."

"Why?"

"Witch business." I frown. "No, I asked them why and their collective response was…" He makes air quotes. "…'witch business.'"

"Okay." I put my legs over the edge of the bed and slip my thick, wool sock-covered feet into my boots.

"You can talk to me," Tony says. He puts his hand on the booklet. "About this kind of stuff, you know?" I smirk. His 'you knows' aren't nearly as endearing as Alex's are. "I…think you would do well in college."

"Well, we may never know." I finish tying my laces. "If this whole saving the world thing doesn't pan out."

"Jamie."

"It's fine, okay?" He bows his head. I move toward the door, and he's there to meet me. "I'm okay."

He puts his arms around me. I freeze. My entire body goes rigid. "You don't feel fine to me. You feel…" He nods against my shoulder. "…depressed."

"Well, I'm not," I say as a complaint. He releases me and steps back. "Happy as a clam."

"You know, they're not as happy-go-lucky as most people think. Apparently."

"Whatever." I step around him and out into the hall. I sigh, realizing how unfair I've been to him. I turn back to my doorway, and he's already gone. It's as if he was never there. I turn back toward the stairs, and Quincy's there, as if he'd always been there.

"What's wrong?" I should probably come clean to him about all the stuff that went down yesterday too, but because I'm a punk, I decide against that and go with…

"Nothing."

He taps his heart. "Ouch."

"Sorry."

"Tell me."

"I…might have kissed…Rais." He taps the center of his chest again. "Okay, so…I kissed Rais." He nods. I stare at him waiting for the explosion of swear words and accusations and…and… Nothing. His stupid gorgeous face doesn't even change. I frown, and the corners of my mouth turn down. "So, no yelling?" He shakes his head. "No scowling?" Again. "Not even a pretend cough to cover up calling me a 'slut'?"

"Why?" he asks with a shrug. "Why would I do any of that to you, Jamina?"

"Because…I deserve it." He shakes his head again. "I-I also told Tony that I'm still in love with him…too."

"Good."

"Good…? Good? How is any of this good? I've kissed your…your brother. I kissed Rais, and I kissed you!"

"Do you love him? Rais, I mean?" I shake my head this time. "Did you kiss him hoping that maybe you'd feel something different from him?" I shrug, and my shoulders slump. "And you didn't, did you?" Head shake. "Is it because you still love Tony?" Shrug. "Well, do you still love me?"

"Quincy," I whine.

"I'm just trying to figure out why you feel guilty about it."

"Because…"

"Yeah, yeah, I know. Lots of kissing…all the kissing." He takes both of my shoulders, and he runs his hands down to my elbows and back up again. "You're young…and you don't know how you feel. You're still trying to get a handle on it all."

I peer into his eyes and put my hands on his forearms. "But…I know how I feel…that's part of the problem. I know that I love both of you. No confusion on that point since…" I sigh. "…honestly, since the day I met you."

He smiles and gives me that look that still manages to knock the wind out of me. "Still," he says with another shoulder rub. "You'll figure it out."

"That's what Rais said."

"So, maybe the furball's not as dumb as he looks." I shove him in the chest, and he laughs, while taking a step back. He steps closer and claims both of my hands. "Have faith…in your magic…in your heart…and in the decisions you've made…they've all told you that you can trust us, right? All of us, even Rais?" I nod. "Then there you go."

I stare into his eyes, and both of mine move from one of his to the other, hoping to find why my heart reacts to his the way it does and vice versa. I shake my head not finding an answer. "Love you," I say as he turns my hands so that their backs are against his chest. I sigh and look at his mouth as he draws his lips in and me with them.

"I…" He groans. "…I shouldn't say that back…"

"What? Why?"

He looks to my lips and swallows a lump. "Because I do…and if I say it…the other thing on my mind will come with it." My eyebrows move down, and I shake my head a little. "…I…really want to kiss you right now." I gasp. I feel the thud of his heart against my hands. His Lust Seal lights up. His jaw tenses. "And," he says as a grumble. "I'm fighting really hard to keep them both in ch-"

"Kiss me." He shakes his head and moves his right arm behind his back. "No…kiss me," I say again with a nod. I move my hands up to the sides of his face. He closes his eyes. "Breathe." He nods. "Breathe."

He bends, and I press my lips against his. He inhales deeply through his nose, and I feel lighter. All the air drains out of me at once and dizziness sets in, but in a good way. Both of his lips move around my lower lip, and I perch on my toes to give him a better angle. His arms wrap around my waist, and he holds his body against mine. He pulls his lips away slowly, tugging my lip with them until we part. I sigh.

He opens his eyes. "Wow," he says.

"How's your seal?" He frowns. He lifts his right arm, and it has gone dark again.

"How did you?"

I shrug and move my hands behind his neck. "I don't know to be honest with you. I'm just starting to realize that like the pendant…how I can just use it with you guys naturally, as if it's second nature…some things just come to me. And so, I go with it."

He hugs me. He trembles…I wouldn't have noticed, but his shiver fell just between two of mine. "You…are so amazing, Jamina." He nods, his nose rubbing against the nape of my neck. "And I do…I love you…I love you more and more every day. I do." We part, and he stares into my eyes. "But because of your heart…because of your big, kind, all-encompassing heart…I can't be selfish with you, and I know that."

My heart skips a beat. "You're not. You've never been selfish with me."

"And I never will…I'll wait for you, Jamina. Whether you're eighteen or eighty…I can wait." He releases me, but I try to hold on… "I can wait and wait and wait…because I know you are worth it." …he steps away and my hands fall to my sides. "You are worth the wait. I feel like I've waited a hundred and eighty years to meet you…what's a few more to be with you." I nibble my lower lip. He vanishes, and I try to collect myself.

I pant, and my hands clench into fists. "You didn't apologize," Tony says behind me. I frown and turn to him. I start to speak… "You didn't apologize to him for kissing him after kissing me yesterday."

"Because I'm done with that. I'm done with the confusion. I'm done with apologizing for how I feel. I'm done with…worrying about the things I can't have…"

"Jamie?"

I shrug. "I…" I shake my head. "…I love both of you, and I'm done apologizing for that."

Tony nods. "I feel it." He takes my hands. "He seems to know your heart, but I feel your heart."

"Yeah?"

"Yeah. You fear that you're hurting both of us, by choosing neither of us, but you're tired of resisting both of us." I purse my lips. My tongue parts them and slips through, sweeping across my lower lip. "And you're worried that that will hurt us more." He is the smart one, isn't he? I nod. He sighs and touches my left shoulder. His hand moves down, and he intertwines our fingers. "But like I told you, let me decide what's fair for me."

I nod and wipe a tear away.

"And I'm sure my brother feels same."

"I know. That's why I want to spend time with both of you." I shrug. "That's a lie…" Quincy probably felt that whopper. "…I want to spend time with you both because I love you."

Tony smiles with a nod. I can honestly say this is the most relaxed I've ever seen him. "Come on," he says. "They're waiting for you." He turns toward the stairs, pauses, and comes right back. "Oh, Amie wanted me to give you this." I frown as he passes me a bottled water. I look it over and frown too. It's just a plain, old bottled water. "She said you'd need it."

He moves down the stairs, and I follow. "I don't mind telling you that she kind of grates on my nerves."

"Amie?"

"Oh yeah…"

He laughs. "She does that with everybody. She has some rough edges…but once you become her friend…" He stops at the landing. "…she'd walk through Hell for you with a smile on her face." I frown. "You know, once you get past the opening awkward part." I smile with a nod. He resumes.

"And what about Rebecca?"

"Now, Rebecca was another story entirely for me. She has this way about her…it's as if it's impossible NOT to like her."

"I could see that."

"She never has an unkind thing to say about anyone…" He stops at the banister. "…but if she does have something bad to say about someone, either she's saying it out of love, or they must've really done something bad." He inhales deeply and nods. "I find the way she views the world both refreshing and endearing."

"And Sara?" I say, moving down beside him.

He does that haughty laugh thing and bows his head. Even with his head bent downward, I can still see a huge smile on his face. I don't know if I should love Sara because she can bring this out of him or hate her for the same exact reason.

"Sara," he finally says. "Becoming Sara's friend…was as easy as breathing for me. I met her when she was very young…she was protecting another witch from me, in fact. A misunderstanding," he clarifies quickly. "The next time I ran into her, before I knew it, I'd already told her half my life story and spent four months in her company. She just…" He nods. "…made sense, being in my life."

I frown and suppress a groan. "You sound like you're in love with her."

"No," he says instantly and with a shake of his head. "It's…not that simple…I…" He nods. "You're not the first person to suggest that either," he says with a point. "A couple of her coven sisters insinuated the same thing…"

"Are you…? I mean, I know I'm one to talk about being in love with multiple peop-"

"She's my friend, and so is her husband."

"Her husband?"

"Gordon. Sara and Gordon…" He said their name together like there is no other way to say it. His eyes narrow. He rests his arm on the banister and leans forward. "Sara and Gordon just fit you know. I love Sara, I love Gordon, but I love Sara and Gordon together. They make sense to me. They have this sort of comfortable romance that I…I would do…anything to protect that…because I envision that sort of thing when I think about marriage."

He peers into my eyes, and I swallow a lump. Did we just suddenly get into a conversation about marriage? I mean, I know we're all admitting our feelings here, but…

"Relax," he says with a hand on my shoulder. "I'm not about to get down on one knee." I release a relaxing sigh. "I'm just saying…one day."

Is he talking about one day with me? I'm too much of a coward to ask so instead, I nod. "So, you want your own little slice of normal?"

"I guess so, and I can have it…someday…just like you can go to college if you want to."

"You just won't let that go, will ya?"

He smiles and shakes his head. I laugh. He tips his head toward the back. "You should go on. They're waiting."

I perch on the balls of my feet and deliver a quick kiss to his left cheek. "Wish me luck." I step closer to the double doors leading to the backyard.

"Luck?"

"Three witches want to meet me outside, and one told me to bring…" I hold it up. "…a bottle of water. What do you think is going to happen?"

"A lesson? A demonstration? Practice?"

"Yes," I say to all three while pushing the door open.

#####

Chapter 27: Spirit

I walk out onto the patio. Sara, Rebecca, and Amie stand in a perfect triangle on the grass. Sara stands opposite me. I hurry down the stairs. "So, what's up, ladies?" I hold the water bottle up. "And why did I need this?"

"I was wondering what was taking you so long," Sara says.

"I bet one her boyfriends slowed her down," Amie says.

"They're not my boyfriends."

"So, that smoking hot older brother is available?"

"AMIE!" Rebecca snaps. Amie shrugs and mouths something back silently.

I stifle a growl aimed at Amie. "Rough edges," I say to myself. "Look, to recap for EVERYONE gathered…Quincy…" I extend my right, water bottle-filled hand. "…Tony…" Left, empty hand. "…are either one of them my boyfriend? No." I bring my hands together around the bottle. "Am I in love with both of them? Yes. Do they feel the same toward me? Yes." I glare at Amie and point the bottle's cap at her. "Got it?" She nods.

"Oh my," Sara says with the purr of a big fuzzy cat. I frown. "Oh, you should've seen how your spirit magic flared when you said that."

"Spirit magic? I don't have any spirit magic."

"Yeah," Amie says. "That's kind of why we wanted to talk to you."

"We wanted to ask," Rebecca continues. "Why your magic is so out of whack?" I frown. "You're a white witch, so…"

"Can we stop calling ourselves that please?" I ask. "I mean, whenever I hear it…" I motion to myself. "…the almond-skinned redheaded witch feels like she's referring to…well, not herself." Sara and Rebecca laugh. "It's a little confusing."

"She has a point there," Amie says. "I mean, I know I feel the exact opposite." I shrug with a nod.

Rebecca crosses her arms. "Anyway, your magic is out of whack. Your spirit magic is weak, and your earth magic is practically non-existent."

"My…" I cross my arms. "My mom…whatever spirit magic she knew, she kept to herself, and she didn't know earth magic. And I learned everything I know about magic from her." I smirk. "Except one thing apparently…I kinda developed that one myself."

"What's that?" Sara asks.

"I can…weave signs in mid-air and make them apply to my magic."

"Shut up!" Rebecca says.

"You what?" Amie asks.

Rebecca takes that step back and nearly trips over her own feet. "How is that even possible?"

I shrug. "Don't know. I just kind of do it. Wanna see?"

"Yes."

"Yes."

"Maybe, later," Sara says as if what I just told her isn't insane or surprising or anything. "We're here to fix your problem, not marvel at your awesomeness and make no mistake you are pretty awesome."

"What exactly is my problem?"

"Jacio," Sara mutters. *Nothing. If you don't take into account the fact that, you can't do this.*

"What?" I point at my head. "Did I…?" I step forward. "Did you just…? You spoke in my mind!

Sara smiles. "It's spirit magic. Your mind was open and receptive, so I was able to communicate with you."

"Wow, that was cool."

"That's a basic spell." I frown and dig the tip of shoe into the grass. "What do you know about spirit magic?" I shrug and play with the Crescent Moon Pendant with my free hand. "Do you know that you have a lot of yours centered on that thing you're holding?"

"I do?" She nods. "I can sense…"

"Quincy and Tony through it…yeah, even more of theirs is focused through it." Sara huffs a laugh. "So, you've been using spirit magic and you didn't even know it?"

"A lot of it too," Rebecca says.

"How do you mean?"

"The three of you have invested so much interest and trust in that object that it has become the symbol of your spirit magic." Sara stares at it with a strange look in her eyes. "…and maybe even more than that."

"Look," I say, while slipping it off over my head. "It doesn't do all the stuff you're saying." I toss it to her, and she catches it. She examines it and then lifts her eyes to me. "See?"

"Yes, I do." Rebecca covers her mouth to stifle a chuckle, and Amie laughs outright.

"What?" Sara tips her head toward me, and I half-turn to find Quincy and Tony staring at me with confused…albeit, handsome…faces from the patio. "What are you guys doing?"

"We…" Tony breaks off and looks away.

"We stopped sensing you through the pendant," Quincy says. "So, we came to check on you."

"I'm fine."

"We see that," Tony says. "Now."

"She won't be for long," Rebecca says. She clasps her hands…fingers intertwining…and her palms clap together. "Solum!" She slams her palms onto the ground, and a ripple appears in the grass…it turns into a crack and rushes toward me.

Tony appears between the fissure and me and drives his knife into the ground. The ripple collides with it and stops instantly. "How did you…?"

"Unda," Amie says before Rebecca can even finish posing her question. I feel a twitch in my hand. The water thrashes against its plastic bottle. The container explodes as a pair of arms wrap around me.

"Quincy," I breathe into his chest. He groans a response. I step back and notice his leg is cut. I glare at Amie. She shrugs in an 'oops' kind of way. I put my hands on either side of Quincy's leg.

"Sano." His wound closes quickly.

"Are you seriously gonna let two guys protect you?" Sara asks. "While you play nursemaid and kiss their boo-boos."

Tony pulls his knife out of the ground. He peers at me over his shoulder with a glower.

I hold out my left hand to him while putting my right hand on Quincy's chest. "I got this," I say to both of them. I march down the stairs and stand across from the trio of witches. "I get it. You wanted to test me…see how bad the imbalance in my magic was…" I take in each of their unchanged positions. "And you're standing in a triangle formation…Sara in the back…which means more than likely she's the least likely to use attack magic…and is the brains of team."

"Very good assessment," Sara says. "Now, what are you going to do about it?"

"Fight fire with fire," I say back. "Or should I say…" I look at Amie. "…water with water…" I come back to Rebecca, and I have to admit I feel a little cocky. "…earth with earth…" Rebecca and Amie ready themselves. I cross my arms over my chest, creating an X. "Amnis," I say toward Amie and quickly draw a pentagon in the air with my left pointer and middle fingers. Sara gasps. "Solum," I say to Rebecca and draw a heptagon in air with my right hand. I slam both hands onto the ground.

"No way," Rebecca returns and clasps her hands again. "Liro," she says quickly and touches the ground…only it crumbles under her hands. "What the…?"

"I guess she schooled you," Amie says. "Aqua," she says with a snap of her fingers. Nothing happens. She looks around curiously. "AQUA!" She frowns. "UNDA!"

I inhale deeply and stand…pulling my left hand slowly up from the ground…drawing all the water around us up with it…the grass quickly turns brown and dry.

"No way," Amie says in a gasp.

"Yep," I return. "I'm pretty much a bad…" Everything goes blurry for a second. "…I'm a…" I shake my head because my thoughts are little froggy…I mean, foggy.

I feel a hand on my arm. "Easy," Rebecca purrs.

"Is she…?" Tony starts.

"What's wrong with her?" Quincy asks sounding only slightly calmer.

"It's…I'm guessing it's her first time using earth magic," Rebecca says calmly. "She probably made the same mistake most earth-users make at first. She put way too much magic into the spell."

"That's what it feels like," I moan. My eyes close lazily.

"Right," Rebecca says. "Well, keep in mind that just because you can see earth a little more readily than the other elements…that doesn't mean it takes any more or less magic to net similar results." I nod. "Get some rest. You'll be fine."

"Fine?" Sara says. "She'll be flippin' brilliant. She used earth magic and a disrupting heptagon to steal the earth from under you and a water spell and an absorbing pentagon to steal the water from you…" Sara laughs. "…she basically took both of you out of the fight without laying a hand on you."

I feel my cheeks go up and fill with warmth. I must be smiling and blushing…wait, now I don't feel them anymore. Crap, I must be blacking ou-

#####

Chapter 28: Return

"So," Sara says with a warm hum to her voice while playing with the straw in her mocha coffee frozen thing. "Is there any particular reason you wanted to come here instead of say, continuing your spirit and earth magic training?"

"Nope, no reason."

"Liar," Amie says.

"Yes, I am."

"Well, either way," Rebecca starts. "I think you're making excellent progress. You're learning to use earth magic on a level that took me years to reach."

"That's because you were in denial about your natural talents, dear," Sara says. Rebecca shrugs and sips her sweet tea. "And you're relying too much on yours." I shrug and sip my latte. Sara sighs. "I'm only hard on you because Tony told me what you have to face…or rather, who…you have to face."

I lower my cup and swallow my sip that suddenly tastes bitter. "And thank you for that, but…" I sigh this time. "…I need down time too, you know?"

"Of course, sweetie," Sara says with a smile. Her warm brown eyes fall to her beverage. "If your mind's not centered you can't do spirit magic properly anyway."

"And if it's not grounded, your earth magic will suffer," Rebecca adds.

I nod as the door chime sounds. I spring up from my seat when I see a head full of awesome crinkly hair march through the door. Zoë looks around and spots me. I subdue a squeal and run over to her. I hug her. "I don't care; you're taking this hug, lady." She laughs. "Oh, I missed you so much."

"I missed you, too," she says while putting her arms around me. "How've you been, little sister?"

"So, much better now."

"I can imagine." She releases me, but leaves her hands resting on my arms. "So, how are you really doing?" I sigh, and my shoulders slump. "That good, huh?" Zoë frowns and looks to her right. "Can I help you with something?"

Sara stands to my left. "Oh, right…sorry. Zo', these are my friends, Sara and Rebecca…" Zoë smiles and nods at them. "…and their friend, Amie."

"Their friend?"

I shake my head and make a cutthroat motion. Zoë giggles.

"Well, aren't you just something special?" Sara says looking Zoë over.

Zoë motions to Sara. "Is she hitting on me?" She turns to Sara. "Because you should know I have a boyfriend…boyfriend," she repeats for emphasis.

"And I have a husband," Sara says, showing off her wedding and engagement rings. Zoë nods. "No, I was commenting on your spark of magic."

"My spark of who to what now?"

"Zoë's a witch?"

"No, but she definitely has a touch of magic running through her family."

"How's that not being a witch?"

"Well, she has no training, and she's never used a spell a day in her life." Sara looks at me. "Fine. She's a witch, but not a practicing one…which means she's not a witch."

"And you are?" Zoë asks with a nod. Sara curtsies. "Nice and I'm guessing Jamie told you all about me?"

"No, Tony did," Rebecca says.

"He trusts you," Amie adds. "That's pretty rare for him."

"Oh, okay…well, can I sit, or should we keep talking in the doorway like a bunch of freaks?" Zoë asks. I cover my mouth and laugh. Sara, Rebecca, and Amie return to their seats. I pull up a chair from the next table for Zoë. We sit down with Sara's coven.

"How was your trip?" I ask.

"It was fine, but I thought for sure I'd see a friend of mine since she goes to school at Georgia State. We made plans to hang out while I was in Atlanta, but she canceled on me last minute." Zoë seems to drift off.

"Are you okay?"

"Yeah, it was just weird. Tracy seemed really out of breath, like she was running or something."

"Tracy? Tracy Harper?"

"Yeah, that's her," Zoë says. "How do you know Tracy?"

"She's my friend Stephen's older sister."

"That's right." She shakes her head. "I'd heard a rumor that Tracy dropped out of school without warning, and I wanted to see if she was okay." She sighs. "I've always gotten a weird vibe from Tracy right before she does something big like that."

Sara reaches across the table and claims Zoë's hand. "Hello?" Zoë says as a question.

"Hi," Sara returns. "This strange vibe that you got from Tracy…" Sara focuses, and I feel a shift in her magic. "…was it like that."

"Like what?"

"She was testing you," I say to Zoë, while slipping her hand out of Sara's. "She wanted to see if you could sense other witches."

"No, nothing like that," Zoë says. "It's just like…her mood would shift big time, and I'd…I don't know, feel it."

"Spirit magic," Sara says. She reaches across the table again and claims both of Zoë's hands. "Relax. I want you to focus on your friend." Zoë frowns. "I can sense that you're worried about her, and I want to set your mind at ease." Zoë nods and closes her eyes. "Remember how you felt whenever you were around Tracy and just let your…" Sara cuts out instantly. "She's here?"

"What?"

"Tracy…your friend is here in town."

"Where?"

"I can't say for sure. I'd need a locator spell and something that belongs to her to get that specific, but I definitely feel her energy localized." Sara frowns. "She's near like spirits though…"

"So, she's visiting her family?" I ask. "They live here in town."

"No, not family like spirits…just people that have a similar energy to hers."

"I should ask Stephen, if he's seen her."

"No worries," Zoë says. "As long as she's okay, I'm not worried about it."

I nod. I come back to Sara and notice her whispering something to Rebecca, who nods in response. She repeats the pattern with Amie and gets the same result. "What's up?"

All three stand at the same time. "We have an errand to run," Sara says with a dismissive tone.

"Should I come with…? You know for training and all."

"No," Sara says, waving me off. "Stay and catch up with Zoë. We'll see you back at the house."

"But I rode here with you."

"I'll give you a ride back," Zoë says. I nod, and the three of them depart without even a wave goodbye. "That was weird." I nod. "Any idea what it was all about?"

"No, but Sara's a spirit magic guru, and she's been teaching me." I tip my head toward the door. "Rebecca's pretty awesome with earth magic and she's been teaching me what she knows too."

"And what about 'their friend.'" I giggle, and Zoë does too. "Has she been teaching you anything or just doing the pouty lip thing toward Quincy the whole time."

"Hey."

"Relax, I know the type. Sweet girl…just gets a little guy crazy sometimes." I nod. "Tracy was the same way when we were in middle school. Probably why I thought about her the minute I sat down."

"Amie's actually pretty good at healing and water magic. She's been teaching me how to use the body to help repair itself using the water inside."

"Wow, that's the most bored I've been while still able to keep my eyes open since Econ 1101." I laugh. "Come on."

"Where're we going?"

"I need some retail, weirdness free shopping."

"You know, I'm not one for shopping."

"Then it's good that you've got me to show you how it's…" Zoë's cell playing an old school R&B song cuts off her statement. "Hold on." She takes her phone out, and the display says, 'Cuddle Bear.' I mouth the name to myself.

"Hey, baby," Zoë answers. "No, just got back and got an invite to meet Jamie for lunch." Zoë flashes a huge smile. "Yeah, I'm in Edenton." She pauses. "You too? When did you…?" She looks at me. "This morning? Awesome. Where are you?" She does a happy bounce in place. "Okay, so I'll see you in a little while. Bye." She ends the call.

"So, no shopping," I say while extending my bottom lip in a faux pout.

"Funny," she says. "But don't think this lets you off the hook." I frown. "Don't give me that look," she says. "Little miss *I'm not one for shopping*, you didn't say that when you asked me to help you pick out a Prom dress…"

"You did, and it looked great and everything was fine."

"Yeah, right," Zoë cuts me off. I scoff. "I want to see pictures." She opens her purse and searches through it. "You had two ridiculously hot guys who definitely asked you, and they would've liked you in a garbage bag."

I forgot all about Prom…we spent the entire night on guard…trying to protect our classmates from whatever it was that Gwen and Alex sensed. I sigh. I feel like I'm missing the entire high school experience while fighting monsters. Plus, Quincy and Alex's cousin, Sora, just graduated, and we didn't get to celebrate after that, because Alex and the rest of them were zapped away to Japan immediately after. I should call Kai and see how he's holding up since he was left…

"Jamie!" I shake my head. Zoë holds up a to-go-cup of coffee. "I was just saying that I still wanted to see pictures of you in your dress. I mean, all you had to do for Prom was look amazing and accept one of their…hopefully, Tony's…offers." I shake my head again. "So, which one was it?"

I open my mouth to respond and nothing comes out.

"Speaking of which," she continues, while moving toward the door. "We're heading back to the estate…because Shay and Mitchell are back from New York."

"Cool. I need to talk to Shay." Zoë freezes and looks at me over her shoulder with a confused expression. "About some stuff…" She arches one eyebrow. "What?"

Zoë says nothing and shakes her head with the corners of her mouth turning down. She steps outside and hurries over to her car. We pile into her adorable little gold tinted Nissan something or other that she keeps telling me the name of, but I forget every single time. She drives it like a bat out of hell, so I guess I should call it that. The Nissan Bat…I giggle.

"What?" I shake my head. "No, really…what's up with you? I mean, you sent me some weird panicky texts while I was away." I sigh. "So, you've been kissing both of them."

"Yes."

"And you're definitely still in love with both of them?"

"Yes."

"And now this Rais guy fancies you?"

"Fancies me?" Zoë laughs. I shake my head. "So, he says…no, he does. I didn't believe him at first, but I don't know." I peer out the window at the houses going by in a blur of acceleration. "The more I talk to him, the more I trust him. He really cares about me."

"Do you…'care' about him?" Zoë asks in a suggestive manner.

"He's okay, but I just don't feel that way about him…ugh," I complain as a migraine comes on suddenly. No, this is worse than a migraine. A needle pierces my temple, while a drill bores into my forehead, and a mallet pounds the back of my head…or, at least, that's what it feels like. I shut my eyes tight and clench my fists over my temples.

"Are you okay?" Zoë asks with a panicked concern in her voice. "Is this some kind of witchy attack?"

"I don't think so. Ugh, but I don't know. I don't know what's causing this but…my head is killing me." I take my glasses off, toss them on her dash, and open my eyes. "Whatever it is…" …I feel a tug… "…it feels like it's coming from…" …back the way we came… "…town. Maybe, we should head back?"

"Are you sure? Wouldn't your headache just get worse if we went back to the thing causing?"

"Maybe, but what if being pulled away from it is what's causing it?"

"Crap," Zoë complains. "Why is witch logic so screwy?"

"Don't know. Didn't get a guidebook." I put my glasses back on and look out the back window. "Just a screwed-up mom to teach me stuff." My teeth gnash together, and my eyes shut tight as the piercing at my temples intensifies. I feel like someone's tightening a vice around the rest of my head. "Ow, ow, ow, ow," I chant while rocking back and forth in my seat. "Come on. Take me back."

"No way," she says. "In the battle of lesser evils…for once, I'm going to side with not doing what you ask me to do."

"Zo'?" I whine. She turns onto the Blackshear estate and sure enough, the second we pass into the barrier my headache vanishes. I open both of my eyes and take my hands away from my temples.

"Feeling better?" I nod. "See? I told you it was the right call. Now, what was causing it?"

"I don't know." I look back in the direction of town. "I wish I knew."

#####

Chapter 29: Sharing

Zoë parks near the willow tree, next to Quincy's car. I sigh as we climb out of the car and move toward the front door. Zoë looks at me as if she just ran over my cat. "Look, I'm sorry…but you just seemed out of it and I didn't want to risk it."

"It's fine. I just can't stop wondering what caused it." I scratch my temple as she lifts her hand to knock on the front door. It opens abruptly and Mitchell steps out. He wraps one arm around her at about butt height, lifts her, and steps back into the house. I hear giggles coming from the foyer as I step through the door.

Mitchell holds her up with one arm and kisses her. She holds her hands to either side of his face and bends to kiss him back. I shake my head and try to shield my eyes while stepping around them.

Shay steps out of the library. "Get a room," she says staring at the 'happy couple.' I laugh, and she does too, not that it slows them down in the slightest. "Jamie, have you seen Tony or Quincy?"

I shake my head. "No. I went out to practice my magic with Sara, Rebecca, and Amie."

"Sara's here?" Mitchell chimes happily, causing Zoë to frown.

"She has that effect on people, Zo'. Don't sweat it." Zoë nods.

"And Amie's here," Shay says like a complaint.

"Not you too?" I ask.

"No, it's just…Amie and I got into a huge fight when I first met her." Shay presses her palms together. "It was stupid and ugly and…I just try to avoid her now, if I can."

"Okay," I whisper. She nods. I do too, and I decide to let it drop. The other thing I wanted to ask her about drops too.

"Well," I start again. "Let's see where the guys are." I put both hands around the Crescent Moon Pendant in a praying fashion. I close my eyes and infuse the pendant with spirit magic. I hum. It's a lot easier to get a fix on them since Sara taught me how to do what I had been doing naturally. "They're close." I frown. "Really close…like on the property close…and they're getting closer."

"How's your headache?" Zoë asks as Mitchell lowers her to the floor.

"It's gone. Whatever that was calling me back to town, the barrier's blocking it."

Zoë nods. "Then it's probably a good thing I didn't take you back."

"Calling you?" Shay asks. I nod which causes her to frown. "And it gave you a headache?" I nod again. "Did you hear anything strange when the headache came on?"

I shrug as the back doors fly open. We peer at the stairs, trying to catch a glimpse of Quincy and Tony behind them. They march around the stairs, carrying…

"Rais?" They walk past us as if nothing happened…as if we're not standing here and like I didn't even say anything. They carry him into the library, and I follow.

They toss him on the floor, and I hurry over to his side. "Was that REALLY necessary?"

"He broke through the barrier," Tony says. "He deserves what he got."

"You don't know that." I put my hand on his forehead and stretch out with spirit magic and water magic. "He's been spelled," I say, finding a huge, magical block lodged in his mind. I hold my hands together and create a pentagon with my pointer fingers and thumbs. "Libero," I say softly, pushing the magic through the five-sided shape created by my hands. Rais inhales deeply but doesn't wake. I sigh. "That was a pretty powerful block." I look up at Quincy and Tony, standing nearby. "Do you think…my mom might've done this?"

"Don't know," Quincy says. Tony shrugs. "We found him near the fence out in the back woods."

"The back woods? You guys don't even go into the back woods…" They both sigh and look away from one another. "…so, what was he doing there?"

"We can ask him when he wakes up," Tony suggests.

I nod. "Okay, but for now, you guys could let him rest comfortably." Tony scowls and looks away. Quincy shoves his hands deep into his pockets. "Please?" They both sigh into matching groans. "Thanks, guys." They lift him, Quincy at his head and Tony at his feet. They move him over to the couch and lay him down.

"So, now we just wait?" Tony asks. I nod.

"Hey, boss," Mitchell says walking into the library with Zoë on his arm. Tony tips his head toward them.

"We need to tell you something," Shay says, stepping out from behind them.

"Sara's here," Tony says with a tone to his voice that says he knows they'll be happy to see her.

"We know," Shay says. "Jamie told us." He nods. "No, um…we have news…"

"About Leon, Brandy, and Phillip?" Tony asks. Shay nods. Quincy and I stare at him curiously. "Vampire hunters based in New York. They're friends of ours. We helped them out on a few jobs." I nod and Quincy arches his eyebrows and lets them fall.

"Well, business has been booming for them since the Chief Magistrate moved to New York," Shay says. Tony grits his teeth and gets that deep, contemplating scowl on his face.

"Chief Magistrate? What's that?" Zoë asks.

"Yeah," I add. "I've heard of vampire senators and magistrates…but a chief?"

"Highest ranking vampire official," Tony explains. "Senators are just like local area heads…like a mayor or governor, depending on how large a territory they cover. Above them are the magistrates…totaling eight in all, they each cover a section of the earth with senators serving under them directly. One of those eight is the Chief Magistrate. Think King…that gets voted in like a president by the other magistrates."

"Queen," Mitchell says.

"The new Chief Magistrate is a woman," Shay says. "Her name is Raven Gregory…and we know that because we had a run in with her sister, Alana Gregory."

"Are you guys okay?" Quincy asks.

Shay and Mitchell look at each other with quizzical expressions. They come back. "More weirded out than in danger," Shay says. "I mean, here Mitchell and I set a trap for this vamp…and in jumps this tiny little dark-haired girl wearing a Catholic Schoolgirl outfit."

"Catholic Schoolgirl?" I cross my arms and frown. "She's not one of those fetish vampires, is she? Because the blood drinking I can actually, almost understand, but the costumes just…"

"No," Mitchell says. "She…" He purses his lips and shrugs. "…well, we did some research before we came back, since she helped us stop the vamp and saved Shay's life."

"Shay?" Tony moans in a voice that I've only heard him use when calling out for me.

"I'm fine. She threw me off, and I got careless."

"The uniform was authentic," Mitchell says, renewing his report. "She attends Middleton Prep one of New York's premiere private high schools…and apparently, she was supposed to marry the Alpha wolf's younger brother as a part of some peace treaty or something, but something happened, and the guy split."

"Can't be," Shay spits, sounding angry. All eyes turn to her. "She was supposed to marry Nathan."

"Nathan's the Alpha's brother?" Tony asks. Shay nods. "He never told us that."

"Wait," I jump in. "Is this the same Nathan that you ran into in New Orleans with mom that was with a girl vampire that sounds suspiciously like

Meghan's missing cousin, Angela?" Quincy nods. "Okay, raise your hand if you think all of this is too weird to be a coincidence." Every hand, except Rais's, goes up in the room.

An explosion sounds off from the house. It reminds me of when my mom came to 'rescue' Siemon. "One of the seals is down," Tony says with his hand on his forehead.

"Is it near the back woods?" I ask.

"No," Quincy says. "That definitely came from the front…near the gate." Quincy and Tony look at each other.

"What?"

Tony turns to me. "Whoever it was weakened the barrier. Not enough for just anything to get through, but anything powerful would have no problem getting through."

"What does that mean?" Zoë asks, while moving in closer to Mitchell.

"It means we should get ready for a fight," Shay returns. I nod. Zoë seems to fret. "Plan?"

"Right," Tony chirps. "Mitchell, you're with me. We'll take point." Mitchell nods, despite Zoë tugging on his arm and trying to pull him away. "Quincy, you and Shay are next…we'll try to keep them from getting to the house."

"Right," Shay snaps at the same time that Quincy nods.

"What about me?"

"Jamie," Tony says.

"Don't tell me you're going to try and protect me, because that is so…"

"No," he interrupts. "I was going to say that you have the most important job as last line…protect Zoë and since the furball is defenseless, Rais." I nod. "Are we ready?"

"Yes," we all say in unison, except Zoë, who still seems to be in shock.

"FAIRIES," Rais barks, while bolting straight up on the sofa.

I move over to him. "Rais?" He turns to sit up.

"Bunny? What are you doing here?" He looks around. "Wait, where is here? How did I get here?"

"We were hoping you could tell us?"

The front door breaks free from its hinges and crashes into the stairs. Immediately after, Stefana, in her human-form, storms into the library wearing red and gold armor with a long white cape…of which, neither is nearly as impressive nor as fear-inspiring as the flaming sword in her right hand. She glares at Rais.

"You get one warning," she says, holding up the appropriate number of fingers on her left hand. "…give our brother back…or be destroyed!"

#####

Chapter 30: Seventh

"What in the Sam Hill are you talking about?" Yes, because when flaming sword-wielding fairies surprise me, I say whatever old timey expression I've heard Mr. Hamish use.

"Our brother was being guarded by two of my sisters," Stefana says. "We lost contact with the two of them and when we finally tracked them down, they were unconscious, and our brother was gone. One of my sisters can make words into pictures. We had both of Tibal's guards describe what they remembered. She created two pictures…one image was of your mother…" She finishes by pointing the tip of her sword at me. "…and one image of that," she finishes, while pointing at Rais.

I half-turn to Rais. "Is that true? Did you kidnap their brother?"

"Of course not," Rais says with a groan in his voice. "You know I'd never do anything like that."

"Do we?" Tony asks.

"Not helping," I say.

"Not trying to. If she wants to carve the furball up, I don't think we should stand in her way."

"Quincy? A little help?"

"Honestly, I can't say if we should trust him or not…but it's your call, Jamina. Whatever you decide, I'll back you up."

I nod once firmly and come back to Stefana. I try to think through this mess logically. "Did either of your sisters actually see Rais take your brother? Did they see him attack them or did they just assume that because he was there and he's a daemon, he must've?"

"He IS a daemon. He WAS there and then our brother WASN'T. What more do we need to know?"

"Oh, I don't know, maybe all that stuff in the middle, for starters?"

"It's really quite simple," Stefana says in what sounds like a snarl. She points her sword at Rais again. "Hand over that daemon furball, and I'll leave his pelt lining my bedroom floor after he tells me where my brother is."

"That's not happening, Stefana."

"Chelsea the 83rd and Jeania the 8th are two or our mother's most loyal and strongest fairies. If they say that that scruff was there, then that's enough to mobilize an army…which is what I did."

"An army?" I shake my head. "This is insane, Stefana. You don't even have any proof."

Her face twists up in a way that makes even her gorgeous features look repulsive. A deep crease moves down the center of her forehead. Her cheeks go up and hide her pronounced cheekbones. Her full lips pull back over her teeth, which grind together.

"I don't need proof. I have twenty of my battle-ready sisters lining this property, preparing to obliterate this house if you don't hand him over." She lifts her sword offensively…looking like she's ready to cut through me to get to Rais. "Now."

I swallow a massive lump and steal a glance over my shoulder at Rais. He sighs, and his head bows. "Faith," I murmur and put my hand around the Crescent Moon Pendant. "Dive in," I repeat my father's one and only lesson on bravery. I take two steps to my right, leaving me standing directly in the path that leads Stefana to Rais.

"Stand aside!" I don't move, but she takes a step forward.

Quincy and Tony appear in the few feet that separate us. Tony has his knife drawn and ready and Quincy takes a fighting stance. Stefana draws a short sword from behind her back and aims it at me too. Mitchell steps forward with his adamant knuckles covering his clenched fists. Shay moves up beside him with two daggers drawn.

I smirk. "Mine are bigger than yours," I say as a jab.

"Over twenty of my sisters are outside…awaiting my command. The six of you don't stand a chance."

"Seven," Rais says. He tries to stand, cringes, falls back into his seat, and his head bows between his knees.

"Nope, we're six," I say. I look at Zoë's concerned face. "Five?" I swallow another lump, starting to get how hopeless our situation is. I know Stefana's strong…probably physically the strongest of all of Devi's fairies. If even four or five of those others are nearly as strong as she is, we're in trouble.

"Stefana," I say, trying to make my voice even…trying to diffuse this entire situation before it gets bloody. "Tell us what it is that you think Rais did exactly. You've been watching him. You know him. You know he's not capable of doing anything that would hurt me." I see Quincy and Tony glance at me from the corners of my eyes.

"No talking! Give him to me, or we will destroy you."

"I can protect them," I bluff. Quincy swallows deeply this time. At least, he was able to hide the sting in his chest. Tony frowns and steals a quizzical look at me. Crap! Even Tony's not buying my lie. "I could cast an anti-fairy spell and send all of you packing." Stefana doesn't budge…point of her sword still pointed at my throat. "At least give him a chance to tell his side of the story." She inches forward a little. "Considering the whopper of a favor your mother asked me for…it's the least you could do."

Her eyes lower to the floor. She lifts them and tips her head toward Rais. They all turn to Rais, but my focus stays with Stefana. She lowers her sword, but only a little.

"Okay," he says with a gruff voice. He leans back on the sofa. "I finally managed to track down your mother…"

"My mom? You found her?"

He nods. "She was outside the barrier and pretty easy to track, plus she was with another witch, who was even easier to follow." I frown. "The two of them were stalking one of the loft apartments just off the square. I decided to wait and see what they were up to, but when I caught the distinct scent of fairy, I decided to take a closer look." He sighs. "When I made it to the apartment, it was an all-out brawl between the pretty redheaded fairy with glasses…"

"Chelsea," Stefana submits.

"…and the tall one with broad shoulders and curly black hair."

"Jeania."

"They were holding their own against the other witch."

"The other witch?" I ask. "You mean my mom didn't fight?"

"Not 'til it looked like they were going to beat the witch with the caramel complexion."

"Caramel complexion?" Tony asks, and his eyes dart over to Quincy.

"Did you get a name?" Quincy asks.

Rais scratches the back of his head. "I think Jamie's mom called her…Selfie? That can't be right."

"Nelfie?" Tony asks. Rais nods. "Nelfala LeBeau," he says with a groan.

"Wait," I cut in. "So, this is where we are…Mitchell and Shay meet the Chief Magistrate for all vampires' sister who was going to marry this Nathan, who's the brother of the Alpha for all wolves'…but broke it off and then you," I pause to point to Quincy. "Ran into said wolf in New Orleans with this Angela, who's a vampire and may be Meghan's cousin…but you also ran into Nelfie, who provided an ambush for my mom only to show up here and kidnap the fairies' brother, Tibal, with my mom?" I shake my head, feeling all eyes on me. "Did I leave anything out?"

"Only the part where Nelfala used to follow Nathan around like a puppy until she finally caught on that that self-serving wolf can't love anyone but himself," Tony says. I have to meet this wolf, Nathan…if for no other reason than to kick his butt. I look at Tony. His jaw clenches, and he stares away from us. I peer at Shay, and her posture matches his. Therefore, it must be…

"MY LITTLE BROTHER IS OUT THERE!" Stefana snarls. "SORT THROUGH THE REST OF THIS MESS ON YOUR OWN TIME!"

"Right," I breathe. "So, Nelfie and my mom were fighting the fairies." I aim at Rais with both pointer fingers. "Go."

"Yeah, I think that was it… 'Nelfie, I'm so disappointed in you,'" Rais says, sounding as if he's mocking my mom. "'…you couldn't even beat two fairies.'"

Stefana growls.

"Sorry. That's when I decided to jump in. Fat lot of good that did. At that point, Jamie's mom jumped into the fight, and it was downhill from there. They knocked out the fairies easily, so it was two on one. The one…that woman Nelfie hit me with a wind spell that held me in the air, and your mom hit me with what felt like a power plant's worth of electricity."

"How did you survive?" Stefana asks.

"I honestly don't know. I thought for sure I was dead. After I blacked out, I woke up here."

"They spelled him." Stefana glares at me before turning her attention back to Rais. "I believe him." Stefana trembles with rage and bows her head. "Stefana?"

She lifts her head and tears pour from her eyes. I gasp. "The dwelling…was spelled too. They left a note demanding that all fairies leave Edenton immediately and forever." She puts her sword back in its sheath and wipes her eyes on her forearm. "…it told us to leave or Tibal would be destroyed." She shivers. "I can't let anything happen to my brother."

I scowl. "We won't," I say. Stefana lifts her head and stares at me. She then looks at the faces gathered around me. I look around the room quickly and come back to her. "We won't." I sigh. "But this is weird. I mean, why would En Quosque resort to kidnapping your brother…and even more than that, why would they try to force all of the fairies to leave Edenton?"

Rais groans. We turn to him. "How man fairies are in Edenton?" I frown. "Think about it. You had three here, watching you alone."

"Five," Stefana says in a whisper. She looks at me with guilty eyes. "Twee didn't know about two of them."

"Right," Rais continues. "Their brother was here…with two guards…and now, this quickly gathered twenty fairies that are on your doorstep."

I come back to Stefana. "I'm guessing you didn't all just arrive when you heard about your brother," I say. She nods. "So, most of Devi's 108 children were here already?" She nods again.

"With that many eyes," Mitchell starts.

"It'd be really hard for anyone to move around freely in this town," Shay finishes.

"It's like your own fairy, traffic cam network," Zoë supplies. "Especially considering that one of you can show images from the others' minds."

I nod as Stefana bows her head again. "Plus," she says with a humble tone, that doesn't even sound right coming from her. "Mother…Queen Devi decreed that we fairies are done being passive observers in the war between the forces of good and evil. That we can no longer selfishly concern ourselves only with our own interests."

She lifts her head, tilting her chin upward. "She ordered that we act in the benefit of not only fae and humankind, but that we would help protect the world as a whole. That we'd be a force for good." She sighs. "It filled my heart with joy to hear mother speak so boldly, but then this happened and this…this…threatens our entire way of life.

"Without the next Fairy King, the next generation of High Fairies will not be born…and the fae world will be thrown into chaos." She trembles again, but this time it's definitely with anger. She draws her sword again quickly and when she does the fire moving along the blade flares out more. "So, as you can see, I cannot just take this daemon's word for it. I can't even just take your word for it, Jamie. I have to take him, even if by force, and make him tell me what has become of my brother."

"Not this again," I say, crossing my arms. "I told you. We won't let anything happen to your brother."

"What if it already has?"

"Then En Quosque lost their bargaining chip early," Quincy says. "And besides, you know he's not dead, don't you?" Stefana twitches. "Fairies can sense the deaths of other fairies…that's probably why Daphne and Nelfie didn't kill Jeania and Chelsea…because she knows the rest of you would've picked up on it instantly, and you would've swarmed the place, right?"

"Yes," Stefana admits. "But…"

"You can't have him," I snap. "End of discussion."

"Then it's war," Stefana snarls, stepping forward.

#####

Chapter 31: Signal

"I don't want to fight you, Stef-argh!" I yell as my headache comes back only feeling like it's tenfold. I drop to my knees clutching my forehead…my glasses fall to the floor beside me.

"Jamie! Jamie," Zoë says, wrapping me in her arms. I barely hear her over the sound of a C-sharp whistling in my ear like one of those stupid air horns, which is…

"…causing my headache," I complain, trying to cover my ears. "IT'S A LOUD WHISTLING NOISE," I shout, but recognizing that I'm shouting doesn't stop me from continuing. "…IT'S LIKE A C-SHARP…BUT IT FEELS LIKE IT'S CUTTING THROUGH MY BRAIN!"

"How can…?" Stefana says but stops talking abruptly.

"HOW CAN…WHAT?"

"Shhh," she issues, while putting her sword away. "That's no strange sound." She nods firmly. "That's Twelana's signal"

"TWEE? WHERE IS SHE? IS SHE ALRIGHT?"

Stefana frowns. She puts her left thumb and pointer finger into the corners of her mouth. She blows and lets an even louder whistle rip free. I stop wincing. Stefana's whistle caused Twee's to cut out. Wait, it didn't cut out, it just turned the volume down.

"Jamie," Zoë says, still holding on to me.

"It stopped…well, stopped hurting, at least," I say in my normal volume. Zoë hands me my glasses. "Thanks. I'm fine now."

"I have a question," Tony says, stepping forward. "Why didn't Quincy, Rais, or I hear the noise? We all have heightened senses." He steals a glance. "I mean, Shay didn't even hear it, and she's part siren."

"Because faux-fae," Stefana says. "Twelana adjusted her pitch so that it can only be heard by those on a fairy frequency."

"Like Fairy radio?" I ask, still rubbing my ears. I replace my glasses.

"Not funny."

"Yeah, but," Quincy chimes in. "Jamie heard it before you did, and she's definitely not a fairy."

"Yeah," Zoë says. "She heard it in the car while we were on our way here."

"You heard it?" Stefana growls. "…and you didn't think to mention it?"

"I just got a headache and didn't know what it was. Twee didn't exactly tell me that she messed with my hearing presets."

Stefana groans and steps away. She comes back just as quickly. "Don't you get it? That's Twelana's cry for help. It's how she sends messages that can't be picked up by any other being."

"She's in trouble?"

"No, she says she has a lead on your mother. She saw her and this Nelfie moving with something large…it looked like a bag."

"Tibal?" Quincy asks.

"She couldn't tell, but she's keeping up her pursuit." Stefana turns toward the door. "I have to go."

"Wait," I call, running after her. "We can help you."

"This is fairy business…"

"This is best friend business," I return. "A little something that I thought you would've figured out about me by now Stef." She glares at me. "I keep my friends close to me…and my best friends are like my family. Twee is my family. I'm going to help her…whether you help me with that or not."

Stefana inhales deeply and exhales loudly. I arch my eyebrows and tilt my head forward. She nods in concession. "Very we…" She cuts out. She tips her head toward the missing front door and listens.

"What is…?"

"Shush," she issues. I hear the much softer tone of Twee's whistle again, feeling thankful for whatever Stefana did. "'They've stopped,'" Stefana says as if repeating someone else's words. "'I'll keep watch until the rest of you arrive! We're at…'" Stefana gasps.

"What? What is it?"

"She cut off." Stefana's eyes become large saucers, and her breathing accelerates. She puts one hand on her stomach as if she's going to be sick.

"Wait," I say with panic in my voice. "She's not…" I tremble. "…dead, is she?"

Stefana shakes her head but continues holding her stomach. "No," she whispers. "…but if she cut out that abruptly, and I can no longer hear her song…then…" She looks at me. "…something has happened to her. She's been knocked unconscious."

Stefana peers over my head. "YOU!" I turn to find Quincy, Tony, and Rais standing in the foyer with us, while Mitchell, Shay, and Zoë stand in the library doorway. "If anything happens to my brother or my sister." She nods as two tears break away from her eyes. "You'll have hell to pay."

She storms out of the open door. Amazingly, she seems a hundred times more upset now than when it was just Tibal's life on the line.

"Bunny," Rais starts. "You have to believe that…"

"I do," I say. "Give me a second to think." I put my hand on my chin pondering the possibilities. More than likely, mom spotted Twee and knocked her out, but then again, because she knew about this fairy bond, she didn't kill her because that would instantly give away where she is. Wait, I wonder if she knows that I'm still working with the fairies. She knows I trusted Twee, but she couldn't possibly know about the rest, especially since so many of them have been assigned to watch me without me knowing about it.

"Jamina," Quincy says, stepping up beside me. I look at him and Tony on my left.

"What do you want us to do?" Tony asks.

I nod. "Okay," I breathe. "First of all, Zo' could you go up to Twee's room and find something of hers…ooohhh," I purr. "That cute little t-shirt that she liked sleeping in with that purple cat face on the front." Zoë nods and hurries up the stairs.

"What's the plan?" Shay asks.

"I'm going to do a tracking spell on Twee. I'm going to find my friend, before my increasingly psychotic mother does something to her." I pinch the bridge of my nose. "I can't believe I just said that…or worse yet, that I mean it." I sigh.

"Hey, sunshine," Sara beams from the doorway. We all turn to her, flanked by Rebecca on her right and Amie on her left. "What's with all the gloomy auras?"

"Oh," Amie says. "And why are there like fifteen fairies hovering around the barrier?"

"Long story short," I say. "Fairies are here. Their brother and youngest sister have been kidnapped…my mom's involved." Sara smiles. "And now, you're kind of freaking me out."

"I guess it was good that we followed up on your hunch," Rebecca says to Sara. Sara nods and renews her smile, which is more of a triumphant smirk at this point.

"What do you mean?" I ask.

"Well," Sara starts. "When I was reading your friend trying to find her friend…" Zoë hurries down the stairs carrying Twee's shirt. "…yes, that's her. Anyway, I felt a very powerful ripple of spirit magic. It resonated in three locations. I'm willing to bet my best bra that that's where they're keeping the fairy boy and probably the youngest sister too."

I nod once firmly. "Can you show us where those locations are?" Sara nods with a smile.

"Did you get all that?" Tony poses. I frown. He tips his head toward the missing door, and Stefana steps into view, still in her human form.

"Yes, I did." She looks at Sara. "Just tell me where."

"Divide and conquer," Sara says calmly. "I can tell by Jamie's aura that she has every intention of helping you whether you want her to or not. If she helps, then you'll get the Blackshear brothers. If they help, then you'll get

Mitchell and Shay. And, we're going along," Sara says, motioning to her coven. "Because I want to meet the fallen witch and help stop her."

Stefana glares at Sara. "Let us help you," I plead.

She sighs, but nods.

"Now," Tony says, stepping forward. "How many warriors do you have with you? Really?"

"Only five of my sisters are close to my level of combat readiness," she admits. "The other 15 have some skill, but they would only slow me down."

Tony nods and holds his chin in his left hand. "Alright," he says. "I'll divide us up." He turns to Stefana. "If that's alright with you?"

"Heard you issuing orders earlier. Go ahead."

"Thank you." He nods. "Alright, Sara…were all of the 'pings' that you got of the same magnitude?"

"No, the one near the center of town was the biggest."

"The one at the high school was next," Rebecca says as if reminding Sara.

"And then there was the one over by the train tracks," Amie adds.

"Good," Tony says. "The center of town is probably the glamour they have over the Voracious Seal." He nods. "I hate to say it, but our largest force should probably go there." He lifts his eyes to Stefana. "You should go," he says sternly. "Take three of the five fighters with you." Stefana nods. "You should also take at least seven of the others with you as support…plus…" He looks over his shoulder. "Mitchell…" He smirks taking in Zoë, clinging to Mitchell's arm. "…and Zoë can go too."

Mitchell pats her hand as if trying to calm her down. "I'll go with that group, too," Sara volunteers. "I'm a spirit magic user…I can get the word out faster if we need back up."

"Good," Stefana says. "The rest?"

"Right," Tony continues. "Jamie, you'll come with me, Shay, and Rebecca to the school. We'll also take five of the remaining non-fighting fairies…to help search, since the school has so many hiding spots." I nod once firmly.

"No, no, no," Amie moans. She points at Rais. "That leaves me with that guy."

"And Quincy," Sara hums, reassuringly. Quincy twitches awkwardly.

"Still," Amie complains.

"Fine," Tony groans. "You can go with Sara." Amie smiles and leans her head against Sara's shoulder. "Quincy, it'll be you, Rais, and the last two combat-ready fairies."

"We'll be fine," Quincy says. "It's the smallest ping…and on the outskirts of town."

"Hmm," Stefana moans.

"What's wrong?" I ask.

"The smallest group," she says. "I'd like to assign our strongest two fighters to that group…" She lifts her eyes to Rais. "…but that's Chelsea and Jeania."

"It'll be fine," Quincy says. "As long as they see that you trust Rais…"

"But I don't trust him."

"Then trust me," I say. "I have felt like I've known Rais since the moment I met him. Despite our rocky start…"

"Rocky?" Tony asks.

"Shut up," I groan. "I still trust him. Twee trusts him."

Stefana nods and lifts her eyes to Rais. "Fine. I'll convey this to my sisters." Stefana snaps her fingers and vanishes into a tiny gold orb of light. She floats out the door and vanishes.

"Are you okay?" Tony asks. I frown and shake my head.

Quincy taps his heart. "Something's bothering you, besides all of this."

I sigh. "The teams…they seem a little…uneven to me." Tony frowns. "I mean, you're leaving your brother and Rais out in the cold."

"Trust me, it's for the best." I cross my arms over my chest, knowing that I probably look just like my mom and not caring. He sighs this time. "Sara is the strongest at using Spirit Magic. Not only does that help her communicate with the rest of us easier, it'll also help them search faster. You're the strongest out of all of us." I shake my head. "It's true, get over it." I huff. "Plus, you've become pretty proficient at using spirit magic yourself. So, we'll cover the largest area and second largest ping. Quincy and Rais have the best tracking abilities even if they have no spirit magic between them. They can search the smallest area and get back to us quickly if they find anything."

"I guess you really did think it through," I say. He nods. My eyes wander over to Quincy. He nods in that way that lets me know he's 'okay with it all.' I hope I'm not giving the face that says that 'I'm not' back to him.

"We should get moving," Quincy says, moving toward me. "Those fairies aren't going to wait all night."

He steps past me, and I catch his arm. He comes back. "Be careful," I mutter. He nods. I perch on the balls of my feet and kiss him on the cheek. I hold there for a moment. I want to kiss him…REALLY kiss him, but…

"I should get going," he whispers. I press my forehead to the side of his face, and my eyes close. Why am I so worried about him? He's strong. Quincy is one of the strongest beings I've ever met. The image of him lying on the sofa when Sara and the others brought him back from New Orleans answers that question for me. It's soon followed by the image of him on the warehouse floor after Siemon attacked him. "I'll be okay, Jamina. I promise."

"You promise?" He nods again. I release him and take a step back. "I'm holding you to that." He smirks.

"Brother," he says to Tony.

"Brother." They both nod and Quincy steps outside. It used to upset me when they'd do that, but I know why they do it now. They've said all the goodbyes that they need to each other over the last two centuries.

Rais moves over to me. "You be careful, Bunny."

"You too…" I bob my head unevenly. "…and I will." He wraps one arm around me. Tony growls.

"And if it comes down to you and Captain Scowl," Rais whispers. "You save yourself and leave his behind right where it is." I laugh.

"I heard that," Tony complains.

"I know," Rais says and steps away. I sigh, thinking that everyone stepping out of this door…has a chance of not coming back. My heart sinks.

"Remember," Sara says, tapping the underside of my chin. "If your mind is filled with doubt, your spirit magic will wane." I nod. "We'll find your friend…and we'll all come back safe and sound. You wait and see."

I smile. "Geez," I say as a complaint and wipe a tear away from my right eye. "No wonder everybody loves you."

"And don't you forget it," she chirps and then walks out the door.

#####

Chapter 32: Twelana

"Ugh," I complain as Tony closes his car door behind me. "This place is even more depressing at night."

"Agreed," Tony says, looking up the front steps that lead to the main entrance.

"Tony?" a tiny orange orb of light says. He stares at it hovering just above his forehead. He nods quickly. "Stefana the 7th told us your plan… and we would like to thank you for assisting us in this delicate matter. I am Brianna the 49th, and I will lead the search along the exterior of the building."

"Thanks," he returns. "We'll check inside. Do you have any sisters among you who use spirit magic or have heightened senses?"

"Yes," Brianna returns. "Samantha the 19th and Kendall the 103rd both have excellent hearing. Also, Amara the 9th can sense emotions."

"Good, they'll come in handy." He nods and steps past her heading toward the steps. "Can one of you communicate with the others quickly?"

"Yes, Amara can also share her emotions with others."

"Empathy as a power, who knew?" Shay poses. I shrug.

"Alright, send her in with us…tell her to stay close, but out of sight. I don't want her putting herself in danger unnecessarily."

"Nope, just the rest of us," Rebecca says. I smirk and cut my eyes to her. She giggles.

"Move out," Tony says and heads up the stairs. The three of us follow him to the front door. He utters a quick unlocking spell, and we're inside.

We reach the break in the main hallway. "We should split up," Tony suggests. "We can cover more ground that way."

"How very Scooby-Doo of you," Rebecca quips.

"Jamie, you and Rebecca…" *Rebecca? …me and Rebecca…? …not me and him?* "…should start by checking the southern end of the building, head for the gym first and call out if you need help. I should be able to hear you.

"Shay," he continues. "We'll head this way." He puts an arm behind her back and guides her in that direction.

"Bye," Rebecca says. She nods for the nonresponse, and we turn in the opposite direction. "That was weird," she says. I frown. "The way he split us up…it almost seemed like he wanted to go off with Shay." I touch the Crescent Moon Pendant and continue walking.

"I also noticed that your heart skipped a beat when he suggested going off with her." I stare at Rebecca. "Earth magic…I can feel vibrations in the earth." She nods. "Shay's heart skipped two beats when he made the call…and another when he wrapped his arm around her. Does she have feelings for-"

"Can we talk about anything else? Like how it'd be awesome if we found Twee and Tibal here, alive, and safe." Rebecca purses her lips, and her eyes swell for a moment then come back down to normal.

I try to ignore everything, but there it is. Shay and Tony's shared past has come back up in a huge way, and it's affecting them. Neither of them would ever admit it, but they're not telling me something. Worse yet, there's something that they're not telling each other. Does Tony really have feelings for Shay...? Am I the only thing stopping them?

"Jamie, are you alright?" I nod. "Do you sense something through your spirit magic?" I shake my head. "Okay, because for a second, I felt your heart rate spike."

"No, I'm fine," I lie. "Just trying to focus my spirit magic." Wow, another whopper. I exhale deeply and do what I said I was doing. I can feel the spirit magic around me...it feels cool and brings me down a bit. It gets me off the 'what are Tony and Shay doing' ledge.

"Jamie," Rebecca says. "I feel something...a weird vibration coming from up ahead."

I look up. "That's the library." I stop walking and peer to my right. "You sure it's not from this direction." She shakes her head. "Weird. You'd figure if something big and evil was hanging around a school, it'd be in the gym."

"You're thinking like a fighter..." She resumes walking, and I move with her. "...or like you've encountered a P.E. teacher." I giggle. "Think like a witch. What's in a library?"

"Books. Shelves and shelves of books..." She arches her eyebrows. "Oh, lots of information with lots of hiding places." She taps the tip of her nose and smiles. "You're really smart, lady."

"Hey, not just a pretty face," she says, motioning to herself.

"Clearly more than a leggy, head turner." She smirks. "Are we rambling because we're scared of what we're going to find in here?"

"Who says we're going to finding anything in here?" She stops walking and looks at me. "Never know until we know, you know?" I giggle. "Sorry, that was one of Drew's things...my fiancé."

I bring the giggle down to soft chuckle. "We should introduce Drew to my friend Alex someday." She nods. "Ready?" I take the door handle on the right. She nods and claims the one on the left. We pull the doors open, stride inside and...nothing. The library looks as plain as it normally does, only darker. The smell of musty old books hangs in the air, and the glow from the exit lights throw deep shadows across the floor from the thick wooden shelves. We look around curiously sliding our feet along the matted, semi-sticky carpet.

"Maybe we should yell, 'Come out, come out, wherever you are,'" Rebecca says in a low voice.

"Trust me, not smart," I return in a whisper. "Careful what you wish for and all that." She bobs her head and continues searching

I walk toward the reference section in the back and Rebecca follows, looking around constantly. "What's that?" I ask about a large shadow falling across a study table. "What is that? Is it…it's…?" We step closer, and I make out… "TWEE!!!" I start to run, but Rebecca catches my arm. "What are you…?" I turn to her and then follow her line of sight to the shadowy figure stepping out from between two rows of periodicals on my left. "WHO ARE YOU? WHAT DID YOU DO TO TWEE?"

The shadow sighs and pulls down the deep purple hood covering her dark curly hair. She lifts perfect caramel skin and a pair of full, puckered, pouty lips. "Just as impatient as ya' mama," she complains.

"You must be Nelfala," Rebecca says. She nudges me with her elbow. I frown.

"One and da same, bebe," Nelfala says and takes a bow.

"Let Twee go," I say. Rebecca nudges me again.

"Does dat ever work, chile?" Nelfala asks.

"First time for everything." Nudge.

"Den mebe I should be askin' you to turn and walk away."

"Did you think that would work?" Nudge.

"First time, chile," Nelfala says.

"Quincy and Tony told me about you, 'Nelfie.' You gave away half of your magic, which means you're probably not even strong enough to be a full-fledged member of En Quosque, so why are you doing this?" Nudge.

"Your mama knows a spell. It'll restore my magic and keep me lookin' dis young for a long, long time, chile."

"You're an idiot." She frowns. "You gave up half of your magic to look younger…" I shake my head. "…why not throw away half your mind, half your spirit, half of your soul…because that's basically what you did." I shake my head again, feeling the frustration build. Nudge. "I'd rather lop off a hand or an ear than give up my magic."

"So, dere's nothin' dat would make you wanna stay lookin' young and beautiful for as long as possible?" I shake my head. Nudge. "Not even say…da love of two handsome, but immortal young men?" I swallow a lump. She laughs. "Puts it in perspective a lil' betta now, don't it, chile?"

"No," I reply. "I love Quincy and Tony…but I'd never give up half of my magic to stay with them for a little while longer. I cherish the time I have with them…"

"Easy to say when you're young, chile." Nudge. "When dey still look atchu like da beautiful, young thang you are…" Nudge. "…but when a few wrinkles set in…" Nudge. "…when some gray hairs spring up. What den?"

"Well, tell me this, Nelfala." Nudge. "Do you really think Nathan would approve of what you're doing now?" She gasps as if something just knocked the wind out of her. She frowns, and her eyes begin to glisten. "I didn't think so." Nudge. "You were an idiot to give up your magic for beauty." Nudge, nudge. "And you're an even bigger idiot if you don't let Twee go right now." Nudge, nudge. I turn to Rebecca. "And will you stop doing that?"

"Maybe you should call for help?" she says through clenched teeth. I make an 'oh' face.

My left hand snaps to the Crescent Moon Pendant.

"I'll prove who da idiot is, chile," Nelfala says and lifts her left hand. A swirl of black smoke rises from her palm and takes the shape of…

I gasp. "The crystal?" She nods with a smirk and holds it for me to see. It's not the whole thing, but it looks like a shard of it about the size of her palm.

"Crystal?"

"My friend Alex and his kitsune girlfriend stomped a bad guy who had a crystal. The crystal absorbs magic and souls. My mom was supposed to be looking for a way to destroy it. Gave it to the bad guys instead," I recap quickly for Rebecca. She nods and sighs. "That's only a small piece of it."

"How does it steal souls and magic though?"

"It…"

"I'll show you, bebe," Nelfala interrupts. She whispers into the fragment, and it releases an inky black liquid. I extend my other arm in front of Rebecca and take a step back. She moves with me, thankfully. The last of the liquid drips away. The puddle moves over to Twee's table.

"No," I moan. I look down at the Crescent Moon Pendant in my hand. "Why isn't this working? I can't sense Tony or anything from this."

"Barrier, chile," Nelfala says. "Special made…nothing gets in or out. Is like dis section of da liberries a whole otha world."

I groan. The puddle rises and takes the shape of one of those bear-dog things that attacked Alex and Gwen. "Rebecca," I say. "Run and find Tony and Shay or any of the fairies." I feel her shake. "Do it. I'll be fine. I promise. Besides, your power would probably bring down my high school."

She sighs but turns and runs.

"GET HER," Nelfala orders. The bear-dog lunges forward in one huge shadow…okay, one huge shadow with sharp although stained-white teeth. Rebecca turns and freezes.

"Capso," I say with a snap of my fingers toward the bear-dog. It runs into the bubble formed around it and splashes against the wall like a water balloon bursting. Its inkiness runs down the inside of the bubble. "Go. I've got it." Rebecca nods and rushes off.

"Oh, yeah?" Nelfala says. I hold my left hand extended toward the captured ink puddle. "Don't breathe easy yet, bebe." I frown as more ink falls from the crystal shard. This puddle separates into two pools and two more bear-dogs rise from them. I grit my teeth as they growl. The first bear-dog reforms inside of the shield and scratches at the sides. I see a tiny light out of the corner of my eye that gives me a little piece of mind.

I huff a laugh. "You givin' up, chile? You done loss yo' mind?"

"Nope. Something just occurred to me. You must be really good to be able to conjure three of these bear-dog things…"

"Hell hounds," she corrects.

I nod. "Well, you must be really good to keep three of them up and running…" I smirk. "…and keep someone as powerful as Twee spelled."

Nelfala gasps, and her eyes dart to the empty table. A C-sharp hits her out of nowhere and throws her to the floor. Twee jumps down from the bookshelf on my right and runs over to my side. I wrap my free arm around her while keeping an eye on the new bear-dogs.

"Don't ever do anything like that again," I say.

She nods against my heart. "I knew you'd come and find me," she says as we release each other.

"Always." She smiles. "Stefana's been worried sick about you."

"She's always worrying about me," Twee says in an 'I already knew that' kind of way.

"Ahem," Nelfala says, while rising to her feet. "Did you forgit about me, bebe?"

I shake my head slowly. Twee takes a step away from me and focuses on the two bear dogs. "I can't believe she's still on her feet," Twee says.

"She's tougher than she looks." The two bear dogs charge forward. "Here they come." Twee inhales deeply. "Extermino," I shout at the left one. Twee opens her mouth and belts out a deep low note that tosses the table and several of the books from the nearby shelf. My bear-dog burns and moves around frantically. Twee's seems to lose a few layers of inkiness.

Nelfala laughs. "What?"

"Nothin', bebe. Jus' somethin' I heard dat I can't believe."

"What's that?" Twee shouts.

Nelfala chuckles. "Dat your supposed to be da next Witch of Light and dat you're supposed to be da next Fairy Queen." I steal a glance at Twee, and she returns my gaze. "Can't believe dat…when you're both too stupid to realize da mistake you makin'."

"Mistake?" Twee asks.

"No," I gasp. I glare at my bear-dog, the one not trapped in a shield, and it lifts its head with a mouthful of fire. Twee gasps as hers stands, and its mouth seems to rumble with a tune.

"TWEE! GET OVER HERE!" She dives over to me. I extend my right hand out to the two of them. "Contego," I shout as a fireball flies toward us. I take the hit and wince. The other bear-dog lets loose with Twee's sound attack. I groan as it repeatedly reverberates against my shield…making my teeth rattle like I'm holding a jackhammer. Oh no, it's slipping…I'm gonna lose it and…

"Eeeeeeeeeee," Twee hums softly toward the near side of my shield. Her song counteracts the bear-dog's tune.

"Thanks." She doesn't respond but keeps up the harmonic support.

"TEAR THEM APART," Nelfala says.

"Nope," I say. I quickly draw a pentagon and heptagon in mid-air. "A little mad at myself for not thinking of this sooner." I point my right pointer and middle finger at Twee's bear-dog. "Capso," I pant and focus on applying the two seals to it. The vibrations disappear entirely from my shield. I lower it and look at the other bear-dog. It prepares another fireball as I draw another pentagon and heptagon in mid-air. "Capso," I say just before it releases its fire…my fire. The fire hits the shield I created around it and is absorbed.

The two bear-dogs squeal and whine in their magic cages. They shrivel into inky little pieces of torn paper-like stuff before crumbling and falling apart. I sigh. Suddenly, my arms feel heavy…so does my head and my eyelids, but that's a whole other story. I fall to my knees.

"JAMIE," Twee says, wrapping her arms around me.

"DESTROY HER WHILE SHE'S DRAINED!" Nelfala yells. I turn to the left…crap, I forgot about the last bear-dog. It rams its head into the shield destroying it…and knocking me to the floor.

"Jamie," Twee says, trying to pull me back to my feet or at least, my knees. I throw my hands up…from a very reclined position. My vision blurs for a second as the bear-dog rushes toward us.

"Capio," I say…knowing any more, and I might pass out entirely. Ugh, keeping that thing under wraps for that long drained my magic and then throwing up four seals that quickly. What was I thinking? "Omph," I whine as my teeth gnash together. The bear-dog hit the shield…demolished is more like it though. He continues toward us. I try to push myself up, but my stupid arms are useless right now.

The bear-dog bites down on… I open my clenched eyes. "Twee!" I sob. The bear-dog sank his teeth into her side, pinning her left arm between its mouth and her body. "Twee, no!"

"Eat…this…," she mumbles. She opens her mouth, and a tone flows out that seems to vibrate softly through the room, through the floor, ceiling and all the walls…and even me. The bear-dog releases her and stumbles back. She falls to the floor and… I gasp! …there's so much blood.

"Twee," I say in a pant while crawling over to her.

"Pathetic," Nelfala says, moving closer.

"SCREW YOU!" Nelfala turns and a piercing howl fills the room. I cover my ears as best I can, but I feel it through my hands. It rattles the back of my teeth and behind my eyes. It makes my nose smell like blood, and my mouth taste like pennies. I try to scream, but I'm sure it's lost in the sound.

"Jamie," Tony says pulling me up to a seated position.

I clutch at him desperately. "Tony…Nelfala…"

"I know."

"Tony," Shay calls. We look to her. She motions forward with a dagger in each hand. "If we don't hurry, she's going to get away." Tony's jaw tenses, and he comes back to me. He steals a glance at Twee.

"Go," I say. "I'll take care of her."

"We'll take care of her," Stefana says, running to her sister's side.

Tony releases me. He stands and runs after Shay quickly.

"Twee," Stefana shrieks as she reaches her sister's side.

"It's okay," Twee sighs. She looks at me. "I'm glad, you're safe."

"Twee," I say in a moan and caress the side of her blood-spattered face. "Why did you…?" I swallow a massive lump and look over her bleeding abdomen. I choke back another sob. "I don't know if I have enough magic to heal you…I didn't realize it was this bad…I…I'm…" I whimper and try to hold back the tears, because I don't want her to see me cry over her sacrifice.

"It's okay," she says as black blood trickles from the corners of her mouth. She forces a smile and lifts one trembling hand. She places it on the side of my face. "You…are my friend…you would've done the same for me."

"Twee!" Stefana sobs on the other side of her, while collect her other hand…her injured hand. She holds her younger sister's hand against her heart. "Twee, please…you can't die…you can't die…"

"Everyone can die, big sis…not everyone can die…for someone they care about."

"Twee, I love you," Stefana says and kisses her on the forehead.

"…love you…too…Stef…" Twee's eyes drift closed, and she goes limp.

"Stefana," Rebecca says, keeping her voice even and maintaining her distance. We look to her. She has one arm covering her stomach and her other hand over her mouth. She looks pale and a little queasy. "Did you…" She swallows deeply. "…did you bring Sara and Amie here with you?"

Stefana wipes her eyes, turns back to Rebecca, and nods.

"That's good," Rebecca says and tries to catch her breath. "I'll go get them…they can help." She turns and hurries away.

A soft light drifts down from the ceiling. I look up and dozens of tiny little orbs of light hover around the roof of the library and from random spaces between books. "The fairies?"

Stefana nods and clutches Twee's hand desperately. "We called for backup." She trembles. I honestly never thought I would see Stefana look this…vulnerable, this helpless. She lifts panicked, tear-streaked, hollow eyes to me. "Her pulse is getting weaker."

"I don't know how much good it'll do…but I'll try." I nod. "I have to try." I put my left hand on Twee's forehead…and trace out a square. "Sano." I feel what little magic I have left leave me and pass over into Twee. She gasps, and her back arches. She breathes deeply although her wounds don't seem to be healing in the slightest. "Not…" My eyes droop. My whole body feels like a lead brick, and my vision blurs into a mess of shadows. "…enough…" The room spins and…

#####

Chapter 33: Sisterhood

"TWEE!" I pant and sit up. "I'm…in my bed?"

"Yes, you are," Stefana says from the dresser. I turn to look at her. Her eyes are closed, and her head is bowed. Her arms cross over her chest, and her big, flaming sword leans next to her…in its sheath, thankfully. "How are you feeling, Witch of Light?"

"I'm fine…" I sniff. "I guess." Given her mood, that's sourer than usual, I almost hate to ask. I have to know though. "Where's…?" I break off as the words catch in my throat and tears well in my eyes. "Where's Twee?"

Stefana's eyes drift open lazily. She huffs and climbs down from the dresser. She collects her sword and puts it back on her hip.

"Did she…?" I weep.

Stefana shakes her head, and I gasp. I cover my mouth to stop from crying aloud. "You misunderstand, girl," Stefana says with a stern voice. "My sister is there…beside you…"

I frown and then turn to the left. I see a mess of silky, black hair and two tan arms wrapped tightly around a body pillow. I lean toward her, and I hear the faint rustle of a light snore as her shoulder rises and falls. I sweep the hair back away from her angelically, adorable little face. The familiar scent of lilacs that follows her presence makes me smile. "Twee," I whisper.

"Yes," Stefana says. "Your…" I turn to her. "…friends managed to heal her wounds." I nod and wipe a happy tear away from my cheek. "They…" Her eyes blink rapidly, and she tilts her head upward as if she wants to keep tears in her eyes. She exhales loudly from her mouth. "…they said that had you not cast that spell…they wouldn't have reached her in time."

"We got lucky. I'm glad."

Stefana moans a positive noise and steps closer to the door, her armor rattles a bit as she moves.

"You…you aren't going to stay and watch over her?"

She freezes in the door. Those tears that threatened escape fill her eyes all over again. She looks at me…no, she looks past me. She stares at Twee, and a tear falls from her left eye. It rolls down her cheek and before leaving her face, another falls behind it. Stefana sniffs. "I have been watching her from the day she was born." She nods, and her eyes move to me. "And for the first time in my life, I feel like I'm leaving her in the only hands that will protect her better than mine." She steps out of the door without another word.

"Her entire life?"

"Leave me alone, Stef," Twee moans…in her sleep. "Mom…Stef keeps trying to make me use her sword…" I turn to her. Her eyes are still closed, although she seems to be wrestling with the pillow more than hugging it now. "Ha," she says, continuing her sleep talking. "That'll teach you."

I laugh to myself. "They act like real sisters…" I gasp. "…Stefana, Twelana…their names, the way they act toward one another. The mocking, the bullying…they ARE real sisters."

"I thought as much," Tony says from the doorway. I come back around to see him. "May I come in?"

"Um," I say while verifying that Twee and I are both decent under the covers. We are. I smirk. Zoë must've put her in that purple kitty t-shirt. "Sure. Come in."

Tony steps inside as I toss the covers and throw my legs over the side of the bed. "How is she?"

"She's fine. She probably just needs some rest."

He nods, steps closer, and motions to the bed. "May I?"

"Yeah." He sits down next to me. I don't even bother wondering whether it's his weight or his presence that draws me closer.

"How are you feeling?"

I shrug, because the truth is, I have no idea how I'm feeling. Here I thought Alex and Gwen stopped the weird bear-dog thing, but because Nelfala was able to summon one…that means those creatures are connected to the crystal. She summoned three of them though. I guess it makes sense. Alex told me that Gwen's uncle, who was human, was able to summon a strong one…and Rich was able to summon one, too. Nelfie probably augmented her piece of the crystal with her own magic, and that's why she could create and control three of them at the same time.

"He hasn't come back yet." I frown and look at Tony. "My brother. Rais either…" He looks at me. "The fairies that went with them came back according to Stefana, but not them."

"Do you think they're…?"

"I don't know. The fairies said that they insisted on sticking around and checking on something." He looks at me. "When you're better…we can go…"

"We should go now," Twee says from the other side of the bed. We look at her. She crawls over to us and leans against us…between us with a hand on each of our shoulders. "We should go and find them. Quincy and the daemon…" She swallows a lump. "…no, Quincy and Rais may need our help."

"Twee, you look exhausted." I motion between Tony and me. "We can handle it."

"I know you can, but whoever has them may also have my brother."

I frown and look at Tony. "They didn't find him?"

Tony draws his lips into his mouth and shakes his head slowly.

"Besides," Twee continues. "They went looking for us, not knowing what kind of danger they'd be in...so..."

"Thank you," Tony says in a low voice and moves to stand. "I'll let you ladies get dressed, and I'll be waiting downstairs." He hurries out of the room.

Twee wraps her arms around me. "You saved my life."

I giggle at the warmth emanating from her and her lilac scented breath. "You saved mine first." She nods against my shoulder.

"Will you be one of my sisters?"

I look at her. "I don't think your mom's looking to adopt."

"I don't care," she says with a tear landing on my shoulder. "I don't know what I'd do if I were to ever lose you, Jamina-Lynda Baggett, and I don't ever want to find out." She squeezes me tighter and begins to rock. "When I saw that thing bear down on you..." She shivers and her tiny, delicate fingers dance along my arm. I put my hands on her left arm to steady her. "...I thought...I thought...I couldn't think. I just moved and..."

I nod and pat her arm. "You know what, Twelana Fairchild?"

"What?"

"From this day forward," I pause to make a tiny circle on her arm. "You and I are linked. From now on, we'll act toward each other..." I make another circle that hooks the first, creating a googol on her arm. I then mark out the words *conjuncta sunt in genere* in the tiny circles. "...as family."

She cries happy tears and continues rocking with me.

"I suppose that makes me family, too," Stefana says from the door. Twee motions for Stefana to join us. She starts but pauses to look at me.

"Get in here, you big, blond goof." She huffs a laugh and kneels in front of me. She wraps her arms around both of us. "You two are kind of awesome, you know that."

"Of course," Twee says.

"Naturally," Stefana adds, and we all erupt in laughter.

#####

Chapter 34: Circle

"Hmm."

"Jamie?"

"Huh?"

"Jamie." I open my eyes and see the tip of Twee's nose, and our right hands intertwined. I frown. "Over here." I turn toward the door.

"Tony?" I sit up. He nods and kneels next to the bed. I wipe my right eye and frown. "Why did you let me fall asleep? I thought we were going to look for Quincy and Rais."

"Shhh," he issues with a finger up to his mouth. I frown. He tips his head to the right. Stefana lays across the bottom of the bed, minus her armor. She wrapped herself up in a big, fluffy crimson robe. She has one arm extended as if she just hit Twee on the thigh, which makes sense because Twee's foot is at the back of her head. I cover my mouth to suppress a laugh.

I motion to the hallway. He nods. I toss the covers and slide out of bed. He stands and gives me a hand up. "You let me fall asleep," I whisper as soon as we step out into the hall. "We need to go and find Quincy…and Rais…"

"Relax," he says. "Quincy called." I frown. "He said he couldn't get a signal out by the old train yard. That's why we hadn't heard from him."

"Okay." I play with my fingers absently.

"Stop that," he moans and takes my hands. "You're still worried about him." I nod. He pulls my hands up near his heart and holds them there. "I am, too. Did you sense anything from him through the pendant?"

I shake my head. "Just out of curiosity, what exactly did they need to check out? Did he say?"

"He said that he and Rais picked up a scent, and they wanted to follow it back to its source."

"What kind of scent?" I ask. "Or should I ask whose scent?"

"They said it was a fairy, but a fairy that neither of them had smelled before." He nods unevenly. "Since the fairies involved in the search were all near the house at one point or another, they assumed that they'd recognize their scents."

"That makes sense."

"But," Tony says with a tone that tells me he doesn't like what he's about to say. I shake our joined hands. "He said they tracked the scent all the way back to the center of town, and it just…vanished."

"They went into En Quosque's barrier?"

"More than likely." I sigh. "So," he starts again, and his tone sinks even deeper. "That's why I came to get you…" His eyes dart to my bedroom door and back to me.

"What is it?"

"A fairy went into the barrier after Quincy and Rais followed it from one of Sara's ping locations."

I stare into his eyes as he waits for me to catch a clue, but I already caught it…I just want to throw it back. "No," I moan. "No."

"You remember what Rais told you? The newest member of En Quosque was a fairy, and that fairy's first task was to claim those daemons Morten and Devon as her vassals."

"No," I sigh again, pulling my hands out of his. "You mean to tell me, that one of the fairies is responsible for helping my mom kidnap, the fairies' brother?"

"It makes sense," Stefana says from my doorway. She yawns and leans her right shoulder against the doorframe. "It would explain how your mother found Tibal so easily considering that Chelsea is good at…" She lifts her eyes to us and slips her left hand into the pocket of her robe. She confirms something there, before continuing. "…barrier seals. Moreover, how would your mother even know that Tibal was here in town?"

"Well, most of your mother's fairies are here so…"

"No," Stefana interrupts. "Tibal does not travel! Before this trip, we'd never taken him ANYWHERE. He'd never left mother's side let alone her home." She sighs. "Have any of the others reported back?"

Tony shakes his head.

"Damn it," Stefana says. She rushes back into my room. I frown and look at Tony. Stefana steps out a second later with her breastplate on and still fastening her lower half. Her robe hangs over her shoulder.

"You dress fast."

She huffs a silent laugh while moving toward the stairs. "I'm off to tell mother about this turn of events. Hopefully, we can figure out who the traitor is by determining who's missing or if there are long periods of absence for any of my sisters." I nod. She hurries down the stairs.

"That has to suck." Tony frowns. "Being betrayed by your own sister like that."

"Worse than being betrayed by your mother?"

"That's different." He shakes his head. "She's never done anything to hurt me directly…just things that hurt me indirectly." Tony arches his eyebrows as if he's getting ready to argue with me. "I didn't say it wasn't a lot of things or that they didn't hurt me big time, just nothing directly." He nods.

The sound of sobbing wanders out into the hall. "Uh oh." I step back into my room. Twee sits up on her knees with her shoulders drooped. Tears stream down her face, and she hugs herself. "Oh, Twee." I climb onto the bed with her.

"I'm worried about Tibal." I nod and wrap my arms around her. "I heard him. He was crying last night."

"That's how they caught you, right? You heard him and got distracted?"

She shakes her head. "No, I mean, I heard him last night…when I was asleep." We separate a little. Her eyes focus on some other place. "I heard him crying in my dreams. He was so scared, and I was worried about him." She shakes her head and looks at me. "I probably sound crazy, don't I?"

"Nah," I say rubbing her arms. "When Alex and Gwen started liking each other, they used to swap dreams…" She wipes her eyes, and her brow arches upward. I laugh. "…he would have dreams about taking on kitsune attributes, and she would have dreams about being a skinwalker."

"Okay, that's weird," she returns. We laugh. She sighs.

"It just means…" I look at Twee. I mean, I REALLY look at her. I focus my magic on trying to get a sense of her.

"What?"

I shake my head and hold back a gasp. Twee's strong…she has power that I don't even think she realizes yet. There must be songs and notes that she hasn't even tried. I smirk. No wonder Nelfala said that she was going to be the next Fairy Queen.

"I just," I say aloud. "I just keep forgetting that you're actually almost the same age as me." She nods.

"Ladies," Tony says from the doorway. Twee tweaks her head and motions toward the door. I shake my head. "If you need me, I'll be down in the library. I want to look something up, plus I want to ask an old friend something."

"Old friend?"

"Mr. Hamish, who runs the general store on the square. He has an encyclopedic knowledge of the town's history. He might be able to answer a question for me."

"Okay, let me know if Quincy calls."

"I will." Tony walks away. "Ladies."

"What?"

"He was talking to us, sweetie," Sara says with her head crossing the threshold. She walks in and stares at us. "We were wondering how the search was going."

"Not well," Twee says, becoming upset all at once again. I wrap my arms around her while still looking at Sara.

"That's actually why we came up," Rebecca says.

"Yeah," Amie continues. "Sara thinks that if we could join in a proper circle, she could focus her spirit magic enough to find the missing fairy."

"A proper circle?" Sara nods. "So, you need five…representing each element." I look at Sara… "Spirit." …then Rebecca… "Earth." …and finally, Amie. "Water." I put my hand over my heart. "Fire." I rub Twee's back. "She uses music…sound…so she could represent Wind."

"It doesn't work like that, sweetie," Sara says. "Even in her human form, Twee is still a fairy. A proper circle has to be all witches…and all of the same affinity."

"So, we'd need five Witches of Light?" Sara nods. A knock comes from the hall. We all turn to the doorway and "Zo'?"

"Hey, girl," she says squeezing in past Amie and Rebecca. "Well, girls," she recants while putting a hand on Twee's shoulder. "How are you two doing? You had me worried."

"We're okay," Twee hums and forces a smile for Zoë's benefit.

"We're better than that," Sara chirps. "We found our fifth."

"Fifth what?" Zoë asks with a scowl.

"RIGHT!" I say, claiming both of Zoë's hands. "You're part witch. You could stand in with us as a member of our circle."

"She is?" Twee asks. I nod. "Oh, can you?" Twee takes Zoë's left hand out of my right. "Please, please, please, please, please." Zoë comes back to me, and I stick out my bottom lip.

Zoë groans and bows her head. "You two are so annoying." She comes back to Twee and me. "What do I have to do?"

Twee and I both release giddy squeals while climbing off the bed. So, weird. I never considered myself a girly girl…but Twee brings it out of me sometimes. We hurry downstairs, bare feet and all, pulling Zoë down behind us.

"Can someone please tell me what we're doing?"

"Okay," Sara starts, marching down behind us. "We've been searching for the Fairy Prince Tibal, right?" Zoë nods. "Well, we haven't been able to find him because more than likely he's behind a very powerful barrier. So, we're going to create a full witch circle…I'm going to use the energy of our full circle to try to pierce that barrier."

"So, you need my energy to help fuel a big spell?"

"Pretty much."

"Will it hurt?"

"Definitely not."

"Cool," Zoë says and as we step into the foyer, I realize, I have no idea where we're going.

"Backyard," Sara says from the second stair, pointing in that direction. The six of us hurry outside.

"You already made a circle," I say taking in the carved-out grass. "Oh, and you tore up the lawn." I look at Rebecca, turning away from the 'plowed' out perfect circle. "Tony's going to be super pissed at you." She shrugs and continue down the stairs. Along the circle, I notice five tiny white saucers.

"We tried just using the elements…you know, representational magic," Amie says. "Instead of a circle, but it didn't take." I nod.

"Okay," Sara says. "Everyone take your place around the circle." Rebecca moves to the saucer with a rock in the center of it. Amie goes to the one with a little splash of water there. I find one with a lit candle in its center and stand behind it. I look at Zoë, and she seems confused. I check the other two saucers; one is empty and the other has a fan. I tip my head toward the fan, and Zoë moves over to it quickly.

Sara takes her place in the last spot and the second she does…I feel it. I feel the circle complete. I look at Zoë, and she seems even more lost now. I don't. I feel like a gentle breeze wafts through my hair tossing it a little…no, pulling it toward Zoë. She feels it too. Amie giggles and blushes. Rebecca holds in a laugh.

"Turn down the heat a little, sweetie," Sara says. I frown. "Oh," she moans a second later. "You don't even realize you're doing it." I shake my head. She looks down, and so do I. The candle's flame stands almost waist high, even though the wicks around my ankle.

"How…am I doing that?"

"Relax," Sara says. "You're the strongest person in this circle, by far, but you need to bring your magic down to a happy medium. Try to match my level." I stare at Sara, and she returns the gesture. I breathe in, cleansing breaths just like she taught me. "A little bit lower." Breathe out. Breathe in. "There." I look down, and the flame is back to normal level.

"Now," Sara starts again. "Close your eyes." I do. "Concentrate on the sound of my voice. Help fuel my magic." I do. "Twee, stand in the center. You have a strong emotional connection to Tibal, so it will help." I hear footsteps on the soft grass. "That's a good girl. Now everyone focus on our common goal." I do.

"Quaerite," Sara says. I think of how happy the fairies will be… "Quaerite." …no, how happy Twee will be when we find Tibal. "Quaerite." I hear Twee humming in the middle of the circle. "Quaerite." It sounds like a lullaby.

"I KNOW WHERE HE IS!" Sara says. We open our eyes. She's already rushing up to the house. Twee and I run after her with Zoë, Amie, and

Rebecca behind us. "We're going to the car," Sara says, moving into the house. "Jamie, grab Tony and follow as quick as you can."

"He's not here," I say as a moan, while holding the Crescent Moon Pendant in my left hand. "He's…" I close my eyes. "…headed toward town."

"He said he wanted to ask Mr. Hamish something," Twee says.

I slip my phone out of my pocket and search for his number.

"Then you'll come with us," Sara says. "You too, Twee. We don't want to lose this. I managed to get through their spell. Zoë, stay put…direct anybody who comes back to the center of town." She marches through the foyer and out the front door. "It's just like I thought. I'll tell you all about it when we get there."

"Wait," Zoë calls from the doorway. I frown and turn to her. She holds Twee and my jackets in one hand and holds our shoes braced up against her body with the other arm. We quickly claim them.

"Thanks, Zo," I say, slipping my feet into my shoes. She nods and shoos us away.

We reach Sara's Jeep and Amie catches my arm. She holds me near the back door. "Are you ready for this?" I frown and shake my head. "This barrier…is the barrier around the 7th Seal…which means more than likely it's where your mom is." I sigh. "I just wanted to make sure you knew that."

"I didn't even think about it to be honest."

"I can't even imagine what you're going through right now."

"Trust me," I say, pulling the door open. "I'm trying not to…" Doesn't stop it from repeating in my head though. I'm going to have to fight my mom…I may have to… A tear falls from my left eye, and I wipe it away quickly.

#####

Chapter 35: Layers

"You brought us to a parking lot," I say, climbing out of the backseat. Twee climbs out behind me and looks around. She's distracted, upset, and I can see tears threatening to break free. She pushes her hair back behind her ears and her lower lip trembles.

"This isn't a parking lot, my lovelies," Sara says staring off into space. "This is the most beautiful glamour that I have ever seen." I frown. "It's not just a disguise. It doesn't just displace matter. It actually tricks the mind into thinking that this is…" She looks at me. "…just a parking lot."

"Then how can you…"

Sara looks at me. "I'm still picking up Tibal…" She points out across the parking lot. "…there." She nods. "No wonder you could never get a bead on him exactly. He's there…and not there…and then there again…and not there." She pauses and bobs her head once. "…and not there and there again." She laughs and claps her hands together. Clearly, Sara has lost her mind.

"But this is a grocery store parking lot," Twee says. She sounds like her frustrations changing over to anger. "My brother's not here! I can't sense him at all!"

"Okay," Sara says with an air of serenity. "Think of it like this…if you want to hide something you put it behind a glamour, right?"

"Of course."

"But the problem with a glamour is that most supernatural beings, like all of us, can see right through a glamour if we concentrate or cast a spell to dispel it."

"Yes…and…?" Twee asks, losing even more of her patience. She sounds like me, when I'm worried about someone or trying to protect Quincy and Tony…even from each other.

"Well, to get over that," Sara says, showing us the back of her right hand. "You put another glamour in front of it or behind it, right?" She puts her left hand in front of her right. I nod. "But suppose, you know for a fact that an extremely gifted and naturally talented witch…" Sara taps her chin with her left pointer finger. "…let's say, she's a young, bespectacled, redheaded witch…" I laugh. "…lives in the same town that you have your double barrier erected…what do you do then?"

"Add another layer," Twee says in my place.

Sara makes a clicking noise with the corner of her mouth while giving Twee the single finger gun. If she wasn't so freaking brilliant, I might point out how lame that was. Who am I kidding? She even managed to make that seem cool.

She turns to Amie. "Amie, my dear, the disguise is yours." Amie nods with a smirk, turns toward the empty parking lot glamour and steps forward. Sara looks at Rebecca. "Rebecca, my lovely, revealing the matter is yours."

"Right up my alley," Rebecca says. "After all, it is a big, brick building, right?" She glances at me. I nod. She steps up next to Amie.

Sara stares at the entire nothing of this faux parking lot and then lifts her head to stare at a sky full of nothing. She sighs. Wait…there's nothing there. There are no birds, no clouds…it's just pale blue sky. I turn around and look at the sun just above the buildings to the west. Gentle, puffy clouds hang in mid-air… I track back to the parking lot. …and cut off into nothing.

"And that," Sara says from right in front of my face. "…is what they were counting on you noticing at some point. Even then…" She returns to the parking lot and takes her place between Rebecca and Amie. "…it would've taken the three of you…" She looks at me. "…Quincy, Tony, and you…" She returns to the nothing. "…to make your way through the glamour, leaving no one who could compete with your mom to go through it and stop her." She takes a deep breath and moves her hands toward her chest as if she were gathering air. "Unfortunately for them, they didn't count on us being here."

Sara peers at me over her shoulder. "Have you heard back from Quincy or Tony?" I slip my phone out of my back pocket. I don't have any missed calls or texts. I shake my head. "Then I guess it's just you two then."

I nod, reach out, and claim Twee's hand. She nibbles her lower lip and turns tear-filled eyes on me. "We'll find him…and we'll rescue him." She nods. "I promise you that, little sis."

"Technically, I'm older than you."

"You're gonna argue this now?" I say, trying to take her mind away from her stress. She smiles and tugs on my hand. "We're ready."

Sara smiles. She turns to Amie and nods. Amie extends her hands slowly. She buries the ruby tips of her fingers into nothing and causes the air to ripple like water around them. She takes a deep breath and pulls. She steps away from Sara moving toward the left. She stops and continues to hold the rippling air.

Sara looks to Rebecca next. Rebecca, in turns, drives her fingers into the same nothing that Amie did, only instead of rippling…the air cracks. Tiny pieces of nothing crumble and fall away with the sound of tumbling rocks. Rebecca pulls the crevice and peels back another layer of the barrier. The building comes into view beyond them.

Sara claps her hands together and rubs her palms against one another. "Get ready to run," she says. "I don't know how strong this last layer is…but I might not be able to hold it open for long." I nod and take a running stance.

Twee snaps her fingers, and her hand vanishes from my grip. A tiny blue orb lands on my shoulder.

I smirk. "Fine. Make me do all the work."

Sara reaches up above her head. Her fingers sink into the air…but the air around her fingers glows. It's a faint golden glow, and a solid note holds as she pulls downward. She kneels and pulls the soft radiance down to her feet.

"GO," she says. I run forward as fast as I can, darting past her. The moment I pass her, the building that mom brought me to, after she flash-fried Siemon, appears clearly with no obstructions. Twee snaps her fingers and appears in human form next to me again. I look back and see that Sara, Amie, and Rebecca have released the barrier. "Jamie?"

"Sara. We made it through."

"Jamie, I probably won't be able to hear you through this thing. Like I said, your mom put some work into this one." I frown. "I'd love to come through and help you, but if even one of us lets our layer go, the whole thing would just switch to the next barrier and let it pick up the slack."

"That makes sense. I guess." Twee nods.

"So, we'll stay out here, and I'll keep texting Tony and Quincy. Hopefully, they'll come along soon, and we'll let them through. Okay?" I nod. Sara turns to Amie and shakes her head. "I'm asking 'okay' like I could see or hear her if she responded." I laugh at myself for being a goof and responding to her knowing that she couldn't see or hear me.

"Come on," I say. Twee follows me over to the main entrance. Twee reaches for the handle, and I catch her hand. "That won't work. There's a whole other glamour over this building."

She looks up at the cube, redbrick building and scowls. "You're kidding, right?"

I shake my head. "Nope. Unfortunately, like Sara said, my mom went a little psycho hiding this place." I shrug. "But then again, since we're standing here, maybe she didn't go bat crap crazy enough."

Twee nods. "So, how do we get in?"

I look the plain white door over and nod. "Like this." I put my right pointer finger on the center of the door and make a swirling motion moving out in larger sweeping circles. I focus my magic on the door and imagine locks unlocking. A thunk comes from the other side of the door, another and another follows it. I continue in this way making eleven spiraling circles. So, many levers, latches, and catches release as I move along. When I finish the last circle, the door clacks one more time and then slowly swings inward.

"Wow," Twee says in a gasping breath. "Yeah, in a million years, I would've never thought to do that."

"Neither would I, if I hadn't seen my mom do it."

"That's pretty amazing that you remembered how to do that after only seeing it once."

I frown and look at Twee. "Yeah. I do that a lot." Which, until this very minute, never bothered me. I mean, I saw Rebecca use an earth spell once, and I reproduced it. I saw my mom do this once, months ago, and I did it as if I'd been practicing it. "It kind of felt like it responded to my magic, too," I say, staring at my right hand.

I shake my head, while pushing the door in. I can't think about that now. I step over the threshold. The large open space is just as I left it…I think. It definitely looks like someone cleaned it a little after that last time I was here. I look around, and the random black doors line each of the four brick walls including the one that we just stepped through.

"What are those?"

"Hell gates," I say, checking each one and trying not to breathe in the awful rotten egg stench of burning sulfur. "Ugh, brimstone…somebody's been using them recently." I put my right pointer finger under my nose.

Twee tugs on the sleeve of my shirt. I turn to her, and she's staring up at the ceiling…or the distinct lack of ceiling that reveals the fading daylight above.

"Yeah. No roof. Mom said that if anyone ever tried to come in here without unlocking the door properly, they'd just see a string of office cubicles." I look at Twee. "I'm guessing that means it'd probably have a roof, too."

"Shhhh." Twee kneels and turns her head from right to left.

"What's wro-"

"Shhhh," she repeats, before I can finish. "I hear something." I nod and let her listen. "It's a low hum…" She swallows deeply and jumps to her feet. I jump with her, mostly because she scared me. "…and it's getting closer."

"Crap." I take Twee's hand and run toward the center of the room. I check each door again, hoping to get some sense of where whatever it is will come from. "Twee, do you sense Tibal? Is he close by? If he is, we can run and get him and get out of here before anyone notices."

"I think they already did," Twee says. "That hum…" She shakes her head. "…it's not a hum. It's a growl."

"Crap."

"You already said that."

"Not helping Twelana." She squeaks as a response. "Okay. Can you tell which direction the humming growliness is coming from?"

She closes her eyes. She turns to the right and points. "That one."

"Okay. Now, focus on finding Tibal…I'll protect you until you do."

She nods again. "Be careful." She gives my hand a squeeze. I release her hand and push her back behind me with a gentle sweep of my arm. I position myself between her and the door that she pointed out. Twee hums that lullaby. Her song is a sweet melody that gets into my head and relaxes me. It feels like I've heard it somewhere before…before she did it earlier, I mean.

The door she pointed to swings open. I swallow a lump as a bear-dog, in all its inky blackness, squeezes through the much smaller door. I extend my right hand. It pulls itself through and regains its size. I grit my teeth. It does, too. It bubbles up at its left shoulder and then its right shoulder.

"What's it doing?" Twee asks.

"I thought I told you to focus on finding your brother," I say, hearing my mom's tone in my voice.

"Right." The humming resumes.

The two bubbles bulge out; they grow to the same size as its head, then take on the same shape, and then grow teeth and eyes. "Crap," I say, realizing where this is going.

"Yep," a familiar and already irritating voice says. "Dats sum, crap." Nelfala steps out from behind the bear-dog with a huge smile. She pats it on the left shoulder right behind one of its head. "…and guess who's in it?"

"Nelfie." I say her name at the same time all three heads growl at me. "What twisted crap have you pulled now?"

"I take it you don' like my Cerberus." She strokes its back, and it seems to purr. "Except dis puppy don' guard da gates a' hell…" She laughs. "…he's dere to send you to it."

Each head opens its mouth. The original starts with a bright orange fire building. The one on the left sparks with electricity. The one on the right drools out a small pool of water.

"Holy crap," Twee says. She wraps both of her arms around mine. "We might be in trouble…" I scowl because…she might be right.

#####

Chapter 36: Last

"Concustodio," I say while extending both hands in front of me. I draw a square on the translucently gold, hexagon that appeared between the three-headed bear-dog and us. I start carving out a triangle next and Twee grabs my wrist. "TWEE?"

"Stop," she says, softly. "Drawing seals is a natural talent, but it also drains your magic faster." She steps in front of me. "Let me." Twee leans forward and emits a warbling, high-pitched whistle. It hits the nearside of the shield, and I can feel it strengthening our defense.

The bear-dog rears up with all three heads and unleashes a rain, fire, and lightning storm down on us all at once. I brace myself for the hit…that feels more like a tickle than the hell I thought it would be. Weird, my shield is vibrating. Twee peers at me over her shoulder and smirks.

"H-how did you know that would work?"

She smiles outright. "You marked me…I'm your sister now. My powers react with your magic."

I huff a laugh. "And here I thought, for once, I was just being cute."

The bear-dog eases off his attack. He sprints out to his right. I grit my teeth and turn toward him, moving my hands to the left with him. Twee catches my right hand and holds it in place. "Twee?" I continue, moving my left hand, and she emits another warbling whistle, but this one seems a few octaves lower than the last one. My shield stretches out, still covering the entire space between both of my hands. The bear-dog fires again and has no better reaction. Best of all, I don't even feel drained from using the shield like this.

"I'll show you," Nelfala says in a grumble, drawing our attention back to her. She lifts both of her hands toward us. I wonder why she's not separating the bear-dogs, or can she? "Quod praecipio tibi victus voco spiritibus…"

"What is she doing?" Twee asks.

"Necromancy…" I try not to bite my tongue, while swallowing the bile she just drew out of me. "…the darkest of dark magic." Twee stares at me with a confused expression. "She's summoning something that's already dead." Twee gasps and turns back to Nelfala.

Nelfala extends her left palm toward us. She drives her right thumbnail into it…blood seeps out from around it. "…et per sanguinem meum…" She moves her left hand making a swipe outward. Her blood splashes across the floor. "…obligo tibi."

The spattered blood sizzles and evaporates…no, it's burning off. The smoke rises and holds in place. It takes the form of six spheres that hold at about nose height. Two dark circles appear about where eyes would be on a human face.

Nelfala steps forward and puts her hand on her hip. "You got it all wrong, chile. Necromancy's not dark magic…and dere's absolutely nothin' wrong wit' it."

"You're wrong," I snarl. "You're worse than wrong…" I stare at the 12 empty eyeholes gazing back at me. I tremble thinking of these spirits, ripped back from their final resting place. "This," I say, tipping my head to them. "…this is just wrong. This is dark…it's evil." I glare at Nelfala. "And if you can't see that you're more twisted and broken than I ever thought you were."

She frowns. "Necromancy isn't dark. It's another form of communing with spirits."

"COMMUNING…is one thing," I say. "Allowing the departed to convey feelings and thoughts of their own…is one thing. THIS…this is horrible. Can't you feel their pain?" I come back to them. "I can. They may not have been in Hell, necessarily, but they definitely feel like they're there now."

I sigh and just my eyes go back to Nelfala. "I get it now." She frowns. "I'm sorry that Nathan never saw value in you."

"SHUT UP!"

"Nathan?"

"I'll tell you later," I say to Twee. I come back to Nelfala. "It's sad that you actually convinced yourself that you cast that aging spell for him…so that you could be with him…so that someday the two of you could be together." I shake my head. "Your own vanity…and lack of self-confidence caused you to cast that spell." I close my eyes. "If I thought for one second that Quincy or Tony only cared about me because of the way I looked…I'd tell them both to kiss my ass."

Nelfala gasps, and Twee laughs softly.

"Because if a guy didn't love every part of me…didn't love me when he was furious with me for arguing with him for the billionth time…" I huff a laugh. "…or didn't love me whether I was eighteen or eighty then, he's not the guy for me." Nelfala trembles with rage. "Maybe if you'd been able to face that reality… What? …forty or fifty years ago, we wouldn't be where we are right now." I point at her. "Your magic didn't leave you because of that spell, Nelfala."

Her eyes widen. "What are you talkin' bout? I cast da spell an' then my magic went…"

"Your magic didn't leave you because of that spell…" I close my eyes and continue probing the edges of her magic with my spirit magic. "…it left you because you changed. It left you because you lost your mind over a boy.

Probably, a really awesome boy…but a boy all the same…and you became someone…" I open my eyes and motion to the six waiting spirits. My eyes cut to the bear-dog that seems to be hanging on my every word, too. "…someone who could do all of this. You became something dark…and your magic…the part of your magic that was light…left, and I can't say I blame it."

"I done heard enough outta you, gurl," she snarls. "GET HER! KILL HER!" The bear-dog renews its three-powered attack. The floating heads spread downward…they generate spectral bodies…that look like bones. The smoke solidifies, and they look like walking skeletons…walking skeletons with sharp finger bones that look like claws. Nelfala examines my shield. "Her…kill the fairy first."

I gasp and look to Twee on instinct. I focus on the shield…hold it in my left hand. The spirits move around the outer edges of my shield, feeling their way around. They smell like death. They carry the scent of overturned earth, mud, and decaying things. I shiver. "She bound you poor souls…" I extend my right hand to the four already making their way around my shield. "…I'll free you." I snap my fingers. "Extermino." The four closest to us burst into flames and fall to the ground.

The other two…only have some minor burning around their forearms and legs. They continue moving closer to Twee.

A crack splits the air. My slip in concentration gave the bear-dog…bear-Cerberus…a chance to fracture my shield. It has three cracks growing out from its center. Twee notes the cracks and turns to the shield. "I got your back," she says. She nods and releases another warbling whistle. The shield stops cracking. Now, how do I deal with these last two souls? Even using extermino caused my concentration to slide enough to give the bear-dog an opening. I'm just lucky that Nelfala doesn't have much personal magic at her disposal.

A shrill wale pierces the air. I wince and fight the urge to cover my ears. My shield…not only is it no longer cracking…the cracks are healing.

I come back to the two souls. Mitchell comes down on top of one, driving his knuckle through its skull, causing it to dissipate instantly. A woman…no, a fairy I've never seen before drives a mace into the side of the other, shattering it.

"Abbie," Twee says.

"Twelana the 107th," Abbie returns.

"Do you fairies always refer to each other like that? Aren't you all sisters? Maybe come up with a last name system…maybe just drop the numbers?"

Twee laughs and motions to her sister, Abbie. "Jamie Baggett, this is Abbie the 75th, named after a brave sprite, who came to our grandmother for help a few millennia ago." She looks at her sister. "She's also known as 'The Hammer.'"

"Hammer…Club…Mace…," Abbie says with a smile. "As long as they stay down."

Mitchell nudges her. "I like her," he says with a huge smile. Abbie laughs.

"Mitchell, where are…?"

"Looks like your shield's holding," Shay says. "You're welcome."

"Shay…? Right, you're part siren…wait, where's…?"

"Where do you think?" she says before I can finish. She points at the bear-dog. "Three-two-one…" As she finishes the one, Tony comes down on the bear-dog's left. His knife is extended out in front of him, and black inkiness covers it. The bear-dog's left head slides off and sloshes into a puddle as it hits the ground.

Stefana crosses over him, coming down across the bear-dog's right head. Her flaming sword flares as she reaches the floor. The right head slides and bursts into flames just before it hits the floor. The bear-dog reels and stumbles backward.

"No," Nelfala pants. Tony stands and throws himself at the rest of the bear-dog. It dodges just before he would've taken its last head. He managed to drive his knife into it though. The bear-dog falls and quickly scampers to its feet. It starts to lose its integrity and the blackness becomes inkier.

"Shay," Tony calls.

"Right." She pulls her daggers from her back and tosses them over my shield. Tony catches them without even looking and drives one into the thing and then the other. He uses the weapons to climb it. Stefana, not taking a beat to rest, swipes at the thing, taking its right front leg with her.

Tony makes it to the ink blob's back and drives both daggers into it. It screeches in pain and sinks toward the floor. It degrades into a puddle and that puddle dries out all at once. It cracks and crumbles before vanishing into nothing.

"AAAARRRRGHHHH," Nelfala screams. She tosses her crystal fragment aside. She glares at me, her bottom lip protruding and quivering. "I'll show you! I'll show all a' ya!"

"Stop it, Nelfala!" Tony barks.

Nelfala smirks. She snaps the fingers on her right hand while pulling out a dagger with her left. The smell of brimstone fills the room. The hell gates swing open…all of them, I think. Daemons storm through them…lesser beings though. Mindless ghouls, some of those porcelain-skinned creatures Tony fought, and even a couple of ornias daemons…the hideously deformed wolf mutations.

"Don't let the little white ones bite you," I say.

"Don't let the wolf-daemons scratch you," Tony adds. He hops my shield and passes Shay back her daggers. She gives them a twirl and holds them in a very stabby way. Mitchell lifts his fists and clenches them tight. Stefana prepares her sword. Abbie pounds the ground with her mace. I'd say it was a warning, but I think she actually enjoys fighting more than Stefana does. Tony twirls his knife around his right pointer finger, and electric sparks dance along the fingertips of his left hand. "Go," he says in a short breath, and the four of them spring forward in different directions. He holds a minute and catches my wrist. I glare at him. "Tibal…you and Twee need to go find Tibal."

I nod. "Twee?"

"I found him." She points to the only closed door on the opposite side of the room…through all the daemons. "He's through there." I sigh.

"I'll clear you a path," Tony says. "Fulgur." He holds a ball of lightning in his left hand and his Avarice Seal flares. "Fulgur," he says again, and the ball grows larger. His Wrath Seal glows, too.

"Tony?"

"Fulgur." The ball grows so big that he holds his hand over his head. He peers at us. "READY?"

I nod. He springs forward. I run behind him as fast as I can. Twee catches my hand and runs alongside me this time.

"HA," he shouts while releasing the massive arch of lightning ahead of him. The bolt strikes the wall just to the left of the door and incinerates everything between it and us. "Go," he says while motioning for us to continue. We hurry past him, and an ornias steps in front of us.

I lift my hand, but Tony cuts him down before I can even issue a spell. We reach the door, and Twee grabs the handle. "Wait! It's a hell gate," I say. "Let me…" I take her hand and draw a heptagon on the back. I cup her hand in both of mine. "Contego." I feel a shield form around her…just her. I repeat the process on myself.

"Are we ready?" I steal a glance at Tony, Stefana, and the others, fighting back the ghouls and daemons…and Nelfala even summoned more of those spirits. I grit my teeth and take a step toward them. "Jamie," Twee says. "I need you…my brother needs you."

I nod, take a deep breath, and grab the handle in her place. I open the door, and the white light on the other side feels hot, even through my shield. I hold Twee's hand with my right hand, and the Crescent Moon Pendant in my left. I look at Tony over my shoulder…knowing that this might be a last look.

Tony swats away one of the venomy ghouls, cuts a spirit in half, and hurls lightning at an ornais…he is every bit the warrior I thought he was. I've never seen him look so, hard to believe, but serene. His seals haven't dimmed yet. His eyes meet mine. 'Go,' he mouths, before turning to two ghouls rushing him.

"Hold your breath," I say to Twee. "And be ready for anything."

We step through the portal, and the heat intensifies. It feels like we're in a metal room in mid-July sun with a dehumidifier set on high. It feels like I should be sweating, but my body won't seem to let me.

I open my eyes, and the white seems to waiver. It seems to lose some of its luster in places and darken altogether in others. The smell of burning sulfur surrounds us…if the heat didn't make it hard to breathe, then it's the smell that's making it nearly impossible.

Sadly, the smell isn't even the worst part. I feel like the energy of this non-space… filters through me. It moves through my body in ever-increasing waves of penetrating heat, but somehow never grows or shrinks in intensity. I feel like it's moving the world around me and not me around the world.

Just as soon as this twisted rollercoaster ride really got started…it stops… leaving us to wonder…where are we…?

#####

Chapter 37: Baby

"Where are we?" Twee asks, and her voice echoes off the white nothingness that stretches out in front of us.

"I don't know." My voice carries the same way. "Are you sure this is where you were getting the Tibal vibes from? Maybe the echoing threw off your…?"

Twee starts humming again. She closes her eyes, perches on the balls of her feet, and throws her arms back behind her. She takes a step forward, still on her toes. If I didn't know any better, I'd swear she was about to fly without her wings. "No doubt about it," she says with confidence. "He's here." She looks at me. "Let's go."

"Where? Everything's white, and it looks like it goes on forever."

That's just what we want people to think.

"What you want people to think…?"

"What?" Twee asks.

"What what? I thought you said something." She shakes her head. I frown and go back to the emptiness in front of us. "It's a big white space that goes on forever…and you sense Tibal here." She nods. "Or maybe that's what they want us to think."

"You don't think he's here?"

"No, I think he is. I doubt this white emptiness just…it can't just go on forever." I take a deep breath, and my magic flares out in a wave.

Twee's hair tosses gently, and she giggles. "That tickles." I nod but do it again. "What are you doing?"

"What you did back at my house," I say. "Only I'm using spirit magic instead of echo location."

"When did you learn to do this?"

"Just now, I guess." I close my eyes and push out from myself for the fourth time.

"Whoa!" I look at Twee…well, turn to her since my eyes are still closed. "Do that again." I do. "Whoa, in the distance…" I open my eyes, and she's pointing at the space straight ahead. "…the white seemed to ripple…like a glamour, but no matter how hard I focus. I can't see through it."

I frown. "That's because it's not a glamour." I slip my hand into my jacket pocket and pull out my spare keys to Alex's apartment. I throw them toward the white nothing. They ripple against the air and vanish. "It's an illusion." Twee frowns. "Think magic for people who can't use magic…it's a hologram or trick of the light." She nods. "Come on."

We run toward the emptiness. I stop just before we reach the threshold, and she stops with me. "What are we waiting for?" she asks with that panic returning to her voice.

"For all we know, another one of those bear-dog things could be waiting on the other side of this. We should be careful." She sighs, and a tear rolls away from her right eye. "That doesn't mean we're not going in…we just need to be ready for anything, okay?" She nods. "Are you? Ready, I mean." She nods again. "Let's go."

We step through the faux wall and find more of the same on the other side. A lot of empty white nothing, but this time there's a definite wall across from us, to our left, and right. I look at Twee, and she looks around in awe at the sterile whiteness.

"My keys," I say, while rushing over to them. I kneel and notice something just beyond the keys. Some object stands directly in front of me. I pick up the keys and extend the same hand outward. "Ow," I complain when my knuckle scrapes against it.

"What's wrong?"

"There's something here," I say, while slipping the keys back into my pocket. I feel it out…moving upward. "It's like a column or something." Twee runs over, kneeling beside me. I rise, keeping my hand pressed against this strange nearly invisible object. "Hey, I think I reached the top," I say as my hand moves over the waist high threshold. "And…" I frown. "…the top is open." Twee frowns and springs to her feet.

"JAMIE!" I jump to my feet, too. Mostly because she scared me again, but also to help if…

"Oh, my God," I sigh, while staring at the beautiful, blue-eyed baby with big black curls all around the top of his head. He sees the two of us, and his little rosy cheeks turn up. He smiles and coos. He moves his arms vigorously showing just how happy he really is. His tiny, pale blue outfit covers down to the bends in his chubby little arms and legs. He rests on a darker blue blanket.

I point to him. "What's a baby doing here? What are you doing here?" I ask him as if he could answer.

"Jamie," Twee says in a low voice. "It's him. This…is Tibal."

"What? Tibal's a baby? The youngest fairy is a baby?"

"Yes, and yes," Twee says while reaching for him. I feel him out with my magic just to be sure, but there are no traps or spells on him. She wraps the blanket around him carefully and lifts him as if he were the most precious of cargo…or, you know…as if he's him. "Hey," she says in a whisper. His face lights up even more, and he stares into her eyes with focus that no child, let alone, a baby should have.

"He's going to be the next Fairy King?" Twee nods. "The one who you're going to marry?"

Twee huffs a laugh as happy tears fill her eyes. "I don't know about me, but yeah, he's going to be the next Fairy King." She holds him closer and nuzzles her nose against his cheek. "He's mother's only child by birth."

"He is?"

She nods. "That's why she's not helping with the search herself. She's still weak from having him." She looks at me. "Twenty of our sisters moved to guard her the second we found out about Tibal."

I step closer to the two of them. I extend my right pointer finger and nudge his cheek. He coos but continues staring at Twee. "Hey, little guy, I'm Jamie." Twee smiles and bobs him up and down.

"We have to get back to the others," I say coming back to Twee. She nods. I wrap my hands around the Crescent Moon Pendant. "Tony seems calm," I say after a few seconds. "Well, calm for him."

I offer Tibal my finger, and he wraps all his around it. I draw a heptagon on the back of his hand…which is not easy, considering how small it is. "Contego," I whisper against the back of his tiny hand. Twee smiles and turns back to the fake wall. I do too…until…

"Mom," I whisper.

"What?"

I turn to the door on my right. I stare at it as if it is the answer to Twee's question. "My mom…she's behind that door."

"Jamie, no," Twee says. She nestles Tibal in the cradle of her left arm and grabs me with her free hand. "No, you're not ready yet…I need you to help me get Tibal to safety."

I shake my head. "Twee, if Tony's calm then the fight's over back there…and he didn't seem sad or anything…" I sigh. "…Stefana and Abbie will help you. Tony, Shay, and Mitchell will help you, too."

The corners of her mouth turn down. She shakes her head vehemently. "Twee, I have to…you knew this day was coming. It's why my mom told you everything she did…she knew what she was going to do, and that I would have to stop her." She shakes her head. "I'll be fine, Twee. Take care of Tibal."

"Don't die," she says in whispered song.

"I won't. I promise." She nods and begrudgingly releases my hand. "Go." She steps through the illusion. I wait… The door opens on the far end of the room and then closes. My protection spells react to the harsh environment of the hell gate…and they're gone.

I walk over to the door and open it. It doesn't feel nearly as hot…the smell of brimstone isn't as harsh either. I step through, and this one isn't like moving through a dusty sandstorm. It's more like falling…it's warmer than the white room, but it isn't unpleasant like the other hell gate. I take another step…or did I…?

I open my eyes and look around again. It's another white space. This one is small though. It's about the size of my bedroom at Quincy and Tony's place. It has four doors, including the one I came through. I sigh. I thought I sensed my mom, but…

The door on my right opens. Mom stumbles out. Her face glistens, her hair hangs damp and wavy around her head, and her clothes seem disheveled. She pants wildly and puts her hands on her knees. She's wearing the fetish outfit again, complete with leather coat and corset. She lifts her eyes.

"YOU!"

"Me," she says with all the casual ease of us sitting in the living room carrying on a conversation over some of my special lemonade. She stands up straight and sighs as if she's just as bored as all that. Her breathing falls back into a regular, slower rhythm.

"How…? Why…? MOM!" I try to wipe my tears on my sleeve. "Mom, you promised…you told me…" She crosses her arms and bows her head. "…you told me you were done with En Quosque…you betrayed Quincy…spelled him."

She looks at me. "Mad about that one, are you?"

"No, I'm mad because…" I tremble. "Mom, you're one of the bad guys." I sniff and try to swallow down the bile building in the back of my throat. "And…" I lift my right hand. "…and I have to stop you."

She sighs again. In fact, everything about her tells me that she's exhausted, not just the sweat on her forehead and throat or the wrinkled clothing. "Yeah and right now, you probably could, baby girl."

"Don't call me that."

She smirks. "You…really could stop me though…" She steps to her left and clears my view of the door behind her. It's just as white as everything else is here. My eyes dart to the door on my right…the one she walked through and then back to her. She glances at the door opposite me. "…or you could save the love of your life." She motions to the door across from me.

"Love of my…? What?" I stare at the door. "Who's back there?"

"You mean with all the spirit magic training you've been doing, and don't think I haven't noticed, you can't tell?"

I frown. My eyes dart between her, the door on my right, and the door behind her. I take a deep breath and come back to mom, the woman who raised me, the woman who is now my enemy. The Fairy Queen said she was asking the impossible of me, but I had no idea. Every spell that I can think of to stop her, she taught me and…I couldn't manage using any of them right now…not one of them. Not against her.

"Oh, I know you. You're debating whether you should attack me or look inside the door." I swallow a knot. "You should pick which one you're going to do soon, baby girl," she says with a serious tone. "Before long, the decision'll be made for you."

"Who's back there?" I ask with a lot of the fight taken out of my voice because of the tears I'm fighting. She nods unevenly. She's my mother. How could I attack her?

"You can capture your own mother. You'd definitely be crowned the new reigning White Witch…"

"…Witch of Light," I interrupt. "Who's back there?"

"…Witch of Light," she says. She nods with another sigh. "So, tired," she says and rubs her eyes. She comes back to me with another nod. "You'd be the next Witch of Light for sure, baby girl. You'd drag me in…last of the great McCabe bloodline in front of the Witches' Council and subject me to their judgment…"

I shudder as the memory spell she placed in my head at the mere mention of Philosopher's Stone passes through my mind. She puts her hands on her hips, exposing her chest more. "…and you know what they'll do to me." I see it again just as quickly…the sallow and empty eyes, pale and ashen skin, thinning and graying hair, and chapped, cracked lips.

Tears well in my eyes all over again. She put that memory directly into my mind as a warning against turning from the role of a Witch of Light, and it stuck. It stuck. That's my mom. Teaching me from the moment I was born and she's still teaching me right now as my enemy. She knew this time would come, and she knew that that memory would keep me from wavering.

"I'm the last of the McCabe bloodline."

"Nope, you're a Baggett witch, baby girl…start of a whole new bloodline; one all your own."

"Whatever. I'm taking you in…I'm sorry."

She shakes her head. "Instead of doing that," she continues. "You could go through this door…" She motions to the door opposite me again. "…and save the man you love."

I scowl. "I love Quincy AND Tony." She smirks. "You said the MAN I love." I shake my head. "They both can't be through that door, because I just left Tony back there…and this…" I lift the pendant with my right hand. "…told me that Quincy was nowhere near where I left his brother."

She rolls her eyes in an 'oh, you know' kind of way that makes me angry all over again.

"You can't mean Rais. You tried to drive me toward Alex and that never took, so you know that my magic, my spirit magic wouldn't react to a skinwalker."

I frown. I turn back the way I came, and that door is still there. My left hand wraps around the Crescent Moon Pendant, pressing its notches and dents into my palm. "Tony's still there." I come back to mom, and she smiles triumphantly. "Quincy? You think Quincy is the love of my life?"

She stares at my hand still resting on the pendant. "You are right-handed, aren't you?" She smiles…not condescendingly or maniacally or even as if she's gloating. She smiles at me with warmth. The same way she did when she'd greet me at my bedroom door for every birthday. The same way she would whenever she'd shove me her extra strips of bacon at breakfast. The same way she did whenever I won some school award. She's my mom. How can I be expected to kill my own mother?

"I have always known you better than you know yourself, baby girl." Tears well in her eyes. "You have to choose now. Him or me…" She sniffs and starts walking toward the door on my left. "…and I already know which way you're going to go." She reaches the door and puts her hand on the handle.

I run toward the door in front of me. I reach it and put my right hand on the handle. I pause and turn to look at her. "Him. Mom, I will ALWAYS choose him over you." My voice quivers on every word.

"I know."

"YOU made it this way though," I sob. "You did this. You did this to us."

She smiles. "I know that too, baby girl." A tear falls and for one second, I doubt my own decision. My fingers ease on the handle.

"For what it's worth," she continues. "I'm proud of you." I shake my head. The anger I felt a moment ago comes back with the force of a hurricane. "You're so much stronger than I am. You're so much stronger than all of this, baby girl." She draws her lips into her mouth, pulls her door open with one clean jerk, and steps through it. The door closes behind her and melts into the wall. It vanishes. I look around and the other two doors disappear too.

I open my door and again the flaming nothingness reaches out for me. It draws me in, and I feel myself moving through time and space. I wonder where it will take me this time.

#####

Chapter 38: Firefight

Where am I now? At least, it's not a blank white space. It's a large, dimly lit concrete nightmare. It smells like dust and stale air, and there are random, exposed gray, rectangular pillars dispersed all around. The white door closes behind me and melts away until all that's there is a gray brick wall.

"No turning back," I say. I nod. "Dive in." I step forward after giving my eyes time to adjust to the shadows. An electric buzz fills the air and large, round light bulbs come to life all around the ceiling. The space takes on a soft glowing golden tone.

"Quincy?" I whisper. I wrap my right hand around the pendant. "Quincy?" I repeat. I don't hear anything back, but I feel him just ahead. I walk toward where I sense him and spot two people lying on the dust-covered floor.

I run to… "…Quincy…? And Rais…? What did you guys do to each…?" I frown, moving to Quincy's side. I pull him over onto his back. He has burns covering his chest, arms…and even his face. They're healing, but still very noticeable. "Rais couldn't have…"

I move to Rais and roll him over onto his stomach…his front is fine…but there are burns on the underside of his arms and along his back. I glance back at Quincy and notice that four slashes move across his left thigh… "Were you guys fighting each other…? …and then someone attacked you…with fire…?"

"Someone, she says aloud to no one in particular," a familiar man's voice says. I jump to my feet. A man with bright reddish-orange hair and green eyes steps out from behind a pillar. He smooths down the front of his gray-on-black pinstripe vest over his matching slacks and white button up underneath. His black tie remains in place.

"Who are you?"

He smirks. "You've forgotten me already? I'm hurt. I guess it can't be helped…" He turns to his right and starts walking. "…although, I will admit…" He places his right hand under his chin. "…it did actually sound like you cared about Rais." He looks at me with a strange, condescending frown. "Not as much as you worry about your pet faux-fae, but it's there."

"I'm not going to ask again." I raise my right hand, palm toward him. "Who are you?"

"How should I say this?" He slips his hand into his right pocket. I get ready for anything…except the pack of cigarettes he pulls out. He takes one and places it in his mouth.

"Smoking is gross."

"Or cool?" He replaces the pack and points to me with his free hand.

"No, it's just gross."

"Eh, suit yourself," he breathes. He holds his right hand up to the tip of the cigarette, and a fire ignites at the ends of his middle and pointer fingers. He lights his cigarette and inhales deeply. I swallow deeply as his fingers go out. "Where was I?"

"You were just about to tell me who you are, or you were about to get a lightning bolt up the butt."

He takes another puff causing the tip of the nasty little thing to glow bright. He blows out a huge plume of smoke, that I can smell way over here, and I was right. Cigarettes are gross. "Right," he says with the cigarette hanging from his mouth. "I'm here to do what Rais couldn't bring himself to do."

"If you're going to try and kill me then…"

He laughs. "Of course not," he says as if it's a complaint. "We knew better than to ask him to do that. Like him, I was sent to retrieve you."

"Retrieve me?"

He draws from his cigarette again. "Yep," he replies. He points his free hand at me. "En Quosque wants you…" I grit my teeth. "…and they sent me to see what was taking Rais so long to bring you in." He glares at Rais. "He didn't have any intentions on bringing you back with him or coming back at all for that matter." He takes another puff. "Unfortunately, he was trying to explain that to your pet when they got into it."

"Quincy is not my pet…he's my-my friend…" I stumble and stammer over the word. "…just like Rais is." Okay, so maybe not just like Rais, but this guy doesn't have to know that.

"I figured as much." He drops his cigarette and grinds it into the concrete with his foot, covered by very expensive looking leather shoes. "I knew there was something in the way that he first looked at you."

…*first looked at me?* He was there…and he can make fire without a spell? "Devon?"

"Ah, now you remember," he says, slipping his hands into his pockets. "Good, that should make this easier. Come with me…now…quietly. Don't resist, and I'll spare your pet and even the traitorous furball, too. What a deal, huh? What do you say?"

"Hell. You should go there. Now. That's what I say."

He sucks air between his teeth. "You barely beat us back with your mother and both of your pets helping you. Do you really think you can beat us by yourself?"

"Us?"

"Morten. Romilda." Morten steps around the pillar behind Devon, dragging his massive hammer behind him. The expression on his face is different though. The last time he seemed…simple, not angry, or vengeful or anything, just simple. Now, he just seems sad. "Oh, get over it," Devon whines. "She betrayed us. She left us for dead, and she has been replaced by a far more suitable master."

"Who is your master now?"

"Oh, she's just full of questions, isn't she?" a woman's voice says behind me. I half-turn and take a step back so that I can keep everyone in my field of vision.

"Yes, she is, Romilda," Devon answers. "And she has refused my very civil request."

The woman looks…normal aside from the sides of her head being shave and the top moving forward in a big swoop of strawberry blond that covers the left side of her face.

"You know what that means, right?"

Devon nods.

She rubs her right thumb against the rest of fingers on her black leather gloved hand while her left arm wraps around her skinny waist. Her leather pants match her frame and hug her in that sense all the way down to her riding boots. I do like the leather jacket though.

"Brother, get your head in the game." *Brother?* Morten lifts his head and hammer at a languid pace. He drapes it over his shoulder. He places its head on the ground again. "Good boy."

Morten glares at me…no, past me…at Romilda. He takes a deep breath and another right behind it. He's seething. Wow, all the sibling issues I've been privy to lately…Gwen and Gavin, Sora and Kai, Quincy and Tony…and now these two. I'm kind of glad I was an only kid.

I come back to Romilda, who's still circling me. I really look at her; that confident bop in her step and all the attitude it portrays.

"I know you." She smirks. "You tripped me in Elizabeth City."

"You're so clumsy, and you were with that delectable looking guy."

"Yay, you just gave me a whole other reason to knock you out of those fake leather pants."

"Come quietly," Devon says again. "These two couldn't take us…"

"You caught them by surprise."

"…and you couldn't beat us last time with your mother on your side…"

"It was five to two then, and I wasn't as practiced as I am now…" I push my glasses further up on my nose and then do the same with my jacket sleeves. "…and that's super smart, by the way. Bringing up my mom, just smart."

"It doesn't seem like she's going to listen to reason," Romilda says.

"And it doesn't look like you three are going to be smart and just walk away, so I guess we're even."

"Crush," Morten says, roaring toward me.

"Wait," Devon says, but Morten doesn't let up.

I extend my hand. "Contego," I say while drawing a square on the newly formed barrier. I move my other hand out, remember his ability, I draw a pentagon around the square. His hammer collides with the shield. I wince and clench my teeth, but it holds…but more than holding, it absorbs his hit and becomes stronger. I smirk.

A hiss comes from behind me. I turn, and a flaming skull with two large horns, sweeping to the back, leaps toward me. "Suffoco," I say and twirl my hand left hand around, while extending my right hand toward Morten. The ensuing tornado holds the skull in the air…blowing out its fiery head every time that it seems to reignite itself. I focus on the skull's skinny, leather pants. "Romilda?"

A fireball flies at me from straight on. Can't move the shield in time. Can't change the direction of the tornado. I dive out of the way, but it breaks my concentration. The shield comes down, and the tornado dissipates. Devon's in his volcanic rock form, holding another fireball ready for throwing. Romilda marches forward with her skull still on fire. No, wait…those aren't flames. That's her hair. Her hair burns like fire. Although, the horns are definitely new.

I scramble to my feet. "Crap." They sent two fire beings after me. Fire is my strongest element…I mean, Quincy even referred to me as the Fiery Witch once. "Crap," I say again, when his ridiculously gorgeous face passes through my mind. "Quincy." I look to him and Rais unconscious on the ground. "Capso." I weave a triangle, a square, and a pentagon on the bubble forming around them.

"Aww," Devon purrs. "And here I was just about to attack them to get you to surrender." He steps forward creating another fireball in his other hand. "I guess we'll have to whittle you down with fire."

"It'd be so much easier just to burn her alive," Romilda says with flames licking forward with every breath uttered. "Rather than trying to take her alive."

"I know, but our new boss wants her alive."

"And who's that?"

"Tsk, tsk," he returns. He crushes one of his fireballs and issues a dismissive wag of his finger. "That'd be telling." His head tweaks. "MORTEN, NO!"

I turn just in time to see Morten's hammer flying toward my head. "Capio," I manage and hold the tiny shield in my hand. I focus because I know I don't have time to create a seal on it. His hammer crushes it and throws me back at the same time… "Ugh," I complain as I hit the ground on my right shoulder. That's a bruise. I roll. My shoulder tweaks. It's definitely bruised. At least, I didn't bump my head. I wrap my arm around it as I tumble to a stop. I put my right hand down…still throbbing from the impact of Morten's hammer. My entire arm trembles, and the pain coming from my palm resonates all the way to my teeth. My left hand scrambles, searching for my glasses…there they are.

"Get your brother," Devon says as a growl as I replace my surprisingly unbroken glasses.

"You know how he gets," Romilda complains. "When he's in this sort of mood, it's best just to let him be."

I manage to get up on my knees. Morten bounces, hammer held horizontally across his thighs. He's like a boxer in a corner…he's waiting to see if the ref counts me out. No, wait. I look at my right hand, still quivering from the hit. My palm is red, but not bruised; it still holds the impression of his hammer and something more.

When his hammer collided with my shield, I concentrated my magic into it, all my magic. I clench my hand into a fist. All the different forms of my magic, and two of them seemed to react to him the most. Fire… I look at him. …which begs the question, why isn't he using his fire attacks like his sister or Devon? The other form, spirit. He doesn't have any. There's no will in his attack. He swings his hammer with nothing behind it, but his physical strength. He's a higher order daemon like his sister, so why…

"Morten," I say with what I hope is a soothing tone. His head tweaks involuntarily. "Morten, I felt it." I stand.

"Of course, you did, stupid," Romilda says. "It was a big hammer that nearly took your head off."

"That's not what I felt. Is it Morten?" He crouches, preparing to spring forward. Another attack. "I hope I'm right about this." He charges toward me, lifting that huge hammer above his head. …wait for it… He gets closer and closer. …wait for it… His hoof beats thud in my ears. …wait for it… He's right in front of me. …wait for it… He brings the hammer down with all his strength. Now!

I dodge to the right, and he buries the thing in the concrete. I tap the top of his hammer with my left hand. "Liro." I feel more magic than I should've used flow away, moving through his weapon. The head of it dips further into the fractured ground, slipping into it like wet cement. I tap my right hand against a very confused Morten's forehead. "Quies."

My eyes close. I see…Romilda. She's in her human form. She's mocking me…well, him. What's that in her hand? Is that a brand? The head of it is white hot. It's an eight-sided shape overlaid with a four-sided configuration.

Binding and strength…? My mind snaps back to the now…my eyes open and lock with Morten's eyes.

"Oh, you poor bastard," I say, taking my hand away as he reaches for me. I hop back and barely get away. My shoulder tweaks, and I grab it. I tremble as it throbs under my grip. He focuses on his hammer, trying to pull it free. He won't seem to let go of it for anything. I glare at Devon and Romilda, watching things unfold. Maybe I should offer them some popcorn.

"She's better than I thought she was," she says.

"Better than you," I snarl.

"WHAT?" she barks with a puff of fire.

"I saw what you did to him…to your own brother. How could you?"

"Family business, white witch."

"Witch of Light," I correct, while drawing a heptagon in mid-air and a hexagon inside of it and for a second, I could swear the shapes hang in mid-air like lines of gold…tiny inscriptions of Latin appearing along the borders.

"What are you doing?" Devon asks.

"Him a favor…and hoping he'll return it."

Romilda's eyes become as big as saucers. "NO, STOP HER!" Devon steals a glance at her panicked face.

"Too late," I say with a smirk. "LIBERO!" Not only do I feel the magic leave my body, I feel it fire at Morten like a bullet through the two seals taking them with it…leaving a golden trail behind. It strikes and throws his head back, violently…

"No," Romilda says. "What have you done?"

"You tell me, but either way, I'm willing to bet he'll be madder at you than me."

"Romilda?" Morten says. I come back to him, and he's on his knees, right hand still holding his hammer. I gasp. He seems smaller…leaner, but still very muscular. His horns are longer and long black hair covers his ears and obscures his face.

Romilda shakes her head, and her hair falls against her neck in a mop of matching black. I guess the strawberry blond was coloring. Her horns stayed though as skin reappears over her skull.

Morten rises. Romilda steps back. Morten's feet aren't hooves anymore either. They look like human feet…bare human feet. He opens his eyes, and they appear gold. No, they look like two tiny flickering candle flames. He looks at me. "Thank you, Witch of Light," he says in a voice like a booming clap of thunder. "I have spent so many years in a fog thanks to my traitorous sibling."

"You're smart?"

"Very," he returns. He places his other hand on his hammer's handle. A burst of fire explodes out of the earth, covering its head. He pulls it out of the ground effortlessly, and it's no longer a hammer. It looks like a scythe with a black blade. "You vermin," he says, turning to Devon and Romilda. "You dulled everything about me with that brand."

Romilda swallows a knot and shivers. She takes another step back, stumbles, and falls on her butt. "Brother, listen…no, you don't understand…"

"What don't I understand?" Morten asks, while marching toward her. He drags the tip of his very long, very sharp scythe along the floor. It carves out a path, leaving a trail of fire behind it. "Should I not understand that you wanted to usurp me and become the next head of our family? …that you wanted to keep me as a pet on a leash? …that you sold me, your own elder brother, into servitude for a cause he cares nothing for?"

"I…," Romilda squeaks. Morten vanishes in a puff of fire and reappears behind her. Romilda gasps as he brings the scythe's blade deadly close to her throat. She sobs. Fiery tears move down her face leaving tiny lava splotches on the blade. "Are…are you going to kill me, brother?"

"No. You, at least, showed enough familial comradery to keep me alive, so I'll extend the same courtesy to you." Romilda sighs in relief, but her tears continue. "Father, on the other hand…" She gasps. "…I doubt he'll be as forgiving."

"No," Romilda shrieks. "You can't…he'll…"

Morten spins his scythe over his head like a baton and then brings it down with a snap of his wrist. He cuts a swath out of nothing. The slice opens wider and fire roars out. He grabs Romilda by the shoulder and shoves her into it. She screams as flames flare in the rift.

"You," he says, pointing his scythe at Devon. "I recommend you NOT follow us…if you value your life." Devon nods. "And you," Morten continues, coming back to me. "You have done me and my family a great service this day. Your kindness will not be forgotten, Jamina Baggett."

"I just did what was right."

He smirks. "Goodbye, Fiery Witch of Light. This will not be the last time you see me." He dives into the portal, and I can't help wondering if that was a promise or a threat. The rift closes behind him, leaving Devon and me.

I sigh. Crap, I'm drained. Devon's as fresh as a daisy though, having just watched Morten and Romilda try to tear me a new one. Hope this works.

"Are we done here? Or do you still want me to take you apart, now that it's one on one?"

"Please." He chuckles. "You look as though you can barely stand. I know that that earth spell drained you more than you'd like to let on and applying that many seals in succession probably drained you even more." I frown.

"Yes, we have a spy in your midst, and she's been reporting on your progress as well as your limitations."

"I don't believe you."

"I don't care. You're coming with me, so be a good girl and give up."

I might have enough left in me for one more spell and one more seal. I had better make it count. My mind scrambles. What can I do? How can I take him down in one shot? He uses fire…my water magic's not strong enough. Lightning probably wouldn't have much of an effect. Wind would only hold him off for so long before…it'd just start feeding him.

"Earth."

"What?"

"Earth. It's the element that's going to put you down for the count."

He smirks and lifts his right hand. A fireball hovers above his palm. "Don't make me burn you. My master wants you unsinged."

"I'm not worried." I focus. Maybe, if I lower the spell protecting Quincy and Rais, I might be able to eke out a little more magic. I sigh. I can't. If something were to happen to Quincy…a-and Rais…I'd never forgive myself.

"What's it going to be, White Witch?"

I nod, slip my glasses off, and put them in my jacket pocket. "That's…" I run toward him and just as I thought, it threw him. He paused…long enough for me to get six steps closer… He draws back. …three more steps… He throws the fireball at me. …two steps…and then I slide as if I'm trying to steal home. Thank you, dad for making me watch the Braves classic games on DVD. The fireball sails over my head. I extend my left hand to Devon. I catch his right leg and use it as a brake. "…Witch of Light."

He looks down at me, and his forearms erupt in flames. "You!" he growls and creates two more fireballs.

I focus on the memory of Romilda sealing away her brother's powers. I draw an octagon on the ground with my right hand. I focus on the earth beneath me and combine it with… "…the first spell I ever learned." I slam my right hand down on the seal while clutching tighter with my left. "Extermino."

"What?"

I feel it. My fire siphons fire away from him, drags his fire downward. The flames around his arms and in his hands recede into his skin. "What's happening to my…?" He groans. I sigh as the last embers vanish. "No," he says, while staggering away. I lift my head. He shrinks like Morten did. He puts both hands over his face and bends over with another groan. "What did you do to me?" he asks, but his voice sounds like it did when he was…

He turns back to me with his plain, human-looking face. I sit up. "I bound your fire." He gasps. I look down at the scorching octagon with my handprint burned into the center. "I bound your fire to the earth…just like I said."

"You…" He walks toward me. Crap. No magic left in this girl…and even if he is just a dude now…he's still way bigger than me. I crabwalk away from him. "I don't need my fire to…"

"I've seen enough," a silky voice with a French accent says. "Take him." I hear footsteps and a lot of them. Six men in black riot gear, covering them from head to toe, rush out and grab Devon. They restrain him. One hits him with the butt of a very big gun. Devon goes limp all at once.

"Put the shackles on him. I want him ready for transport as soon as possible," the woman says, stepping out from behind a pillar. "Oh, we've got one hell of a catch this time."

I take my glasses out of my pocket and put them on in a fumble of motion. I stare at the gorgeous woman with pale skin, pouty red lips, and long black hair almost as silky as her voice. She sighs. Her eyes move over to me. "Take him away," she says dismissively. The six men do just that.

She strides over on ridiculously high stilettos underneath a tight, black pencil skirt. "Hello," she says, offering me a hand. "You simply must be Jamina Lynda Baggett, known as Jamie-Lynn by most of your classmates except one very special young man who simply calls you, Jamie. Alexander Garner, who is supposed to be the next Alpha of the Garner clan of skinwalkers."

I frown and stare at her outstretched hand. "And you're…" I search her aura. "…a vampire with an absurd amount of information about me and my friend."

"It's what I do, dear. My name is Duchess, and I know your magic is flat lining, so rest assured that if I wanted to hurt you, you'd already be dead."

"Thanks? That's…oddly comforting." I take her hand, and she pulls me up.

"To set your mind at ease, I believe you know a Witch of Light in my employ by the name of Bedlam."

"You're Bedlam's employer?"

She nods. "Furthermore, I came to help, but you were going up against three fire wielding daemons, and I'm good, but not that good. Also, I came to tell you something, Witch of Light." She looks me over and throws her hair over her shoulder. "A man named Rex is holding onto something important for you."

"Rex? Why do I know that name?"

She shrugs. "He will present it to you on your eighteenth birthday."

"That sounds a little sketch and a lot of pervy."

She huffs a soundless laugh. "It is important. You have to keep it safe. You'll need it to fight them."

"How do you know so much?"

"Like I said, it's what I do." She sighs and stares at me the way my mom's cousins do whenever they come up from Florida. "Jamina Baggett…" She laughs in that weird soundless way again. "The Baggetts and McCabes…" I frown as she nods. "…now that's a story."

"What are you talking about?"

"Funny how some old-world families always manage to find each other."

"What are you talking about?" I repeat, feeling on edge and at ease at the same time in a weird way.

Duchess tips her head toward me. "Your friend's waking."

Quincy moans. I come back to Duchess…and she's gone. I look around. She's REALLY gone. I run over to Quincy and snap my fingers, releasing his shield, while sliding on my knees.

"Quincy? Quincy, are you okay?" I move closer until I'm on top of him, literally. He sits up, and I sit back to give him room.

"Yeah. I'm…" His head bows. "…fine."

"What?" He lifts his left arm. "No," I say, taking in the new seal on his forearm. "That's…that's…"

"Indolence," he says, tracing the strange writing along the inside curves.

"The other one…it didn't…" I take his right arm, and his Lust Seal has similar writing…and more lines to it.

"They become more…pronounced as they come in. I'm sure Tony's seals look like this now, too." He looks at me with guilt. "I tried to call you."

"Cell reception must be bad."

He takes the Crescent Moon Pendant in his right hand. "I mean, 'call' you." I nod. His hand moves to the side of my face, and I tremble.

"When I came in and saw you on the ground, I…" I throw my arms around him and hold him tight. "Quincy, I love you so much…and almost losing you once was horrible…and then almost losing you again…" I can't talk because I feel a horrible lump in my throat.

"You'll never get rid of me, Red." We part, and he sweeps the tears out from under my eyes. My eyes dart to his lips and back to his eyes. I kiss him. I inhale deeply and tug on his bottom lip before parting my lips, only to bring them together again around his top lip. The kiss ends, and I sigh. I hold my forehead to his.

We part, and I stare into his eyes. Is it true? Is he…?

"Ugh." We turn to find Rais, lifting himself up on his hands and knees. "I am so going to kill that…" He looks at us. Quincy continues holding me, and until that moment, I didn't realize I was straddling him. "Oh," Rais says with a frown. He stands. "I'll…" He takes a step back. His eyes meet mine and dart away. "…give you two some space." Before I can respond, he vanishes.

"We should get you home," Quincy says. I nod and wrap my arms around him again. "The sun will be up soon."

I hold him tighter. "Just…a few more minutes, okay? Just…" I try to swallow down the huge lump in my throat as my mother's word run through my mind again. Did I choose and didn't realize it? Is Quincy really THE love of my life? I renew my hug. "…give me a few more minutes of this. Okay?"

He reciprocates while stroking my hair.

#####

Epilogue

I step out of my closet and check my clothes over. "So, glad I finally got the smell of brimstone out of my hair." I push it all back and then wrap a hair band around it. "It's only been what…two weeks since I went through those hell gates?" I fling my towel over the open door and step into my bedroom. Stefana leans against my dresser. I check the door…that she closed…and come back to her. "And it looks like I'm going to have to add a new smell to it…burning fairy."

She smirks. "Easy there, Witch of Light." She uncrosses her arms and reveals a gold armor breastplate over her surprising amount of chest. She stands and raises her hands in surrender. "I didn't come to fight."

I sit on the edge of my bed. "So, I haven't heard from any of you fairies in weeks and then you show up, and you're not looking to fight?" She inhales deeply. I pull one boot on, just in case. "No?"

She shakes her head.

I slip my foot into the other boot and stand. "Then why are you here?"

"The exact opposite actually." She sighs an exasperated breath and steps closer. That flaming sword of hers rests on her hip. My eyes come back to meet hers. "I came to…thank you. You saved my brother's life…kept your word to my mother, and…" She swallows deeply. "…you…um…saved Twelana's life when I couldn't."

"She's my friend…"

"But she's my sister." Golden tears accompany Stefana's words. "Twelana, unlike ALL my other sisters, is my actual sister. I love her like no other. The only person I love as much as her is our brother, so as you can see…" She takes my right hand. "…you have done so much for me personally."

"You're welcome."

She shakes my hand and then wipes her cheeks. "But…this is not the only reason I came here today." Here we go. "You have done as my mother asked and you kept watch over your mother although it was at great personal difficulty to you," she says in a stern, official sort of way. "As such, my mother wants to make good on your arrangement. She would be here to tell you this in person, but considering recent events, she has chosen to stay close to Tibal…so has Twelana.

"Furthermore," she says, preparing the next part of her speech. "Because you saved Tibal and Twelana…" She nods. "…who will most likely be our next Fairy Queen…" So, Twee really will be the next Fairy Queen. "…I have been authorized to offer you a second boon."

"Look," I say, waving her off. "I didn't do any of that so that your mom would owe me a favor. I did those things because they were the right things to do…by my friend and you know, saving the world and stuff."

"Be that as it may," she says with a sigh, sounding more relaxed. "My mother feels she owes you a great deal. I do, too."

She reaches for her belt and pulls out a small gray stone. "What's that?"

She shows me the tiny sigil stone with two markings that I recognized as *bind*, with its intersecting swirly lines, on one side and *transport*, with its two wavy lines that could easily mean water, too. "One of the fairies guarding Tibal, when your mother attacked, is our greatest sigil-maker and sign weaver. During the attack, she managed to get close enough to your mother to lay a hand on her."

"She…touched my mom…? So, what? My dad did that about a thousand times…and I just almost made myself throw up a little in my mouth."

"Well, you might want to stifle your vomiting." Her tone's serious. She presents the stone again. "You see, when she touched your mother…she placed the corresponding sigils to this stone on her skin…unbeknownst to your mother."

"You mean…?"

Stefana nods with a mischievous grin. "That's right…whoever uses this stone will go directly to wherever your mother is right now." I swallow a lump and stare at it. I extend my right hand, and she closes hers around it.

"Witch of Light, you may not know this, but the 4th Fairy Queen, my mother, Devi, is exactly like her mother, the 3rd." I shake my head not getting her meaning. "She, like Sharon before her and like…Twelana after her, has the ability to grant any wish made to her." One intrigued eyebrow arches. "That's right. She can grant any wish, but she has limited her wish granting to when she owes someone a boon as not to upset the balance of the world."

"Then, couldn't she just grant her own wish and fix whatever someone does to…?"

Stefana shakes her head. "If she were to grant her own wish, like Sharon, she would be destroyed by her own power." I nod. "Nor can she grant the wish of any fairy, even if they're outside of her clan."

"I guess that would explain why fairies don't rule the world." Stefana nods. I lift my eyes to meet hers. "And…now, your mother owes me…not one, but two of those wishes…I mean, boons, right?"

Stefana's playful smirk returns. "Yep."

"And I can wish for anything I want."

"Within her power…which is vast and just short of being able to stop Eden herself."

I try to pretend that I need to think about what either of my wishes are, but I don't have to. "You're authorized to convey my requests to your mother, right?" Stefana nods. I open my left hand. "First of all, give me that stone. That is my first wish."

She smiles outright and opens her hand. "Before you accept it, you should know that my sister Chelsea was only able to apply enough magic for one…this stone will take one and only one person to your mother. No more."

"I'm sorry," I say with a bit of a snarky tone. "Did I stutter?" I extend my hand more. "I said, 'give me that stone.'"

Stefana laughs. She drops it into my hand. "I knew you'd say something like that." I nod and hold it between my thumb and pointer finger and look it over. "And your other wish? Or do you need time to think it over?"

The sigil stone feels warm and smooth in my palm, and I actually get a bit of mom's magic through it. "No." My head bows. "I know exactly what I want my other wish to be."

I lift my eyes to Stefana. "I want your mother to break the curse on the Blackshear brothers. I don't want them to be forced to love me. Is that clear?"

She takes half a step back. "Are you sure? I mean, even if she does…there's no guarantee that you'll be freed from the curse, too. More than likely that would equate to two separate wishes." She ponders for a moment. "You may end up still in love with two men who don't love you in return."

My free hand moves to the Crescent Moon Pendant…my right hand…and I feel both their hearts through it. I smile absently thinking of my boys…my stern and angry, Tony…my playful and subdued, Quincy. "I'll risk it. I love them too much to keep torturing them like this…especially if it's all a lie."

Stefana sighs. "Very well. Mother will hear your wish by midday, and it will be granted at one minute past the hour." She points. "You know how to use that sigil stone, right?"

"Pretty simple. Apply magic. Sigil activates."

"Witch of…" She breaks off. "Jamie, you're a woman after my own heart. So, I know what's going to happen the second I leave you."

"Then maybe you should get going so that it can happen."

"May I…hug you?" I purse my lips, but nod. She steps forward and slips her arms over my shoulders. I put mine under hers. "You have done so much for those I love that I now regard you as family. Be safe and return well."

"You too." We part. "And if I come back from wherever alive, maybe we can keep up the being civil with each other thing."

"Don't hold your breath, Witch of Light. You're like family…and while I love all of my one hundred six sisters…I only like about fifteen of them." I smirk, and she smiles outright. "Goodbye, Jamina Lynda Baggett."

THE FAIRY QUEEN | 229

"Goodbye, Stefana, 7th Fairy of Devi."

"Would you like me to say anything to Twee? Or the Blackshear brothers, in case…?"

"No. They…they know how I feel about them."

She sighs and snaps her fingers. She vanishes into a tiny golden sphere of light. It soon fades too.

I open my hand and look at the sigil. I go over to the nightstand and collect my glasses. I pull the Crescent Moon Pendant over my head, just before I put them on. I place the Pendant on the bed and stare at it for a moment. I place my left pointer finger on it…two tears fall on it. "Goodbye, Tony. Goodbye, Quincy. I love you both so much…and if you never see me again…know that that will never change." I remove my finger from the pendant. "…even if the way you feel about me does."

I step back, wipe my eyes on my sleeve, and move over to my closet. I take my jacket and quickly pull it on. I check my shoes, jeans, shirt, and jacket. I'm ready…as ready as I ever will be anyway.

A knock comes from my door. "Jamie?" Tony calls. "Jamie, are you alright?"

"We can't sense you through the pendant anymore," Quincy says. "Is everything alright?"

My face scrounges up and more stingy, hot tears threaten escape. If I answer them, I'll give myself away, and they WILL stop me. I inhale deeply and focus my magic on the sigil. They knock again. Wind rushes up around me. A sound like a high-pitched whistle follows it.

"JAMIE!"

"JAMINA!"

My hair bounces in its ponytail…like the puff of curls it is. My magic creates a tempest of power, but more than that, I feel my mom's…her magic flows around me like a warm feather down blanket. A bright white light threatens to swallow me up. My bedroom door opens, but it's too late…I'm already on my way. The whistle becomes a deafening screech, and everything brightens to an all-encompassing white nothing. And suddenly, I

End.

THE CLAIMED SAGA
FOX FIRE: THE KITSUNE
CHAPTER 1

MIDNIGHT PRINCESS: THE KNIGHT WOLF
CHAPTER 2

FIERY WITCH: THE CURSED BROTHERS
CHAPTER 3

FOX FIRE: FAMILY TIES
CHAPTER 4

MIDNIGHT PRINCESS: THE NEW BLOOD
CHAPTER 5

FIERY WITCH: THE FAIRY QUEEN
CHAPTER 6

FOX FIRE: REIGNING SUN
CHAPTER 7
(COMING JULY 2021)

MIDNIGHT PRINCESS: THE ALPHA BLOODLINE
CHAPTER 8
(COMING NOVEMBER 2021)

FIERY WITCH: THE VAMPIRE HUNTERS
CHAPTER 9
(COMING MARCH 2022)